CH00867226

If At First

CRIMSON *Cove*

Book One

Tara Brown

Copyright © 2015 Tara Brown
All rights reserved.
ISBN-13: 978-1514151839
ISBN-10: 1514151839

This book is dedicated to my daughters.
My girls.
You are the very first people I loved unconditionally.
You and the cats.

Thank you, Andrea Burns and Lori Follet.
You have both made this book series my favourite.
Love you to pieces.
Not like Crimson Cove pieces, where you end up in pieces, but like like
lots.
Loads.
There.
I love you loads.

Once upon a time, in a crappy little town ruled by deceit and treachery, there were six girls—six princesses. Each one more spoiled and entitled than the next.
For nearly two decades they dominated the seaside land with parties and indulgences galore.
Unbeknownst to them, they each represented something—a season of my life.
But it isn't my turn to talk.
As much as the story is mine, this isn't my version of it.
This is theirs.
But don't worry, I will be heard.
No matter what.

Anonymous

CHAPTER ONE
Mission Impossible

August 3rd

The maple trees lining the streets always made me feel like I was home, no matter which part of town I was in. They were our calling card and namesake, Crimson Cove. A cove of red maples.

The East Coast had maples everywhere, but only Crimson Cove had the red ones exclusively. We were famous for the drive into town along the shores from Stamford, Connecticut. We were the small cove just between Stamford and Darien, a red splotch on any aerial map. It was small with only 18,733 people and even that number was dependent upon who you asked. I know my father didn't count the laborers or the service workers as residents of our town. Even if their families had lived here longer than ours.

I leaned my head out the window, wondering what kind of treasures I would find in Vincent's bedroom today.

Maybe I should feel guilty for snooping in people's things but I didn't, and Vincent's room was my favorite.

I considered it boot camp-style training for being an investigative journalist. There was nothing like the real thing to teach you how to do it, and I was in the perfect place to learn. There was no town with secrets as good as ours, or scandals that ran as deep in all of the United States, including Hawaii.

Andrew, my partner in grime, gave me a look from the driver's seat of our work truck as he drove down the highway. "Lindsey, earth to Lindsey!"

A scowl crept along my face as I stared at him, realizing he was talking. "Did you say something?"

1

"A few somethings. You wanna grab lunch first or after Vince's house?" He chuckled.

I sighed and turned to look out the window at the downtown core passing by me. "Whatever. I don't care. What are you in the mood for?"

"Well, to be honest, I really want some sushi."

I turned back and laughed with him. "We don't have time to stop for sushi. We still have the country club to do."

He nodded as he offered up his adorable dark stare. "I know, but I was thinking maybe we could be too long at sushi and Vince's house and the other team could do the clubhouse."

"I like where you're going with this." Neither of us said it, but we both were ashamed of the fact we worked for my father. It was so far beneath us we didn't really know how to protest it. Andrew had been hired on because of a drunk driving incident two months ago. I had been forced into it with a "learn some work ethics" spiel from my father, most likely spurned on when I rolled my eyes and told him I planned to be a journalist and didn't need his money.

Andrew's dad had insisted he work for my dad to learn what happens when you behave like a commoner— you get to work like one. My dad wanted me to see how bad it was being poor.

It sucked that we had both landed ourselves here, working for the summer for the first time ever. But we tried to make the best of it by slacking off and doing the bare minimum. Every house belonged to someone we knew, and usually they felt sorry for us. So we swam and ate and napped, a lot. A lot more than my dad knew about.

The part that pissed me off the most was that my father had never done any physical work at his own company, not a day in his life. He had never gotten his hands dirty before, whereas mine were covered with dirt marks and cuts.

"So which first, sushi or Vince's house?"

"Vince's," I answered him, certain I could clean up there before we went to eat. The dirt under my nails and the bruises and scrapes on my arms weren't going to come clean, but at least I could get the majority of the mess I was scrubbed off. And I did plan on heading inside to snoop, just a little.

Andrew Henning wasn't a big talker. He wasn't a big anything, except pothead. He was a huge pothead. We didn't have that in common. Being a fan of control made pot low on my list of things I enjoyed. But Andrew clearly didn't mind being constantly in space.

As we pulled up to the largest house in the cove I growled inwardly. I had known Vincent Banks my entire life, and I wasn't big on him either. His father was easily the richest man any of us knew, and therefore a friend of my father's, to whom the importance of wealth and breeding outweighed every other aspect of a person's character.

Vincent's mother had left when he was eight. She remarried some European dude and never came back. He visited her in the South of France every summer, usually around this time.

I crossed my fingers, hoping he was in France and not at the house to torment me the way he always did. He liked to pretend he found me attractive and teased me about us hooking up. I was a safe person to bug; his girlfriend was one of my best friends and she was better looking than me by a lot.

At first I had found it funny that he always hit on me, even if deep down I knew a guy like him would never be interested in a girl like me. Girls like me dated political science nerds or accountants. He was exciting and crazy and careless. But after a few years it got annoying, like the joke had ridden its course and I was done.

In our group of girls in Crimson Cove, Rachel had me voted the least likely to ever get laid, which was fine with me. I didn't want some drunken teenaged boy conning me with insincere compliments and a bevy of drugs and alcohol, just so he could ply my pants away from me.

I shuddered, imagining it. It wasn't hard to either—all my friends had lost their virginity that way. My actual best friend Lainey and I were the only virgins left and everyone knew it. She was worse off than I was. I could at least look like I fit in, but she always struggled. If she wasn't pushing her glasses up on her nose, she was squinting because her mom had taken her glasses away. Her mom was the socialite of all socialites. Her getting Lainey as a daughter proved God had a sense of humor.

Andrew pulled up to the massive gate that made everyone else's gates seem paltry in comparison, sort of like the Banks' family fortune. "Good afternoon, Master Henning. Master Banks is not home at the moment. Would you like to come in and wait for him?" the guard asked over the camera. "I am expecting him shortly."

I winced. Vincent would be home shortly?

Andrew shook his head. "We are here with Crimson Cove Landscaping, Barry. I'm working for Mark Bueller this summer."

"Excellent." He buzzed us in.

"So excellent," Andrew muttered.

We both rolled our eyes, probably in perfect sync.

"You wanna do the gardens and I'll mow?"

I shrugged. "Sure." The gardens were the worst job but mowing was harder work. You had to check the oil in the mower and drive around in the hot sun and empty the clippings. The gardens just hurt the neck and back from bending over. But it was the better job for my true passion— creeping in people's shit and sniffing out their secrets.

I hopped out of the truck and strolled to the gardener's greenhouse where the tools were for the weeding and clipping. Since it was done every week, the work never got to be anything beyond a few moments in every garden. It was the fact that there were over a hundred gardens. I grabbed the shears and the mini rake and threw them into the cart, pushing it out into the hot sun. I dragged my tee shirt off and walked around in my strapless bikini top. It was the only way to avoid the weird tan lines I had started to get. They infuriated Louisa, my stepmonster.

After I had finished most of the gardens, I headed for the ones just outside Mr. Banks' office. He wasn't there or he was being silent, maybe reading. I stood, peering in the window and sighing when I realized he clearly wasn't there. I slipped around the side of the office, lifting my phone from my pocket and using my thumbprint to unlock it—the only option I used, rather than having a password. I sent a text to Vincent: *You almost home?*

He responded right away: *No. Do you need me to be home?*

I rolled my eyes. *No.*

He sent his usual torment: *Have dinner with me tonight and we can talk about all the places I was instead of home, and you can tell me why you fight this so hard.*

I grimaced and texted another one-word answer: *Gross.*

He sent a winky face and I entered the office. The house was silent when I crept past the desk, walking like I had a reason to be there. I would say I had to use the bathroom or needed a drink. Mr. Banks knew me well enough that he wouldn't care. And the house was so large I could live there and he might never notice me.

His office was a series of sealed and locked chests, drawers, and cupboards. He never left anything unlocked. It was a waste of time trying to snoop in there; I'd learned that the hard way.

He was a closed off man with a closed off office who was never really home much. I might have felt sorry for Vincent if he wasn't such a pervert.

I slipped past the door and into the hallway where I made my way to the stairs. I hurried up them, knowing I was heading so deep within their house that I wouldn't be able to explain why I was there if I got caught.

My heart raced and my breath hitched as I crept up the stairs, making no noise. The rush of being in someone else's house, touching their things, and seeing their secrets got me high. I never needed drugs or alcohol or petty theft. I needed to see things no one else knew about.

It was wrong and I knew it, but I compared myself to the staff. It was no different than having a maid or butler.

When I got to the top of the stairs, I knew where I was headed. It was the room I had been nearly busted in last time. I had managed to escape down another hallway before the maid found me snooping.

With excited hands and a racing heart, I turned the knob, cracking the door and listening for a single stirring.

The large suite was empty so I stepped in and closed the door behind me, resting my back against it and sighing.

The room was beautiful but tidy in a weird way, like no one lived here amongst the white furniture and white walls. I knew Vincent slept here; all the living was done in the parlor downstairs or the games room, just like at my house.

Out his window, the royal-blue sea swelled in the cove, complementing the stark room and adding some balance.

I clicked the lock and crossed the hardwood floor to the computer and sat in Vincent's white armchair. I was about to run the computer in safe mode when I smiled.

I couldn't help but shake my head, seeing that he had his password on auto save so I could just log in as him. His password was a sad four digits—no doubt a date. It was probably something lame like the moment he lost his virginity. If I had to guess, I would say he was likely about eleven years old when it happened, and it was definitely to an older woman.

He was depraved and obsessed with sex. My mother's voice in my head reminded me he was also a seventeen-year-old boy so it fit him well.

Andrew driving past the window on the mower below made me recall when Vincent had slept with his mom. Andrew had laughed it off when he found out, thinking it was nasty but still funny. Maybe having a dead mother made me a bit sensitive, but I wouldn't have laughed if Vincent had seduced my mom. I might have stabbed him in the eye and then the balls. Or vice versa. But maybe that was an overreaction. I did seem to overreact when he was around.

Although Andrew's mom wasn't exactly a pillar or virtue like my mother had been.

I looked back at the computer, scanning the emails but was disappointed at the lack of awesomeness in there. It was mostly stuff his dad might have forced on him like response letters from the Yale Club in New York welcoming him as a legacy.

In my heart of hearts I didn't see him as the sort of guy who wrote any of the letters in the outbox. They were all polite and professional, and he hadn't even added innuendos or obscene jokes as colorful flavor.

Not in those ones. The ones he generally sent me were fairly dirty. I opened an email he had sent me a week before, and nodded at the repellent humor and filthy images. I had laughed when I opened it the first time but only a little, and I *was* offended, even if I didn't look it.

Okay, not offended but aware that a joke of that nature was inappropriate to send to a girl you weren't dating. Or just any girl in general.

I scrolled a little lower, about to give up when I saw it: an email from a girl named Sasha. We went to school with her but had never hung out together. For lack of a better term, she was a giant ho.

Her father had landed himself in hot water with insider trading and was doing five hard years at the cushiest of prisons—a place my dad called Club Fed. Its real name was the Otisville Corrections Facility. Her mother hadn't divorced him, but she was actively seeking a replacement. And as far as I was concerned, Sasha was actively seeking her future Mr. S. Daddy by hitting up every rich guy in the cove.

I clicked on the email, sitting back with my jaw on the floor when I saw the nasty photos and dirty requests being made on her part. "Asshole," I whispered.

I deleted it, noting he hadn't even opened it yet. Sage, his girlfriend, would thank me later for that. I searched Sasha's name in his account, wrinkling my nose when I saw there were plenty of emails he *had* opened. It had been going on for weeks.

"Gross." I closed the email app and walked away from the computer to check out the other things in his large suite. His walls were bare; not even artwork graced them. But on the wall opposite his bed, he had a large white case of shiny silver and gold football trophies. He was the running back for the Crimson Cove Cruisers. Not because he wanted it, but because he was told he would be.

I ran my finger over the glass case, streaking it with a wide smudge. It gave me a sick amount of pleasure to do it. Everything about him was always immaculate, especially the way his room was. I knew the smudge would torment him.

I bit my lip and turned around, narrowing my gaze on his extra-large king-sized bed. A wrinkle crossed my nose as my lips lifted into a sneer.

It was akin to walking into Hugh Hefner's house and seeing the den of sin he called a bedroom.

Certainly that was the iconic symbol Vincent strived to pattern his life after and imagined himself most similar to.

Well, maybe not on all levels. He did have impeccable manners and was always dressed like he was meeting someone of importance. Even his casual clothes were overly dressy. He suited Sage in that respect perfectly. They looked like a couple from a Hugo ad.

When I got to the bed, I sat but I didn't look down, for fear I would catch a glimpse of something unholy that one only bought at a filthy shop on the bad side of town. I hoped that was the only thing I caught. The thought made me stand and shudder as I bent forward to look in the drawers instead of sitting. God only knew if crabs could jump that high.

One couldn't be too sure with a guy like Vincent.

I rifled through his drawers, noting how tidy they were. A sign of a very sick individual. In *my* drawers you could lose a hand. You could hardly walk in my room most mornings, until Lori got there. Then it was eerily clean.

The bottom drawer seemed shallower than the top one. I pushed them both in and paused, seeing that from the front of the bedside table they were the same size. I opened the bottom one again and pushed on the wooden base. It pressed down like it was connected to a spring and then lifted.

A slow grin crossed my lips as I slipped my fingers in the sides and pulled the bottom out with the few items still sitting perfectly on the board.

Below was a gold mine of things I desperately wanted to unsee the moment I saw them.

Naked Polaroids of girls I recognized either from TV

or school, lubes, condoms, two burner phones, and one gold key. I slipped the key into my pocket and picked up the phones. I turned them both on and sent myself a text from each, and then deleted the text I'd sent and turned them back off. I put them back and checked the numbers on my cell phone. I didn't know either number.

I reached in and dragged my hand over the Polaroids, scanning the photos of the young women flashing their goods for the camera. I pulled back, my stomach tightening as the pictures got less like selfies and more like creepy H&M ads. The girls seemed despondent and sad, like someone had taken the photos against their will. And Polaroids were not like pictures sent with texts. You were most likely there when the photo was taken.

Nauseated and disturbed, I put the board back and closed the drawers, knowing I had been inside for far too long and those were a sign from God telling me I needed to stop snooping in people's houses.

I slipped my phone back in my pocket and headed downstairs, trying to find my usual sense of fulfillment and excitement about the fact I had a key to something I would have to solve.

But the images I couldn't surpass flooded my mind.

"Linds!"

I jumped when I got to the office and heard Andrew calling me. I closed the door to Mr. Banks' office and hurried in the opposite direction of Andrew's voice. I curled up on a bench in the backyard, facing the ocean, and closed my eyes.

"Lindsey. Where are you?"

I fought seeing those images again as Andrew came around the corner. "Are you shitting me, dude? You fell asleep? Come on, I want my sushi." He shoved me lightly on the shoulder.

Ignoring him as if I was waking from a real sleep, I waited a few moments and stayed perfectly still. But then he went silent. Cracking one eye, I jumped, screaming, "Ahhhhndrew!"

He was sitting on the ground, staring right at me. I sat

up as he laughed. "I got you so bad."

"You did." I blinked and breathed. "What do you want?"

"Sushi."

I nodded. "Okay." Leaving the Banks residence did sound quite good actually.

"Did you even finish?" He shook his head.

"Nope. But no one will even know. Let's go." I got up and grabbed the gardening supplies, trying to still my rapidly beating heart and twisting stomach.

The key felt like it was burning a hole in my pocket. I couldn't stop thinking about what it might unlock and where the pictures had come from. If I knew one thing about Vincent, it was that he didn't need pictures of sad girls. He had every girl we knew throwing herself at him.

So why would he have them?

I had considered his house to be like all the others in Crimson Cove—a trial run for my future days when I would be a reckless journalist in the field—but that notion was gone.

I had a firm sense that my days as a local snoop were over. If Vincent had taken those pictures or had any part in them, he wasn't who I thought he was.

A desire to solve the mystery roamed about inside my mind, offering explanations that it was some kind of role-play or he had found them. I realized I wouldn't rest until I knew where they had come from. It bothered me that Vincent had them, but it bothered me more that he might have been the one pointing the camera. I always thought he was a playboy, but I never imagined it went to this level of depravity. He was a harmless annoyance I could shoo away, not a psychopath I had to fear.

Or so I had thought.

CHAPTER TWO
High-cut shorts and low expectations

August 4th

I walked out into the yard, strutting just a little because my theme song was playing over the speakers: "Do I Wanna Know?" by Arctic Monkeys. It was my summer jam from last year, and I still wasn't ready to part with it, so it was fast becoming my summer jam for this summer. The beat and the cool sound of the lead singer's voice had me in its clutches.

It was Friday, a day that had taken on new meaning for me. It was the weekend, which meant I was free for two whole days.

The end of this wretched summer couldn't come fast enough. My father trying to teach me a lesson about being a good socialite was killing my back. I was nearly ready to break and resign myself to being a soulless mooch like the stepmonster.

I stood at the edge of the pool, stretching and rolling my aching neck back and forth before I pulled my sweats off and picked the Sabz high-waist bikini bottom out of my butt. I didn't understand why I had listened when Sierra, my fashion-dictator friend, demanded they were the only bathing suit bottoms any of us would wear this summer. Classic cut was what she had said, but it meant classic wedgie in my books, and in my butt.

I dragged off my shirt and tossed it on one of the new lounge chairs the stepmonster had bought. Seeing them made me wonder what she and Father Dearest were fighting about. It was the only time she redecorated, except for when she had first moved in with us. That was the summer of renovations as she had torn up the whole house. There wasn't even a tablecloth left when she was done erasing Terri, my dad's first ex-wife, or Number Two, as I liked to call her.

These new chairs were cream-colored fabric on dark wood frames, which seemed risky to me, almost like she dared me not to eat lime popsicles and chocolate cake on them. Not that I had to bother with ruining the furniture—two younger brothers would take care of that. Aaron and Matt were at summer camp, but they would be back and those chairs would be ruined.

"Lindsey, is that back in style? The old-lady bottoms from bathing suits in the sixties?" Louisa offered up a smirk from behind the wide Ed Hardy shades she had lowered so she could give me the look.

I grinned back at her, not sure which way we were going with this. The stepmonster and I usually avoided each other, and the pool had always been a safe zone—a neutral territory.

I liked the neutrality of the pool, so of course that forced my answer to be one that might deescalate the situation instead of answering her the way I wanted to. My honest answers usually made things much worse between us.

I took a deep breath and reminded myself I was above her petty taunts. "Yes." I pointed my ass at her as I popped it for her viewing pleasure. "See how the high-cut top shows off my narrow waist and it lifts in the bottom part so my butt cheeks show a bit. It's this season's super sexy bikini—or so Sierra says—and she does usually know this stuff."

She lifted a perfectly manicured eyebrow at me, still grinning wickedly.

It had been a perfect retort until a little evil slipped from my lips, as it always did, "I mean super sexy for the younger generations, obviously. So the ladies in your group wouldn't know that—being why you weren't aware of it." I grinned wide, loving it when her jaw dropped.

I had no self-control. The Doritos under my bed were

proof of that.

My inner Diablo relished in the fact I had a "screw you, Louisa" point on the board before noon, and said point involved calling her old. Hitting thirty was hard for her.

Turning back to the pool, I tossed my short hair about and dove into the cool water, breaking the surface and pretending to ignore the little voice that suggested I should try not to be hateful to her.

My inner dialogue always sounded like an argument between my mother and me. She was the ghost of common sense to my whiney teenaged brain that always insisted Louisa had started the fight.

But there was a common denominator that I always refused to admit to. I had been the exact same with Terri. In fact, I had been this way with the women my dad had dated in between my mom, Terri, and Louisa.

I hated it when I brought up that point, even if it meant hearing my mom's voice again.

I felt the subtlest amount of guilt for calling Louisa old, which thankfully didn't last long.

By the time I surfaced, the water was so refreshingly cool that I couldn't even force myself to feel sorry for saying it. My remorse slipped off my shoulders like water off a duck's ass.

I bobbed, enjoying the sun beating down on me as I scanned the deck for Lori; I needed a drink.

When I turned back to the stepmonster, I caught a glimpse of a sneer. Luckily her eyes went over my head when she gave her annoyed sigh and spoke like she was being inconvenienced, "Marcus, stop. Seriously," she demanded, using his big-boy name which meant he was in trouble. Most people called him Mark.

I grimaced and turned around to see what my father was doing to aggravate her.

He stood on the deck, one hand in his chestnut hair and the other holding his phone. His dark-blue eyes looked like they could shoot flames from them. "What do you mean the Blacks know Gerry Allen sold the market property to the Van Harkers? How the hell did they find out? If they decide to pull out before the Van Harkers have an idea of what's going on there, we are screwed! We promised the Van Harkers we had taken care of their first sale." My dad's voice barked over my head as he lifted his face and scowled at the white fluffy clouds. "This better not become something. We have a firm deal with them over the land—I do not need this today! Do you have any idea who the hell Jamison Black is? Or better yet, who his father is? You better fix this, Janine!" He thumped the screen of his phone and tossed it on the lounger, sighing and giving Louisa a look. "Don't start."

She didn't. She didn't even breathe. No one liked it when Mark Bueller got angry, not even me.

We both sat in awkward silence, feeling sorry for Janine, his secretary. She was an unusually nice lady, especially for this part of the world.

He shook his head and bent forward, picking his phone up. Just as he had it in hand, he caught me in his peripheral. I took the face he made as my cue and sighed my breath out, letting my body sink back under the water. I opened my eyes as I submerged, and grimaced seeing his hard stare lowered to me. His lips moved fast, making me glad to be under the water, where I could pretend he was saying anything to me, and the haze made the lies possible.

His version of coping with conflict and failure was to strike out at everyone else.

And I knew what he would attack me for. I knew Andrew wouldn't keep his mouth shut. He was such an imbecilic moron when it came to knowing when not to talk. If he wasn't such a nice person I would hate him, but his genuine indifference to everyone was a bit endearing to me. He wouldn't even have bitched about me napping—he would have just said it nonchalantly, not understanding that my dad would kill me for it. His dad was pissed about his drunk driving, but his sentence of manual labor was to appease the sheriff far more than it was to make his father happy. His father was less aggressive than mine.

But there, floating in the water and watching my father shout, I didn't care about the fact I'd been busted napping at work. Instead, my head rang with the name Black.

The Blacks were buying something new with Lainey's dad? I thought they had just moved into their new house last summer. They owned a beautiful estate on the water, like all of us did. I knew this because we did their gardens—*we* as in me and Andrew, the rat.

The Blacks?

Maybe it was a different Black family. The last name was a bit of a Smith or Brown or Jones. They were everywhere.

I wished I had Lainey's ability to catalogue all the things she saw and read.

I kicked off the bottom of the pool, surfacing and gasping for air as the shadow of my father turned and huffed into the house.

Treading water, I glanced back at the teary eyes of the stepmonster, wincing and wondering what vile sentiments of love and respect they had spewed at one another while I was under the water. She lifted her drink and pulled on her sunglasses again, this time with her wide-brimmed hat.

This brand of denial was the key ingredient in the recipe for a successful marriage in Crimson Cove.

And Louisa was the queen of making it work.

What I wanted to know was how she had gotten a drink in the time I'd been underwater and where the hell Lori was. Lori was Louisa's maid and loyal to a fault—just not to me. She had come with Louisa which meant our old maid got fired.

I still missed our old maid. *She* was loyal to me.

I swam to the stairs and climbed out, grabbing my towel. My eyes drifted in the neighborhood of the stepmonster, and I contemplated just ignoring the sniffles, but I knew it might be worth something later. An ounce of kindness went far with wicked stepmothers, possibly because I hardly ever showed it. When I did, it was in public. I found acting like we were BFFs in front of others bought me more with her. "You all right?"

"Yes." She sniffed and smiled. "Fine. He's just temperamental. You know how he is when a deal is falling apart and tomorrow is the big event. He's just stressed. Jamison Black is a powerful man in the Senate and his father is a chairperson on some zoning committee or something. It's a big deal if we screw the Blacks over."

What I wanted to say was that my dad was an asshole and she deserved better. But she didn't. So I shrugged and played along. "He kicks it into high gear, Louisa. He acts like he hates all that work drama, but when he has to earn a buck, deep down he's in heaven. This is his jam. He and Mr. Allen will figure it out." I smiled and wiped my face and body. "I'm going to the Shack. You want some pastries?"

She pressed her lips together and shook her head. I saw the look in her eyes and almost thanked her for not commenting about how I didn't need a pastry. She didn't understand my body just as I didn't understand her getting Botox at thirty as a preventative measure.

My mother had been Italian, so I had a pear shape like all the women in her family. My breasts were smallish but my trunk had junk. Thankfully, Nicki Minaj had made junk in one's trunk akin to winning the genetic lottery. I wasn't ever overweight. Being five foot four and one hundred and thirty pounds was respectable. Being a size four or a six wasn't bad to me, just to the rest of Crimson Cove. But I was the last girl to care.

I left my wet towel in a mound on a chair and hurried inside before I convinced myself that I should stay and talk it out with Louisa. Being nice to her scared me.

What if we had a moment?

Then I might have to overdose on something later while wearing far too much mascara and listening to nineties grunge. I even had the blonde wig to go with the depression I would be forced to fake.

I made it as far as the kitchen with my thoughts distracting me. I almost didn't see him, but when I did, I skidded on the large tiles to halt myself while gasping in shock. "What are you doing here?"

Shit.

Did he know I had his key and had snooped in his

room?

Did he know I'd seen the vile photos?

No, how could he?

It was weird timing for Vincent Banks to be standing in my kitchen with a drink. He was dressed in a pair of beige dress pants and a pale-blue dress shirt. He belonged in a men's cologne commercial.

I hated how attractive he was.

"Hey, princess." He seemed weird or cockier than normal. I had to tell myself there was a slight possibility he knew I had his key. He winked and sipped his drink. "I have been thinking about you, a lot."

His broad shoulders and thick muscles were hard not to notice, even with hateful thoughts roaming in my head. And his chestnut hair was shaggy instead of slicked back, maybe because we weren't at school, in proper uniform. It was the one feature he had that I adored. It made him look sweet, which was contrary to his actual personality. I reminded myself about the Polaroids.

"What are you doing in my kitchen and how the hell did you get a drink? Where is Lori?" My eyes scanned the kitchen for her.

He cracked a grin, lifting one side of his lips. "I suspect she doesn't like you. You're too nice to her; she doesn't dig that. She, however, was very attentive to me. I think she likes me." He lifted the straw to his lips, sucking and swallowing with great emphasis.

"All older women like you, Vince. Ask Andrew's mom."

He flinched but recovered quickly as his green eyes trailed down my body, nauseating me. "I like the swimsuit. It's a little less than you normally wear, isn't it? I almost prefer you dressed like a nun, the way you always are. I like imagining what's in there. I feel like it's a game we play, no?"

"No. We don't play games." That was a lie—we always played games. But since the pictures in his drawer were haunting me, I didn't want to play anymore. In fact, I almost covered myself, but I knew that's what he was going for, so I stood there, nearly naked. "You are so nasty, Vincent. The very worst of the very best people." I wanted so

17

badly to say I knew about the photos.

He laughed, loving it when we bantered back and forth. His eyes narrowed but remained filled with humor. "Oh, I assure you, princess, I am the very best of the very worst."

The name was ironic and I knew it. I was the last girl to be called princess in this neck of the woods.

I swallowed hard, thinking I wasn't sure I wanted to be having this conversation with him.

He stepped forward, leaving the nearly full drink on the counter as if to taunt me with it. I wanted to run but I didn't. He made my stomach twist in knots when he was near me. It was the oddest feeling.

"Oh, Lindsey." He sauntered to me, making my nerves light on fire. "Why don't you let me show you just how good I can be?" He looked down on me, his green eyes lit with that look he always had. I hated it. It was like he was undressing you or imagining a dirty scene being played out. "Make me be good."

I shook my head and brushed past him, walking to his drink. I plucked the straw out and left it on the marble counter before lifting the drink to my lips and sucking it back. I swallowed the last of it and smacked my lips. "You know what your problem is, Vince?"

He grinned wider. "That I have somehow let you slip through my fingers at every opportunity?" His answer was mocking and cocky.

"No. You have never actually had an opportunity. That's all in your head." I took another sip. "Your problem is that you always forget you have a girlfriend. You are truly notorious for forgetting this fact. But luckily for you, your girlfriend is one of my besties. So I can remind you and keep you on track. Like a nun might." *And you have dirty pictures I don't want to talk about.*

"Too bad for you, I have a thing for modest girls." He shook his head, his eyes sparkling in jest. "One day, princess. One day you are going to be begging me to take that v-card." He walked past me, leaving the kitchen and intentionally brushing the back of his hand along my thigh as he did it.

I shuddered and fought the urge to stab him with something.

The door closed and he was gone, but I could smell him in the air. Cologne and confidence and whatever that sneaky smell was that girls couldn't resist. I hated that he smelled good. I knew it was a trap. I imagined even the Venus flytrap smelled good to its prey.

When I got to my room, I checked on the key in my secret stash. It was still there and the room was a complete mess. It was unlikely he had been in here or knew about me sneaking around his room.

I jumped, hearing my phone vibrating with messages and pics from Sierra, Sage, and Lainey. I grabbed it and scanned through them, wrinkling my nose at the invite to her party that had been sent in a group chat among the five of us, started by Rachel of course.

I fell onto my bed dramatically, wishing someone were there to see the effort I put into it. "Noooooo," I moaned.

I couldn't fight the wrinkle becoming more of a glare. Rachel was the one girl in our crowd I would rather not spend warm summer weekends with. Especially since I was spending my weekdays destroying my manicure by working for my father. Weekends had become a bit sacred.

And the rituality of it all started on Fridays.

Rachel's attempts at being a ringleader of sorts for the sophomore girls all year were unbearable, but I tolerated it at school. However, summer was my time.

If I wanted to get drunk by the pool, reading and relaxing, that was my choice. I liked being quiet. I didn't have social ADHD. I didn't need to have a plan for every night of the week.

I pressed a name on my phone and made duck lips at myself as my FaceTime made the ringing sound.

"Hey." Sage smiled sweetly from her makeup table. I saw the banner she had painted in art class hanging above her bed behind her. She was all sugary until she saw me, then she scowled. "What are you wearing? We have to be ready to go at seven. It's five and you look frumpy. Is that pool hair?" Her ruby-red lips—might I add *naturally* ruby-red lips—pursed. "Why do you have to be the annoying one? Just stop. Whatever you're thinking—stop. You're making those wrinkle lines again. You are actually going to age badly. Just stop." She said it like stawwwwp. It was a new thing for her. Everything I did or thought or said, she answered with a STAWWWP!

"I have other plans tonight," I lied. "I can't go to the beach party."

"You're going." She forced a glare but the FaceTime froze with her glaring. It made me laugh. She didn't have very many mean bones in her body. But if she and her brother got into it, she turned into something else fast. And Vincent genuinely brought out a sort of dragon lady in her, but she wasn't the only female with that response to him.

Regardless of how she treated her brother or Vincent, she was one of the sweetest and most giving people I knew.

When people met her, they assumed she was either a ditz or a mean girl. She had all the features of either. Tall, blonde, tanned, blue-eyed, perfect boobs, and leggy. And of course there was the name Sage. It had sealed her fate as the typical dumb blonde or tyrant-esque mean girl.

Getting to know her though, you learned fast that she wasn't exactly what she appeared to be.

Yes, she looked like a cheerleader or an Abercrombie and Fitch ad.

Perhaps she acted like she didn't really have much of a voice to contradict that appearance.

But none of that prepared you for the fact she had low self-esteem, something I blamed her stepdad for.

Her beautiful attributes didn't give you a reason to suspect she was the best photog you had ever seen, instead of the usual model, which everyone assumed she was.

Nothing about her hinted at her ability to draw anything she saw, or that she spent at least ten minutes of every weekend at her father's grave. It was always on Sunday morning. If you slept over at her house it meant you were also going.

And nothing about her warned someone just meeting her that her life wasn't as perfect as it seemed. Mostly because her stepdad was sort of a dick, which said a lot about him to me.

I read once that the mark of a true gentleman was how he treated someone who could do nothing for him, or to him. I think it was Austen who wrote it, and I probably bastardized it. But either way, Sage and her sister Emily could do nothing for their stepdad Tom, and he treated them terribly. Her brother Ashton was the golden boy in Tom Rothberg's mind. The girls might as well have been the maids or nonexistent.

No, everyone assumed they knew Sage by looking at her.

But I would have to say no one knew Sage, not even Sage. She was far wiser than she let on and much less confident than she acted. I had seen the other side of the coin with her many times.

And Vincent didn't seem to be helping any of that. He was a cheating bastard with a nasty picture collection.

The phone unfroze and she closed one eye as she started applying mascara. "Stupid FaceTime. Dude, your face froze with you looking all crazy. I wish I'd been able to take a picture of it for you. You know you have to get ready now, right? It starts soon and we have to go early."

"I don't want to go," I muttered, hoping she might let me off the hook.

"You're going." She opened the eye she was doing, dotting her lid with mascara from her long lashes. "Damn, Linds. What the hell? You made me screw up. I can't do my mean look with one eye." She dabbed and cleaned the dots, but I saw them faintly when she looked at me again. "I am picking you up, and you are going to have fun. It's a beach party. Don't be lame. It's better than the bullshit we have to go to tomorrow night. I am dreading that event. I mean, I have a cute dress and new shoes, but I still don't want to go."

"I know." I sighed and nodded. None of us wanted to go. "Is everyone going?"

"Tomorrow night? Don't tell me you already forgot about the gala?"

I squeezed my eyes together. "No, I mean tonight. Of course, I can't forget about the gala. My dad is stomping around here like a dictator because of it." It was also likely the reason her boyfriend was at my house. His dad had probably asked him to stop in and drop something off. They were all bosom buddies when it came to Crimson Cove Inc.

"Oh. Yeah." She lined her eye, staring at me with one eye and making a weird O shape with her lips while speaking. "You know Sierra wants to go—any excuse to be a slut. Lainey is going since I told her that guy she has the crush on was for sure going to be there because Rachel has invited everyone."

"Her mystery man?" I asked with a wry grin.

"I swear it's Ash's bromance, Jake. If he's anywhere she's going too. She's so obvious."

"He's hot. I would have a crush on him too. But he's not my type."

"He's super hot. What *is* your type?"

I shrugged. "I don't know. I haven't really met it yet." Jake was my type, but he was way too hot for me. All the guys we knew were too hot. I was the plain Jane in the group. Lainey was way hotter than me—even with her thick dork glasses that she swore were a bold fashion statement. She just played down her hotness by wearing weird clothes and slouching and never doing her hair.

"You know you thought Gunter, the German exchange student, was hot."

"Yeah." I didn't want to talk about Gunter.

"He was into you." She smiled as she opened her eyes, again dotting her lids with mascara. "Oh snap. I gotta go. This is brutal. I'm going to look ridiculous if I don't stop talking and doing this."

Again I pursed my lips. "Fine. Pick me up at eight."

"Ten to seven, dick."

"Whatever." I tapped the phone as she said something else, but I didn't care. I was annoyed that I would be spending my night with Rachel herding us about and telling us how fabulous the year to come would be. A year she had been planning for far too long. Eleventh grade was going to be epic. I could hear her voice in my head.

I hated plans and I hated Rachel, and I HATED beach parties. Sand in my shoes, sand in my shorts, sand in my bra, and sand in my hair, all combined with sticky drinks and stinky fires.

My life was already horrendous with the dirty fingernails and the weird tan lines from my job.

After a long week of landscaping like a minion, I didn't want to spend my time out of doors unless it meant being on a patio with a drink.

I didn't even need friends for that. I could read or write and be by myself just as easily.

I still couldn't believe I had a job. It was so pedestrian.

Getting up, smelling the defeat in the air, I hauled on a tee shirt and jean shorts and dragged my jaw-length brown hair into a pathetic ponytail. I wrinkled my nose at the sad little stump at the back of my head. "Why did I ever cut my hair?" I asked the mirror as I shoved my cell phone into my back pocket. The girl in the reflection had nothing. She seemed as disappointed as I was. She had liked the long hair too. I pulled the ponytail out and let my hair fall back to my jaw so it could dry naturally.

After texting Sierra back, I grabbed my keys and bolted. When I got down the stairs, I almost sprinted through the house to avoid the angry version of my father lurking about like a dragon in a keep.

Hanging with Rachel was bad enough, adding my dad being a dick wasn't necessary. Worst weekend ever.

I closed the front door with a slam and hopped into the Maserati GranTurismo—my sweet sixteen prezzie! The engine purred, even when I skidded the tires and squealed out of my driveway. I had tried awfully hard and still couldn't make this car angry. The back end slid a little, declaring my recklessness in case my father missed any of it.

When I got to the end of the driveway the gate was randomly closed and it didn't open. I pulled up really close, hoping the sensor might be on the fritz.

When it didn't even think about budging I sighed.

Slamming that door had been a bad idea. I was

always acting and then thinking—or regretting as it was in this case.

"Shit!" I sat in the car and tapped my fingers against the wheel as I contemplated my options. One being abandoning the car in the driveway and taking my keys. I could climb the fence and walk to the Shack. I wrinkled my nose at that option and jumped out of the convertible, leaving it running with the door open, and walked to the monitor at the gate. I bit my lip and pressed the button. "Daddy, something is wrong with the gate!"

"Linds, we talked about the driveway. We talked about you marking it up. What did I say about that?" His face wasn't present, just mine, thank God. His voice was scary enough.

"Not to," I answered weakly and rubbed my eyes like I was tired. "Daddy, I'm sorry. I was just trying something out from the movie I saw last night. It was that one with the racing drivers—" My lie got higher pitched and died a painful death mid sentence. *Why didn't I watch more racing car movies?*

"And what did I say about the goddamned door?"

That made me flinch. His spicy attitude hovered just under the surface, ready to launch itself at anyone close by. "Not to slam it?" My answer came out like a question.

"And what did I say about sleeping on the job? Andrew was telling me a fabulous little tale about scaring you, while you were sleeping."

And there it was.

I bit my lip and went for the one thing he hated the most. "Uhm, well. I got my period at work. It was really bad. My cramps were awful. I tried working but it just made it worse. And I kinda threw up a little. After I finished my work I took the nap. And I didn't want to tell Andrew so I—"

"Okay." The gate buzzed as he panicked, always avoiding the fact I was a girl. "Don't do it again."

I waved, beaming at the camera. "I totally won't. I'll take Midol next time." An evil chuckle slipped from my lips as I rounded the car and jumped back in, skidding the tires and peeling out, cutting a vehicle off on the main road.

I waved a hand at them as they honked and skidded to a halt.

My car was a dream to drive. I could almost let it do all the work. I had learned to drive on the gardener's beater, a Toyota truck. I nearly killed myself and the gardener eight times learning to drive in it.

Had my father gotten me that instead of this beauty, I might not be alive to piss the people off behind me.

I sped along the coastal highway, my hair flipping about in the warm breeze as I contemplated the many reasons the Blacks might be selling their house.

Was it a divorce?

I loved Crimson Cove divorces. They brought the llamas to the drama and made the gossip so much juicier.

I got lost in thought on the drive, noting the familiar gates of the estates that lined the highway. If you paid attention there was a pattern to them. Every fourth one was the same.

All the beautiful houses were developed by a company my father was a partner in, Crimson Cove Inc. They had started it when I was six, and in the last ten years it had become the vision they had told us all it would be. I smiled, remembering the way I was obsessed with the model they had made, though it was more of a diorama. It came with people, cars, bushes, and flowers—all demonstrating how beautiful Crimson Cove could be, if only it was cleaned up and repopulated with the right kind of people.

The rich kind.

And not just the regular rich—the old-money rich. Those were the preferred people.

Some bits of the original downtown core lingered amongst the newer, fancier versions of everything. But if you looked hard enough, you could still find mom-and-pop restaurants and shops. And if you went to the north, you'd also see a few of the old houses where there was no ocean view, just a bog.

The Shack was one of the long-standing established businesses my father hadn't managed to run out of town. It was a local coffeehouse on the waterfront, right in the cove.

It was my favorite place to hang out. None of my friends liked going there. They preferred to represent in finer establishments.

I often chuckled, pondering if a rich girl drank a coffee in a regular restaurant but didn't have her picture taken, had it even happened?

Maybe it was the reason I came to the Shack, knowing none of my portentous friends would be caught dead here, except Lainey. And even she towed the line of expectations rather tersely.

As I pulled up to the small building and the smell of coffee wafted over my head, I sighed. "Heaven."

The car made a subtle beep as it locked when the door closed and I sauntered inside. Hailey, the slightly emo-looking barista, offered a wave. I smiled at her, walking past the lineup of desperate java seekers. The tension in my neck eased and the possibility of a headache vanished when the full scent of the shop permeated my pores.

I loved coffee.

"You back again?" Hailey asked, almost flirting with me. She was just the type of girl I wanted to flirt with.

Firstly, she wasn't a lesbian so she wasn't ever going to expect this, whatever it was, to move beyond the subtlety it had peaked at. We laughed like little girls and teased each other, but there was no pressure or expectations.

Secondly, she was stunningly beautiful but in all the indirect ways, ways that attracted me. Dark hair with a hint of beachy wave to it. A deep dimple in only her left cheek. Her skin was pale, contradicting the beachy waves, and her smile wasn't always real. Sometimes it sat there on her face, lingering and left behind while her eyes had already changed to a subject she didn't share aloud. Whatever she was thinking, contradicted the smile on her face.

Her eyes were amazingly bright blue—the kind you wished you could borrow, like you did a sweater.

And thirdly, she was super cool. The kind of cool that required zero effort. She didn't try. Her personality wasn't exaggerated or fake, which around here was unheard of. She was just mellow and sort of poor and a little humble in the way people who don't expect anything are. If I had to set her up with someone, it would be Andrew. I think in a world without expectations, they would be the perfect coupling.

He could smoke pot and tell her his weird stories, and she would have zero drama for him to bother with. But she did have a boyfriend. One I hadn't met yet. He lived out here somewhere, along the shore. I assumed it was in one of the small houses in the North.

Her piece-of-shit cobalt blue Ford Taurus was exactly how I imagined Andrew's room looked, just chaos and yet an invisible system was in place. It was how my room looked. I nearly died, gleaning information from the car the one time I was in it. I suspected she lived in the car, maybe randomly sleeping at her boyfriend Zack's when she needed to, but otherwise she was in the car. Her purse was in the car. If you wanted floss or lip gloss, it was on the floor. Her bank card was in the glove compartment. Her ID was strewn about in amongst the clothes. That cardigan she wore last week that I liked, lay on the back window.

Had I been given the chance, I would have sifted through the debris, finding it all disturbing and yet tantalizing, like reading an interview with a bomber or mass murderer.

My assumptions from what I had seen were listed in my mind like a to-do list:

- She was an only child. There were no photos in the car of her and family and no phone calls when you were mid conversation, which made me think there was no one but her. My dad hounded my ass a lot.
- Her parents were clearly not part of her life. She never spoke of them and when asked she changed the subject as if she hadn't heard me. Also her financial situation screamed she had no daddy she could call and beg money from. I got the distinct impression they were people she wanted nothing to do with. My imagination whispered that she might have fled, maybe in the night, making her all that much cooler.

- She liked the color black far more than any girl I had ever met and not in the glamorously slimming way. It was in a way that told me she wanted to blend or not be noticed.
- She looked over her shoulder when she talked. I questioned whether she might actually be wanted, like by the authorities. As in maybe she wasn't really nineteen and maybe if someone recognized her she would have to go home to her horrid parents. I mean, she did look younger—more like my age.
- She was a hard worker, the sort who possibly grew up with a job or a ridiculous amount of responsibility. I had seen it in a few kids at school. When a common sense moment came at us, they were always the only survivors. The rest of us rich kids sort of stood there, baffled at how they had responded so quickly. But in our defense we had maids to clean our mothers and fathers up off the floor and cooks to ensure there was a meal when our parents were still sleeping at four in the afternoon.
- She didn't throw away anything. She had mixed tapes from the nineties. I had seen them stored lovingly in her glove compartment, instead of on the floor next to her deodorant.
- She was my first girl crush. Not in a sexual way, but in the sort where I wanted to see what was inside her head. Every choice she made was the opposite of mine. Every idea she had was contrary to what a regular girl would say. A regular rich girl, that was. I had once seen her wash tinfoil. It was insane.

My cheeks flushed as I watched her fill orders and smile awkwardly at people who forced eye contact from her. It had taken me weeks to get her to look me in the eye, like meeting a skittish animal for the first time.

Her pale skin glowed as her eyes darted nervously away from the person in front of her.

I grinned, biting my lip and wondering if she inspected me as closely as I did her. Or if anyone had ever inspected me this closely.

When it was finally my turn at the counter, my drink was waiting for me. She tilted her head and toyed with her lip ring, flicking it with her tongue. "Did you see there's a solar storm tonight? Should be fairly badass."

"Let me guess, you have a telescope in your car?" I mocked her but nodded internally because I did know about the storm and already had my telescope pulled out of the pool house.

She snorted, pushing the drink at me and shaking her head. "I wish."

"I have one." I nodded. "It's not the Hubble but it works. Wanna meet at my place, at say one? I have a beach thing to go to, but I can escape, I'm sure."

"What's the beach thing?" Her smile widened, dragging my eyes to her pink lips. She didn't even have lip gloss on. Her lips were just a pretty color of pink.

"Party. Beach party." I rolled my eyes as I slid ten dollars at her. "Everyone will be paired off for the evening, thinking themselves so clever at not getting caught climbing into the wrong sports cars. I should be able to get away."

She leaned forward. "You don't plan on climbing into the wrong sports car?"

"Have you seen my car?" I cocked an eyebrow. "It's amazing. I don't cheat on it ever." I lifted the drink. "Thanks." I left without my change, wondering if I was being too cheesy by overtipping and if she would see that as portentous.

I didn't know how to act with her. She was out of my league.

A league I imagined I was alone in.

Because deep down I always sort of thought I was out of my friends' league in a lot of ways. Maybe not looks but in smarts, definitely.

CHAPTER THREE
Kiss my Manolos

"Why are you wearing that?" Sage plucked my tank top and scowled at me in my mirror as I smeared some Buxom lip plumper on. "Is it cotton?" She wrinkled her nose.

I glanced down in the mirror. "Stop." I used her STAWWP. I even made the weird voice she always did when she said it.

She rolled her eyes. "Can't you at least try to throw on something remotely close to sexy? You have the nicest arms. Why not showcase those shoulder blades?" She ran her hand across the top of my chest softly, making me feel weird.

"Dude, seriously? Stop."

"Look, you have muscles." She pinched my bicep.

"It's called hard work. My dad thinks I came over on a boat and need to work for basic human rights. He's a slave driver."

She chuckled. "That's not a very politically correct joke."

I cocked a dark-brown eyebrow. "Careful, Sage. Your smarty pants are showing. Dumb blondes don't know politically correct is a thing."

"Whatever."

"Sage, can you do this? My mom always does it, but she isn't here. She's not back till tomorrow night." Lainey looked up at us from my bed. Her blinking and tearing eyes were red from trying to get her contacts in. Normally, she didn't bother with them, unless we were going out and her mom was in town. Her mom always demanded she wore them, hating the fact Lainey had glasses.

"You have to get used to doing it. Just wear the contacts every day." Sage sighed and slumped on my bed. "Why don't you just do the laser?"

"My prescription is still changing. They won't do it until it's done changing. The doctor said closer to nineteen." She winced but kept her eye open as Sage slid it in. "And if I wear the contacts every day my eyes will be worse candidates for the laser."

"Better?"

"Much." Lainey sighed softly; it was the way she did everything. She brushed her lush chestnut hair behind her ears and gave Sage another look. "Uhm—"

"Oh my God, you need me to do your makeup too, don't you?"

"I can't see as well close up with the contacts." Lainey blushed, looking sweet. She had the finest cheekbones in the world, normally hidden by thick black-framed glasses. Her skin was pale from a serious lack of sunlight and an even more serious gamer addiction. She and I were the two oddballs in the random group of friends. All our parents had been part of the same social group since we were very little, which had made it easy to become friends, but hard to actually hang out as we were growing up to be so different.

To the rest of Crimson Cove, we were *the* exclusive country club kids. To them we didn't have personalities or differing lifestyles.

From a distance we appeared to be everyday rich girls, sporting Fendi bags and clothes or shoes from a designer no one had heard of yet—this week it was Kim Haller.

But in reality, when no one was watching, only Sierra, Sage, and Rachel looked that way. Lainey and me were the shame of our households. Lainey for the way she looked and me for the way I looked and spoke.

"Have you met Marguerite yet?" Sage asked. "Though she prefers Rita for some ungodly reason. Rita! Can you imagine?"

Lainey shrugged. "We had a cook named Rita once."

Sage nodded. "My point exactly. It's much nicer don't

you think, as Marguerite?"

"No. I don't know." I shook my head, not sure which question I had actually answered but liking the name Rita and not caring either way. "I heard she and her mom are finally moving here this summer. Her dad has been the mayor for seven months already. You'd think they would have come sooner."

"They're here now." Sage grinned. "And they *are* interesting. Marguerite is Rachel's new BFF. They have been doing everything together for like a week. And I even heard she talks with a Louisiana accent like her dad when it's convenient for her, but she's a New Yorker through and through. My cousin went to cotillion with her. Says she can flip it back to Jersey if her crème fraîche isn't fresh enough, but when guys are in the room she is Miss Southern Belle."

Lainey sighed. "Great. Another Rachel. At least that means they'll think they're too good for us and not expect us to hang too much."

"I hate the way if I don't message Rachel back fast enough, she gets her mom to message the stepmonster and then suddenly I'm on a scheduled playdate." And I hated nothing like I did hanging out with Rachel alone.

"Like tonight," Lainey added bitterly.

"Raid night?" I asked, cracking a grin.

"Maybe," she sneered. "Don't act like you didn't already know there was a solar storm and that the sky is going to be remarkable tonight. Even *we* might see the northern lights. Which, I know I don't have to tell you, never happens down here."

We both looked mournful as we sighed, but Sage snapped her fingers. "Stop! Dork out later. Sierra is meeting us at my place in like ten minutes!"

"We're going to your house?" Somehow that lit a fire under Lainey's butt. She lifted her face, closed her eyes, and didn't move again until Sage said it was okay.

When Sage was done with Lainey's makeup, we sauntered from the room, each texting up a storm on our phones as we walked down the hall.

I read over the message to Rachel, finally responding

that I was *totally coming!!!* Ugh.

When I looked up, the stepmonster was just getting up and putting on her "company" face as we walked past the parlor. "Girls, you going to Rachel's festivities tonight?" Her eyes landed on me and her nose wrinkled and away went her pleasant face for company. "Lindsey, darling, what are you wearing? Is that cotton?"

I glanced down at my simple gray tank top from Calvin Klein and a Ralph Lauren flared black mini skirt. "What?"

"It's awfully casual." Her green eyes darted to Sage. "Is that Dolce & Gabbana?"

Sage nodded, looking confused. It was a dumb question. Sage only ever wore D&G, Dior, or Valentino. She went everywhere looking like she might be walking a catwalk at any given moment. Her clothing always had to be the very best. Sometimes I wished I had her style, but then I would be elbow deep in a plate of nachos and a sundae and remember I am a human who needs cheese and carbs and accepted a size six quite easily.

"Beach parties are dirty and I like casual clothes. I have on Manolo Blahniks. That should satisfy even you." I narrowed my gaze. "And besides, Sage doesn't have to dig for a living so she can wear whatever she wants. Her entire life is spent lounging and grooming. Whereas I have to think about the fact the dirt under my nails might not match my Dolce & Gabbana dress."

Sage parted her lips, but I shot her a look. She snapped her mouth shut and nodded.

"Those are flats. No one wears flats with a mini skirt. Your legs would look much better in a pair of heels." Louisa gasped again, glancing at Lainey smoothing her cute Kim Haller sleeveless dress. It was the one I loved. It was cream colored and covered in words written in differing fonts and colors.

I had a cream-colored summer dress from Kim Haller too, but I hardly wore it because she was an up-and-coming designer, and therefore not to be worn to any of the functions I might actually wear dresses to—according to the rules of the Bueller household. But only since the new regime.

My last stepmom, Number Two, hadn't made the same demands of me socially. She was more concerned with not getting caught having sex with the staff.

"Honestly, Lindsey, some heels wouldn't kill you and maybe a different top?"

"I'm being ironic wearing flats and being short," I lied, hoping she wouldn't understand the word ironic and let it go before I ended up trudging around Rachel's yard in heels.

The stepmonster relented with an eye roll. "Fine. Dress down like a commoner. Just don't come home before midnight though."

She knew me too well.

I offered my "screw you" smile and headed for the door, even more determined to be home before eleven. I didn't skid on the drive out; I didn't need my two closest friends to see me getting reprimanded by my father through the camera at the gate. I didn't need anyone to know that was how he parented most days.

As I turned out onto the road, I opened the car up. The wind in my hair made me smile, but I was the only one smiling.

"Why do we have to have the top down?" Sage shouted as she pulled up her Pucci scarf to cover her hair. In the rearview I laughed as Lainey suffered through trying to hold her long dark locks in place.

"I like the top down." My short straight hair had few perks. Being able to ride with the top down was one of them.

I parked in the driveway of Sage's house, noting her older brother's Jeep was there. I prayed Rachel wasn't. I didn't need an early start with her. I hated that they were dating and she was always at Sage's house.

As we got out of the car Sage's older brother, Ashton, walked out of the house. He offered us all a grin and nod of the head. "Ladies." He was the hottest guy at our school, which said a lot. We didn't have a single homely kid. Some might have started eighth grade a little frumpy or weird looking, but by tenth grade they were downright beautiful or handsome. Some kids had the summer of "travel" plastic surgery or fat camp while others just started to outgrow their awkwardness.

"Ash!" Sage offered back a middle finger.

I waved, frowning at Sage. She never came in hot and heavy, not first anyway. He usually provoked her—well she called it provoked, I called it joking.

Ashton was the nicest guy in the senior class. He was smart, kind, brave, and undeserving of a girlfriend as evil as Rachel Swanson. But he was a sheep to Rachel's wolfish behavior. Watching her parade him around, flaunting the fact she was dating a senior who happened to be the star quarterback, made me queasy.

"Sage, why you gotta be so rude?" He shook his head.

"Why do you have to be so dumb?" She scoffed.

I swallowed hard, hating it when they fought. My eyes darted to Lainey who looked down at her nails to admire the fresh paint and pretend not to listen to the sibling war.

"You coming to the beach?" he asked me, maybe trying to be friendly and ignore his sister.

"Of course we are. Her Highness has beckoned." I chuckled.

"I'm sure she did." He laughed and nodded as he walked up to his huge Jeep. "She's not so bad. You need a ride?"

"Please—like we would ride with you. We're going with Sierra's driver. Just tell me that you're still planning on breaking up with Rachel tonight?" Sage folded her arms and smiled wickedly.

"Stop listening in on my conversations." His dark-blue eyes narrowed.

"Stop having them so loudly. You have more white-girl problems than any of my friends."

"You're a real asshole sometimes, Sage." He seemed pissed as he jumped in and started the Jeep, driving off in a huff.

Lainey offered a confused look. "He's dumping Rachel tonight?"

Sage shrugged. "I friggin' hope so. But I think we all know she'll smooth talk her way back in. He intends to try, as far as I heard him say, but I don't think he has the guts to break up with her. You think we have it bad with Mrs. I Rule The Roost? You should see how she treats him when no one is looking." She turned and stormed inside.

If ever you wanted to see the worst behavior out of Sage Miller, it was when she and her brother fought. It wasn't often but it was always heated. Otherwise, they were both some of the nicest people I knew.

"I told you, Rachel reminds me of Louisa. You watch, we'll all turn thirty, and my dad will start dating her after he divorces Louisa. He'll be sixty friggin' years old and still looking for that new young 'thang' to be mean to him and spend his money."

Lainey laughed but Sage still seemed annoyed. "You all right?" I asked her as Lainey sat on the couch.

Sage sighed and gave me a look I knew to mean she was not okay. She eyed Lainey and then me. "You guys can't say it was me who told you. Swear!"

I crossed my heart as Lainey nodded.

Her eyes stopped on me again. "I was driving over to your house yesterday when you got off work, and I saw Rachel. She was on the side of the road, leaning against her car with some guy, leaned up against her. I have never seen a guy like that, not here anyway. And I have never seen Rachel like that, all plain looking. It was so weird. He was—"

"Older?" I thought I'd be helpful.

"Gangsta?" Lainey jumped in, also helpful.

"Hip-hipster." Sage shook her head and shuddered as if the words she had whispered made her sick. "Like he just got here on the bus from the Village."

Lainey and I both leaned back in disbelief.

"What?" I asked, knowing deep down hipster was my dream fantasy, if I ever found a guy I wanted to date. But how many future bankers were hipsters? My dad and Louisa had compiled my list of men to date and hipster dudes were not on that list.

But as much as I fantasized over a boy who could

quote sonnets and sing like Damien Rice, Rachel did not. She had practically written the list of boys I was to date, with my parents. And every one of them was a Young Republican.

"Seriously. He was wearing a wooly winter hat and a knitted sweater that was layered over,"—she paused and took a breath—"layered over a white extra long tee shirt. I think it was a ladies' shirt. And he had low-slung skinnies on with Chucks."

Basically, my dream guy.

"And he had a beard. In the summer."

Not my dream guy. At all. Abort!

I had seen that CNN report about the filth in beards. A little scruff was one thing but a full beard, no. No bueno.

"A wool hat in the middle of summer?" Lainey wrinkled her forehead. "That is the true sign of a douche nozzle. It's the douche nozzle calling card. Wow. And a beard. Maybe he's in a boy band."

I shook my head, mystified and speechless. Even Lainey didn't approve, and she was pretty chilled out about guys and fashion.

"And they were making out. I saw them in my rearview. His hands wrapped around and were cupping her butt." Sage cringed. "Did you see the CNN report on beards?"

Lainey held a hand up, waving the words off. "Shhhhhhh. No. Stop."

"Dude." I fake gagged. "Stop!"

"She's cheating on my brother, *my* brother, with some scungy Greenwich Village loser. I can't even—I don't even know what to say. I mean, I knew she was sleazy, and I warned Ashton when they started dating, but this is a whole new level. It's just too much to take. The very insult of it is over the top." She turned and walked into the kitchen to get us a beverage. "My mom would lose her shit. Ashton is at Yale next year, and he doesn't even have to apply. He's a catch, a total catch. He's the star quarterback for God's sake, so even if we lived in a normal town, he would be the hottest guy there. I don't know why he wasted his time with a girl like her. I could kill her for what it will do to him. She was never going to be anything respectable. I think we all saw that."

And that was officially the meanest thing I had ever heard her say.

Lainey narrowed her gaze. "So you're not mad at Ash then?"

"No. I'm pissed at Rach. She's a ho. I mean, I'm mad he's dumb."

Lainey raised her eyebrows again. "I agree. I just—" She paused. "Nothing."

"Spit it out, Lain. No one wants to listen to you do the sputtering thing!"

My jaw dropped but I didn't have to defend Lainey, she jumped right to it. In fact, she lost it. "Screw you, Sage! You were a bitch to Ash, and I don't understand why, if you're mad at Rachel and not him. I could kill her too for what she did to him, but you don't have to take it out on me, or Ash." Her face was flushed and sort of sweaty. She lifted her finger to push up her glasses, but they weren't there and she looked at her finger, confused when it didn't make contact.

"I can yell at my own brother whenever I want!"

I lifted my hands. "Whoa. Whoa, ladies. Easy, Sage. You're kinda needing a Snickers right now. Stop."

She breathed heavily through her nose for half a heartbeat before she sighed and walked to Lainey, forcing her into an embrace. "Sorry, Lain. I just hate that she is pretending to be so into my brother so she can have all her invites to be with the seniors and act so much better than us. But really she's slumming with some random and making my brother look like a moron."

Lainey nodded and I was shocked to see she was nearly as angry as Sage was. She didn't ever give two shits about Ashton or any other guy, except her dream man who she refused to name. But she did hate Rachel on the same level as I did, so maybe that was it.

"What are you two hugging it out for? Lezzzz go to the party, bitches!" Sierra walked in, interrupting the tense moment. She winked and laughed. "Are we ready to go or what?"

Sierra always looked like a movie star. She was tall and skinny everywhere, except the places that mattered. She had actual junk in her trunk, but not too much, and huge boobs.

We all believed God was on her side.

No matter what, she always landed on her feet, looked hot, and managed to never get caught for anything. And her parents didn't give a damn about what she did. If my father saw me in the dress she was wearing, he would lock the gate and never open it again. But her dad probably wasn't even home to care.

Tonight her tight white mini dress was so nineties chic it made me think she might bust out some coke any second. Or do the Sharon Stone leg-crossing thing all night. Lord knew Sierra wasn't wearing any underwear either. She never did.

She wore huge white stiletto platforms to match the dress, and pinkish lipstick to go with the blush on her alabaster skin. Not that she needed it, or accessories. She had fiery red hair to her waist with beachy waves and slight blonde hints to bring out the color.

She flashed her bright-blue eyes at me and nodded toward the door. "Leaving before all the hot guys are taken by the townie sluts I know Rachel invited?"

"Townie sluts?" Sage narrowed her gaze. "Did you see a hipster guy in that mix?"

Sierra nodded, primping in the huge hallway mirror. "Yeah. What was up with that? Rachel brought him to Andrew's house last night. It was awkward as balls."

"As balls?" Lainey asked. I too was confused as to the reference and it's relation.

Sierra laughed and reiterated, "*As balls.*"

I sort of wished I had gone to Andrew's when he invited me so I could have seen the hipster beard dude.

Sierra snapped her fingers as she walked out of the house. "Move, ladies!"

She was the feisty one.

We always joked that if we were ever to become the next set of Spice Girls, I would be Beefy Spice because I am shorter and stalky and get muscles. Lainey would be Nerdy Spice, obviously. Sierra would be Feisty Spice. Sage would be Spacey Spice. Rachel's name depended on if she was with us. If not with us, she was Bitchy Spice. If she was with us, she was Sexy Spice. She actually named herself that after we had all joked about our own names. *Of course.*

I got up and followed Sage, who was over her rant as fast as it had come on, and Lainey who still seemed out of sorts. She kept blinking and looking down.

"You okay?" I asked.

She shook her head. "How could she do that to Ashton—Rachel I mean? How could she cheat on *him*?" She said him with a lot of emphasis. She wasn't even mad that Sage had snapped at her. "She's the luckiest girl and she doesn't even know it." Lainey was my best friend, in the entire world, but I didn't know what she was on about. She was officially the last girl on earth I might have suspected had feelings for Ashton. But in that moment I wondered if he could be her mystery man.

Not that she would tell me. She wasn't like that.

"I don't know. Ashton is pretty awesome. Maybe he will break up with her and be free." I nudged her.

She nodded but said nothing. That was her way. She was soft-spoken in nature, which made some people overlook her, but I adored her. If you knew her well enough, you knew she was funny—witty.

She was smart, really smart. And she was pretty, in her own way. She had a slim build, the exact opposite of Sierra. She had no junk at all. Her trunk was in the negatives. It drove her insane to be so skinny.

It drove the rest of us nuts that she could eat whatever she wanted and never gain weight, except in her boobs. They were actually all right for a skinny girl. Not like "Sierra all right," whereas most people assumed hers were fake.

The thing I loved the most about Lainey was her eidetic memory. It was fascinating to watch it work, like reading about a serial killer to find out how or why they do the things they do.

She could read anything or see anything, and it was there in her mind for life.

Some things were bad to remember forever, and she had plenty of those.

"Not that it matters to us, right? We don't have to clean up Rachel's messes." I linked my arm in hers and leaned my head on her shoulder. "Who is ready for a fun night?"

She sighed. "Me."

It was about as convincing as the "me" going on inside me . . .

CHAPTER FOUR
Arrrrrrr, me matey

The driver took us the long route. When Sage was clearly deep in a text or something on her phone, I leaned into Sierra and whispered extra quietly, "Is Vince meeting us there? I thought he would be our ride or at least be with us." I was grateful he wasn't, but it was weird they weren't together. They hadn't been hanging out much all summer—if at all. I, on the other hand, had been seeing tons of him.

She shrugged and spoke so softly my ear tingled from her breath on it, "I don't know what's up with him and Sage. She hasn't said a word to me about him since I told her he was being a douche. I doubt she will now. She's pissed with me but doing the thing where she pretends it's fine."

Sierra and Sage were complete besties. Before Sage's dad died, he and Sierra's dad were best friends—almost brothers.

The two girls had been inseparable until recently, and I blamed Vincent. I didn't have any proof that it was him, but I just liked to grumble his name as *Vincent* in my head and blame everything on him.

I did know though that Sierra blamed Vincent for the friendship dying off a little and Sage blamed Sierra.

I stayed out of it but had listened closely enough to safely assume Vincent was completely to blame.

He was a cheating, lying, disgusting excuse for a boyfriend.

"I did his yard yesterday and found a bunch of nasty pictures in his room and on his computer. He has totally been cheating on Sage, I think with that disgusting whore,

Sasha." My voice was hardly a whisper.

"I know." Sierra nodded. "He tried his shit with me. We were crazy drunk like two weeks ago, and he totally came on to me. Sage was sleeping. I kicked him in the balls. Now he hates me. I tried to tell Sage what happened but she thinks I hit on him. He must have lied to her. She's been really cold with me since, not mad but just like cut off sort of." Catching Sage's eyes on us, Sierra pressed the button and spoke demandingly into the mic, "Where the hell are you taking us? Why is this taking so long?"

"Sorry, miss. I heard on the local radio there was an accident on the other road. So I thought we might avoid the delays. Apparently, a tree came down over some lines," the driver spoke back softly. I could hardly hear him.

Sierra groaned. "I hate long car rides. Do we have booze back here?" She leaned forward and opened her dad's bar. A grin spread across her face. "Yes, we do." She pulled us each a tiny bottle of tequila and passed them out.

I wanted to say no thanks, but I knew the odds of me not drinking with them weren't good. No one argued with Sierra, except Rachel. They were always toe to toe, bickering about something.

Sage lifted her tiny bottle and smiled wryly. "To Rachel, may she rot in hell."

Sierra coughed. "That is my kind of toast. Screw you, Rachel." She looked longingly at Sage, smiling.

We all clinked our little bottles and sucked back the shot. I winced and Lainey fully shuddered.

Sierra shook it off. "Why are we toasting her demise this time?"

"She's cheating on Ash with that dude with a beard you said she brought to Andrew's," Lainey offered up with another shiver.

Sierra wrinkled her nose. "The moment I saw him all I thought was, who has a beard in the summer? Like is he a pirate or a captain?"

I laughed at Sierra. "No. I think he's from the East Village."

"Ugh, of course he is." She made a face. "Gross. We

need to get close enough to see if he smells like weed and patchouli. I hate that combination. I like them both separately but not together." She fished out another bottle for us all—this time vodka. "Well, I say good riddance for Ash. I wish we were rid of her that easily."

Lainey sighed. "Yeah."

There wasn't one of us that would argue that point. But how did you get rid of someone who all your parents loved and forced upon you? Even worse, we constantly had our family gatherings. Ditching her as a friend would make it awkward. College would be my escape. I planned on Brown and I was alone in that choice.

We all drank our next shot as the driver finally pulled off the road, stopping just before the large house in the circular driveway.

Rachel's house was sizable. Not as fancy as Sierra's or Sage's and not as enormous as mine or Lainey's. But it was somewhere in the middle of them all. It was a waterfront estate, the very feature Crimson Cove was known for. Well, except of course, the trees all turning red in the fall and lighting the entire cove up with crimson colors.

We climbed out when the driver opened the door. He kept his hat on and head down, with his eyes to the road. I didn't trust people who wouldn't look you in the eyes.

Sierra grabbed my hand and dragged me away from the car. "Let's get drunk and see if we can't accidentally fall in love for an hour or two."

I wanted to protest, but I didn't.

Music boomed from the back of the estate where the sea and sand provided the backdrop for a dusk-filled skyline with overly dressed teenagers having fun. I knew it was too much of a draw for Sierra and played along.

The music was loud but the crowd was louder. There had to be two hundred of our closest friends here.

Sierra let go of my hand, throwing her arms into the air and hugging a dark-haired girl. I leaned forward and grimaced, seeing it was Sasha.

Sage had her head high, scanning the crowd, no doubt looking for the douche-bag pervert she called a boyfriend.

Lainey came and slipped her arm into mine again. "Hey, don't leave me, kay?"

I shook my head. "Don't leave me either."

We strolled out into the sunset and the chaos. I remembered what I wanted to ask her. "Dude, I meant to ask you. Why are the Blacks buying a new house? They just bought a house."

She laughed. "They're insane. They think their house is haunted. Such morons. They actually got my dad to list it, like last week, and they want to buy one section of the market property, but our dads have rich Europeans building a gated community there. The Van Harkers have already bought the land. My dad said today that the Blacks are pissed because they heard about the sale. They think they had the request in to buy the land before Dad sold it, which is true. So they're upset and feeling cheated. But they were only buying one lot and the Van Harkers would only buy it if they got all the land."

"That's disappointing. I thought it was something juicier than ghosts. I figured Mrs. Black got caught for that affair she's been having with that high school kid who plays hockey for Notre Dame. I really thought they were getting a divorce."

"Oh my God, you have to stop snooping in people's shit. You're going to get caught one of these days."

"Maybe." I winked at her.

"Lainey! Lindsey! Drinks!" Glasses were shoved into our hands as the giver, a blonde girl, ran off again. I didn't even see her face, just hands and shouting and then a drink.

I shrugged and lifted the red liquid to my lips, but Lainey snatched it, dumping them both out. "Remember when we were at that party in eighth grade and that Nathan kid put Ecstasy in everyone's drinks and we were high as hell, in New York City?"

I opened my mouth but my frown gave it away.

"How do you not remember that? I threw up outside that barbecue place and the man chased us with a broom."

"Oh yeah. I remember that. I had that weird hot dog

with the cheese in the middle, and I kept stroking your hair and saying that I loved you. That was awkward."

"I called it death on a stick—the hot dog."

"Right." A smile owned my face as I laughed. "That was horrible." I looked down at the drinks. "Good call."

She sighed and walked to the bar. "Two vodka and cranberry juice with a squeeze of lime and a splash of Perrier."

The bartender nodded and got to work. He seemed familiar but I couldn't place him.

"Where do I—?"

"That time we all went boating with the Frasiers and you got seasick. He was the bartender who cleaned you up and hid you so Louisa would stop shouting at you."

He winked at me from behind the bar.

"Right." I winced and remembered how vile that felt as well. "We have a lot of throw-up stories."

"Try recalling them all as if they happened only a second ago. Sometimes I get sick when I think about it too much."

"Gross."

"Yup." She gazed into the crowd and sighed. "I wonder if Ash broke up with Rachel yet."

I cringed. "Oh, she is going to be heinous to be around until she finds a way to get him back or finds something better to replace him with."

Lainey laughed bitterly. "You mean something she can actually parade about the club, something she would be allowed to date."

"Not the bearded dude."

She agreed. "Not the bearded dude."

"We should see if one of our parents wants to take us somewhere, like tomorrow. Like France. We can hide out there for the last few weeks of summer."

"Seriously?" She gave me a look. "You forgot about the gala already, didn't you?"

I opened my mouth to say no, but I nodded and laughed. "I really don't want to go."

"Me either. But our fathers are the forefathers of this

great and amazing town."

I rolled my eyes and took my drink from the bartender as he put them up. He offered a huge smile and another wink. I frowned and took my drink, desperately hoping he didn't remember me and that was why he was being friendly.

"So, if I tell you something, can we never speak of it again?" I needed to tell her about the terrible pictures so she could rationalize it for me. I hated Vincent, but I didn't want to *hate* Vincent.

"I won't bring it up again, but I'll likely never be rid of it. Is that the sort of promise you are looking for?"

I shook my head. "Forget it."

"Oh, now you have to tell." She nudged me and took a sip.

I opened my mouth to say no but a scream made me jump.

"ASSHOLE!"

We both turned to see Rachel shoving Ashton at the docks. She screamed again, like she was hurt but she looked fine, apart from the screaming rage.

"Oh, sweet Jesus. He just did it."

Lainey's jaw dropped as she turned her head. "Oh snap."

Rachel shoved Ashton again before storming up the dock to the patio and across the grass. Her chestnut hair bounced behind her as the most evil look claimed her face. Ashton appeared upset running after her. I leaned into Lainey and muttered, "He is a dead man."

"Hopefully not." She looked worried for a second until we saw Ashton leaving and not running after Rachel at all.

"Come on, you two. You are taking forever." Sierra interrupted and grabbed our hands, pulling us into the crowd to dance just as the DJ started a new song up.

I sucked back my drink and started dancing, letting go of everything.

Ashton and Rachel were not my problem; I didn't need to solve them. As much as I wanted the gossip, and I wanted to know the "who, what, where, when, and why," it wasn't actually my problem.

And I had somewhere important to be in a few hours. The solar storm was going to be better than the one a few years ago. But that wasn't the best part. The best part was Hailey. I was sort of excited to hang with her again, and maybe I was excited because I was curious about how I felt about her.

I knew everyone had called me a lesbian behind my back—or even better—a dike since I had cut my hair to my jawline. And I had never been with anyone so I wasn't sure if I was able to classify my interests.

I'd kissed a couple of guys, but they were more like frogs and less like princes. So while the idea of being with a guy who loved me more than anything in the world was intriguing, I wasn't one-hundred-percent sure if I just had a girl crush on Hailey or if I had feelings for her.

A small part of me sort of wished Hailey was the real deal for me.

And I honestly didn't know what I would do if she was.

My world didn't have room for extremes like that.

CHAPTER FIVE
This brings a new meaning to CRIMSON Cove

The evening flew by, filled with drinking, dancing, and laughing.

The sun faded and it got dark, taking away the royal blue and then the midnight blue of the sky as the light vanished completely.

Before I knew it I was a little buzzed and a lot tired of dancing.

I wiped the sweat from my brow, grateful I had used my makeup setting spray on my face. The party had turned out to be more fun than I had anticipated, mostly because of Sierra and Lainey who were still dancing.

Rachel had been scarce, her night no doubt ruined.

I wasn't sorry for her. She had made her bed.

I wandered down to watch the sea from the railing of the deck for a moment, not sure whether I was ready to go home or not. It felt like a huge decision to go. Like I was making the choice by leaving the party.

I dismissed the thought and told myself I needed to leave because it was close to midnight, and I would need to assemble the telescope. The stepmonster had felt it clogged up her chi in the feng shui and had shoved it into the pool house.

I didn't even know what she meant; our house was surrounded by a giant patio with heaps of space for everyone and everything. We had seven conversation pits set up around the backyard.

Clogging was an extreme word choice.

I had already dragged it out onto the deck, but it was

in a couple of pieces so I had to assemble it quickly.

The music stopped long enough for me to hear screaming. I turned back, seeing the power had gone off. Everyone moved in amongst the solar lights, calling to their friends. The lights flashed once and then came back on, bringing the music with them. In the shadows on the dock I noticed someone near me. I held my breath until I heard his voice.

"Hey, princess. What's going on?"

"Seriously, stop calling me that." I glanced over, wrinkling my nose as Vincent—a wasted version of Vincent—nestled in next to me at the railing. From a distance he was absolutely gorgeous. Dark hair, tanned skin, green eyes, and a smile that always suggested he was thinking something naughty about you. He was a tall drink of water, but the water was vodka and up close he reeked of dysfunction and alcohol.

"You look lonely." He nudged himself closer and slid his arm around me, pulling me into him while looking down on me with that smile. I shuddered and leaned away from him as the stale alcohol breath seeped into my space when he spoke, "Why don't we go for a walk and you can tell me about your summer. I saw you laboring away yesterday," he muttered as he lifted his hand into my hair. "And why did you cut your beautiful hair off? It was so nice and silky. Perfect hair for a perfect princess."

"Where?" I pulled back, startled. "I mean, where's Sage?" *Oh God, did he see me at his house? Where had he seen me laboring?* "Stop calling me princess. I will cut you, I swear it!"

He flung his free hand and motioned like he was lost on words. "Gone. She was yelling at Rachel because Rachel was yelling at Ash and he left hours ago and hasn't come back so Rachel's even more pissed about that. It was a hot mess. They were in the bushes. I'm wearing Gucci. I don't trek about the woods in designer shoes. Anyway, it was tedious and pathetic." He leaned back into me, pulling me to him. "You look like a hot mess. I like this skirt, princess." He brushed a hand on the back of my bare thigh, lifting my skirt just slightly while saying princess with even more affect.

I shoved him back. "Stop! Dude. You're dating one of my best friends and you're a pervert. And I am the *last* girl to be called a princess. If either of us is a princess, it's you."

"Everyone is a pervert, Linds." He shook his head. "And no one actually dates Sage. She's more of a trophy you carry around for a bit, claiming your conquest, and then moving on." He laughed and pointed a finger at me. "But you—you are trouble. I saw that from a mile. Just let me see if this is what I think it is." He leaned in closer, moving fast and pressing his lips against mine.

My heartbeat increased as he pressed my chest into his and squished me, stealing all my breath.

My knee came up hard, before I even had a chance to wrestle with the idea of doing it. I didn't like kneeing boys in the balls. It was a committed choice once you went in, so I didn't ever want to do it unless absolutely necessary.

He groaned as I made contact and his knees buckled. "Oh, shit. You wanna play rough?"

I laughed and stepped back. "You have some serious issues. I wanna play slap you around for a while if you try that with me again."

"We can do that too," he spoke through a groan.

"You are such a pig."

"And you are such a virgin." He winced again, cupping his balls. "Let me fix that for you. Let me help you loosen up," he slurred and I wrinkled my nose.

Stepping back more, I shook my head. "Night, Vincent. Get therapy."

"I've always liked you, Linds. Even when everyone said you were gay I said I think that's even hotter."

"You're an asshole, Vince! Clean your friggin' room and stop taking pictures of poor helpless girls." I waved over my shoulder and stalked up the dock away from him. I regretted the words the moment I spoke them.

The wind off the ocean was picking up, the way it always did at night, making me cold and bothered by the fact I'd told him I'd seen the stupid pictures.

A flash of red hair caught my eye. I narrowed my gaze

to see Sierra sneaking out of the bushes next to the stairs up to the dock, by the large barbecue pit. She stepped out and glanced around and then disappeared into the crowd on the dance floor.

I waved but she didn't see me. She was too far away.

I had lost them all in the crowds and drama.

Lainey wasn't in the spot I'd left her.

Sierra had clearly been doing something she didn't want anyone to see, in the woods and in heels no less.

Sage was obviously caught up in Rachel's drama of the day.

And I could still taste her boyfriend on my lips.

Gross.

I trekked up the yard, thankful I was in my flats. Vincent's mouth on mine had sealed it for me—I was ready to go home.

"Linds!"

I turned to see Sierra calling me from behind the pool house. She waved at me and called again, "Come here."

I spun and looked back toward the water where the dancing and partying was happening, wondering how she had gotten up here so fast without sprinting in her heels. I shook my head and assumed I had hallucinated and hurried to where she was hiding.

But as I rounded the corner she wasn't there.

I blinked and listened, hearing sobbing from close by. As I got around the next corner, I jumped, startled at the way Sierra's makeup ran down her cheeks. Her lips trembled as black mascara tears rolled down her face. She reached for me with bloody hands.

I stepped back. "Sierra, what happened?" She hadn't looked like this a moment ago.

Her breaths ripped from her in jagged gasps as she tried to speak, "Rach—Rach—Rach—" She shook and gave up, succumbing to the sobbing.

"Something is wrong with Rachel?" I asked but she didn't say anything, she just cried.

How had she been so calm moments before? How had she been down at the party, sneaking from the woods?

It didn't add up.

My heart pounded in my chest. Clearly something horrible had happened. I scanned her body for wounds that would explain the blood, but she had none I could see.

"Where is Rachel?" I grabbed her arms, shaking her and noting the crimson color was smeared across her white dress. "What is happening?"

She sobbed, turning and pulling me through the yard where no one was. I couldn't get my breath as we rounded the pool house and walked to the guesthouse on the far side of the property.

I continued to try to get something from her. "What is it? Are you hurt? Is Rachel hurt? Was there an accident? Did you idiots try to drive?"

She dropped to her knees, shaking much worse than before. She bawled and heaved, just pointing at the forest behind the guesthouse.

I let go of her, leaving her there.

I didn't know what to do or what to expect.

I didn't have any sort of training for a moment like this one, no first aid even.

So I licked my lips and walked—holding back the storm inside me.

As I cleared the grass and the building, I stopped. Horror climbed up my legs, freezing them in the spot they stood. It paralyzed my waist and chest, keeping my breath from me. I lifted my hands to my lips, in shock and confusion. There was no way the thing before me was what it appeared to be.

It was a lie.

A mistake.

I gasped my breaths into my hands as a montage of horror movies I had seen took over my brain, creating an obvious hallucination.

"No!" I gasped as a sound escaped my lips, either a moan or a cry. I couldn't be sure.

I couldn't be sure of anything.

My brain was also frozen, stuck on the image that was so obviously staged.

I twitched slightly, shaking my head back and forth in denial. "No."

Lainey matched me in motion and horror and possibly outdid me in shock. She stood across the bodies from me, as if she was my mirror reflection but a more ghostly apparition than I was. Her cream-colored dress was also coated in blood, as were her hands. She had been processing the scene longer, or she had created it. There was always that option.

I dropped to my knees, not sure of exactly what I was seeing. My friends were dead on the forest floor, but my brain refused to allow that in.

Pain stabbed into my knee but I ignored it. I knew it was there, like the vision of my bloody friends before me on the ground, but I didn't feel anything.

Lainey too dropped to her knees, shaking and sobbing.

There was no explanation. She offered no words.

"No," I said again as I stared at the way Rachel's body was twisted, as if broken that way on purpose.

Maybe she had fallen and her back was broken?

I gazed up into the trees above us and knew there was no way she had been up there. And even if she had been, that wouldn't explain how her head was twisted so disgustingly that I hardly recognized her. Her dark hair was shiny, like it was glossed with something, but I knew it to be blood. Her dress, a pink Marc Jacobs, was soaked and more of a crimson color.

A gasp slipped from my lips as I looked at Lainey again. "What happened? Did you call the police? We need to call 9-1-1! Did you check their pulse?"

She shook and stared at Rachel whose eyes were open. I peered down, noting her palms faced the sky, regardless of how unlikely it was she had fallen that way with them twisted so. First aid might not help her.

My brain refused to feel a thing as it processed the scene, explaining it all away. I leapt forward, finally making the movement I knew I should. I checked Rachel's pulse, watching as the blood oozed slowly from the fresh wounds in her midsection. I gagged, noticing the warmth still in her skin. "Call 9-1-1! Call! Call them!" I snapped at Lainey but she didn't move. She just stared at Sage who was on the ground next to Rachel, their hands almost touching like they had died reaching for one another.

Only Sage's hands were coated in blood and her lip was swollen.

I stared down at her long enough, knowing she must have killed Rachel in a fit of fury, and suddenly realized she was still breathing.

Where Rachel was not.

"She's alive," I whispered.

Lainey lifted her eyes to me, shaking her head and still in shock.

"She's breathing."

Lainey frowned, looking at me like I was a monster for saying it. "SAGE IS ALIVE!" I shouted.

Lainey jumped and Sierra appeared next to her. They clung to each other.

All three of us gaped down at our friend as she coughed and blinked, coming back to us from whatever place her horrific deed had put her.

CHAPTER SIX
Daddy's girl?

I looked in the rearview at Sage and wanted so badly to ask why we had run, but the way she shivered constantly told me there was no point. She hadn't said a word from the moment she opened her eyes. She had seen her hands and then Rachel's body and screeched. She was clearly still in shock.

I drove us in Rachel's car to Sierra's house. It was only a five-minute drive along the shoreline and Sierra's driver had ditched us.

None of us spoke.

When we got to the house, the gate opened and I drove in and parked at the guesthouse in the back. I jumped out, grabbing the door and helping Lainey from the car. When I got her inside she was still twitching and shuddering. I stared into her dark eyes. I knew what she was seeing. It sickened me. The whole scene was likely to be on replay.

Sierra grabbed Sage from the car and dragged her in.

Once we were all there I couldn't look at any of them. I didn't know why we had done what we had done, but they were clearly guilty of something.

I walked back out to the car.

I would have to take it back. How would I explain? Why did we leave?

The moments after Sage woke were blurry with confusion, and I knew we had made the wrong choice. It was the illegal choice.

Sage had woken and instantly gone into shock. She had seen Rachel's dead body and made a high-pitched sound before scrambling backward, desperate to get away. She started to have a panic attack, and for whatever reason, Sierra panicked too. She had grabbed Sage by the arm and dragged her from the forest. I didn't know why they were running, but I wasn't going to be the one left standing there with blood on my hands. I took Lainey's hand in mine and followed Sierra as she bolted for the garage. We stole Rachel's car and drove off before anyone saw us—before we even talked about what we should do.

There had been no words. No explanations. No confessions.

Obviously, one of us had killed Rachel, and all I knew for sure was that it wasn't me.

I stared at the car, completely lost on how to solve this. I was about to go back inside when a figure appeared in the driveway. I jumped, about to run, until I saw it was Ashton. He walked to me and paused, tilting his head to the side. "Is she safe?"

"No. Rachel's dead," I called out, feeling weird about speaking for the first time in so long and even weirder about the sentence I had said.

"Sage—is Sage safe?"

I nodded, lying to us both.

He walked to Rachel's car and looked at the door, speaking in a low tone, "I'll take care of this. Burn all your clothes and wash everything you have touched with bleach. Soak phones and keys and everything in bleach. Scrub under your nails in the shower, washing everything three times and bleach the shower when you're done. Burn the towels and bleach the floors." He got in and started the car, giving me a look. "NOW, LINDSEY!" he snapped at me out the window before driving the Mercedes away and leaving me there to wonder what the hell had just happened.

There hadn't been a drop of blood on him. He clearly hadn't killed Rachel. Her death had been a bloody one.

Maybe he knew it was Sage and he was covering it up for her. Unless he had washed up already. But I could swear I saw him leave the party long before Rachel must have been killed.

I turned and closed the door, seeing the three of them sitting on the leather couches and staring at the wall. They mirrored the girls in a horror movie—the kind you always roll your eyes at because they make all the wrong choices and somehow live through it all.

"Don't sit," I said. "We have to burn all these clothes and the shoes and bleach the couches. Bleach our hands and our phones and our keys." I looked at Sierra. "Bleach?"

She frowned, like she didn't hear me or understand the words I was saying.

"BLEACH!"

"Pool house," she muttered, stammering the rest, "It-it-it's in the p-p-p-pool house." Tears started rolling down her cheeks again.

Sage looked at me blankly and whispered, "I toasted her rotting in hell." Her words turned to sobs, "I-I-I-I toasted h-h-her—" She broke down, falling from the couch onto the carpet. I closed the door to outside behind me and observed the rug where she was touching it with her bloody hands, wondering how long we had before we would run out of time to clean this all up.

Lainey started to cry again.

I realized then I had to be the common-sense girl, the survivor in the crowd. I had to be the reasonable one. I walked to Sierra and grabbed her blood-coated hands and lifted her from the ground. "Come on." I forced her to stand and walked her to the large walk-in shower. I pushed her inside and turned on the water, making it so hot it was just bearable. I lifted the garbage can. "Put your clothes in here."

My mind screamed; it begged me to stop and let the authorities do their job. It told me I was in the wrong, and I was choosing the thing that would end my life before it had even started. I was aiding and abetting.

But my mother's voice whispered that they were my family.

So I did it.

Sierra started to strip and I turned and went for Lainey, dragging her in next. I pushed her, blubbering and incoherent, into the shower with Sierra. They already resembled inmates as they shivered and stripped. "Put your clothes in the garbage can."

Walking back into the living room I jumped seeing Sage was already standing and no longer crying. She just stared at the wall but then turned sharply, and gave me a pained look. "I don't know what happened."

I didn't either, and I almost didn't want to know. I was scared to be alone with her there so I offered her my hand, forcing it to stay still and not shake. She lifted her hand, caked in dried blood, and dropped it in mine.

I pulled her to the bathroom and pushed her inside the shower that had seemed so large a moment ago. "Take everything off, every scrap of clothes and jewels and put them in the can." I stepped back, seeing the caked blood on my hands.

My eyes lifted to the mirror, realizing the horror of the scene before me. A thousand things ran through my mind, but I had one response. I dragged my cell phone from my pocket and called my dad.

He answered after a few rings. "You all right?"

My lips trembled then and tears flooded my eyes. When I spoke my voice cracked and ended as a whisper, "Come to Sierra's guesthouse. Hurry. I need you." I pressed it off, not sure what else to say. Not sure what was true and what was in my head. I had small tidbits that were roaming around and making things up, based on assumptions and the things I had seen.

In reality, one of us or none of us murdered Rachel.

For whatever reason I was more afraid that it wasn't one of my friends.

I stripped my clothes off too, putting them in the basket and stepping into the shower with my friends.

Brown water, consisting of mud, dirt, leaves, grass, and of course the blood from our dead friend, ran from our four naked bodies.

We had never showered together before, but I would remember this for the rest of my life. I would never be free of the image of the four of us, huddled and shivering. The air wasn't cold and the water was scalding, but we were cold. It was a cold that comes from within. The kind that grows, starting at your heart and spreading out until every bit of you is numb.

When I got out and dried off, I was emotionless. I wrapped myself in a towel and walked to the door, standing there waiting for the lights from my father's Benz to roll up.

I had never needed my daddy in my life the way I did in that moment.

Her blood was still on me.

Her dead eyes still looked at me.

Her scream still rang in my head.

But, ironically, her mean words were gone.

She was a saint in my mind.

I didn't know how or why, but I could no longer think a mean thing about her.

I felt sick for ever wishing bad things for her.

I was a bad person.

I had wished this.

That rotted inside me, making the cold worse, like I was dead with her. Like I too was lying on the ground in the woods, with the sound of the party all around me and the blood from my body underneath me. That blood was the last warm thing she had felt. Or was it the hands of her killer?

I shuddered and blinked, seeing lights. My heart jumped, and for one beat I feared it was the police. But the moment it got close I knew who it was. I opened the front door and stood there, soaking and wrapped in a towel.

All the times I had pretended I hated him and imagined I didn't need him and acted like I couldn't have cared less about him, this was the moment that shoved all those others away.

His car skidded to a halt and his door hung open as he sprinted to me, shaking me. His words were either too slow or too fast, or I just didn't have answers. I knew I should speak but I couldn't. What could I say? How did I say it?

"LINDS!" He shook me, snapping me out of it with his biting fingers and loud words. "WHAT HAPPENED, BABY?"

I blinked as tears filled my eyes and words fell from my lips, "Rachel is dead. We have her blood on us. I need help."

"Was it an accident?"

I shook my head. His eyes widened, and I could see his reaction was going to be bad. But he held it back. He swallowed it down and nodded. "Did you kill her?"

I shook my head, blinking tears so thick they blocked the truth and the world from my eyes.

"Did one of the girls?"

I nodded, shaking and stepping into the warmth of my father.

He paused, biting his lip and then became the man I knew he was—deep down I knew he was this man. A man of action and a man who knew what to do in a terrible moment like this one. A man we needed.

He released me, stepping back and pulled his phone from his pocket, pressing someone called Hendricks, a name I didn't know. The man answered, sounding groggy.

"Hendricks, I need you. Now. The Casey residence. Haul ass and prepare to burn." He hung up before he said anything else. He swallowed again and glanced past me into the guesthouse. "Is she—Rachel here?"

I shook my head. "Her house." My voice was weak.

"Good." He breathed with relief and still somehow looked worried though he didn't sound it. "That's good. Okay, this is what we are going to do: You and the girls are going to walk to Sierra's house. Get cleaned again. Someone will come and fetch the towels you are wearing. Before you go, leave every effect you have on you in this guesthouse. Touch nothing else. Not even one earring goes to Sierra's house. I don't care if your mom gave it to you, do you understand me?"

I nodded, glancing back as the other girls came into view from the bathroom, each in a white towel and dripping wet.

"You girls go to the house now. You swim in the pool for a couple minutes, bring the towels in with you, and leave them in there. Get Sierra's clothes on and take her car. Go to our house. Don't answer your phones and don't talk to anyone until we speak to you. Don't cry and don't talk about this; the staff will hear you. Do not speak and do not call anyone." His tone was grave. We all nodded. "Now, go!"

I jumped and stepped away from him, walking to the big house. As each girl passed by him, he checked her face for earrings. Not one of us had a single thing. Everything was in the can in the bathroom where we had left the blood of our friend.

We walked in silence to the backyard where the pool overlooked the ocean. I held on to my towel, like it was a baby blanket, and jumped into the pool, letting the cool water pull me under.

The lights of the pool told me when each of my friends jumped into the water, but I didn't need to look at them to know what their faces looked like. I knew already.

The image of each expression would haunt me until the day I died.

CHAPTER SEVEN
Frogs in boiling water

We as a group had never dressed silently. We didn't do anything in silence. We had never been uncomfortable with each other before. We were a discombobulated mess of people who didn't fit, but we were friends. We were family. We were not uncomfortable or awkward. If anything, we were the opposite.

But in that moment, we were every one of those things.

We sat silent in the car on the ride over to my house, all feeling out of place in clothes that didn't fit right or feel right.

I felt like we had once been something, and we were not that thing anymore. I couldn't find the word for it, but I knew we were never going to be whatever it was again.

Lainey reached for me in the dark, slipping her hand into mine as Sierra drove us to my place. Sage sat in the front, not speaking and shallow breathing. But Lainey squeezed me, maybe checking to see if I was okay.

I wasn't but I didn't want to tell her that. I didn't know if I trusted her anymore.

I didn't trust me.

One of them was a killer and I was an accomplice. It wasn't snooping and it wasn't innocent. Someone was dead. Rachel was dead.

When we pulled up to my gate, the guard let us in. I lifted my free hand and waved, trying to be that girl. The one who waved at the night guard. The one who was normal.

"When we get inside, let's go in the hot tub," I

muttered. "I think we need more chemicals."

None of them spoke.

Sierra parked out front and we got out, silent as mice. I watched Lainey as she climbed out of the car. Her cheeks were flushed and she appeared to be tired. She blinked like she fought to stay awake."

We were never this way when we arrived after a night of partying.

The staff might know something was wrong.

I nudged Sierra and nodded at the door. "Be normal."

She smiled wide, pushing her cheeks up into place. "Hot tub sounds great. I'm aching everywhere."

Lainey made a sound like she was laughing but it was horrible. "Me too."

Sage couldn't do it.

I suspected it was because she had killed Rachel, and she might never laugh again as a result.

Of the four of us, she was the least likely to kill anyone. She was always all talk when she was mad. Her temper was bad, but I had never seen it go beyond mean words followed by an instant apology.

To me that meant something dastardly had occurred between the time we had arrived at the party and the very moment Rachel died. My inner Diablo blamed Rachel. I knew what she was capable of.

We stalked through the house silently, slipping past the rooms, one at a time. Somewhere in the dim lighting and heartbreak, we had given up on the fake laughing and carrying on. We opted for sneaky, which to me suited teenaged girls just fine.

Each step became lighter and eventually we were looking over our shoulders and slipping into shadows.

When we finally reached the back door, I took a breath, squeezing the lock slowly and opening it so it wouldn't creak. It was a noisier door than most in the house.

I tiptoed across the deck, lifting the lid off the giant hot tub. I didn't look back at my friends. I just stepped in, fully clothed in Sierra's version of pajamas—men's boxers and a silky tank top.

She didn't even flinch when the silk hit the warm water. I sat in the steam as they too climbed in, each nestling into a corner.

"Lindsey?" A voice filled the foggy air. I jumped, looking around as a shadow appeared across the pool. I bit my lip as Sage started to whimper. "Lindsey, it's Hailey!" the voice called again as she walked to us.

I had completely forgotten about us hanging out.

I sat in the dark, surrounded by steam and wondered what the hell I should do. "Hey," I said in a panicked voice that didn't sound anywhere near as calm as I tried to make it. I sloshed out of the tub, wrapping my arms around myself the moment the cool evening air hit me. "I'm so sorry. I totally forgot. Can we do it again another time? We just got back from the party and my friend isn't feeling so hot." I was rambling so I forced my mouth shut.

She looked like she expected that when she nodded, her eyes darting to the silhouettes of my silent friends in the steam and dim lighting. "It's cool. I'll see ya 'round." She turned and walked away and I didn't stop her. I didn't explain why I never introduced her or why I never asked her to join us. I let her think I'd ditched her, and I was the mean girl who was too cool to hang out with her.

I hated treating her that way, but I didn't want to drag her into this mess. She walked off and I turned back to the hot tub.

We sat in silence, not a single one of us offering an explanation or a confession or a word of remorse. We took turns crying so softly the others in the bubbling hot tub barely heard it.

I couldn't say how long we were in there. I only knew that it was a man's voice that snapped me out of the haze I was in. I had been stuck, reliving every second of finding them all the way I did. So when he spoke, I jumped and turned fast. I couldn't stop my hands from coming up defensively. I didn't realize I was covering my face with the backs of my hands, recoiling from the manly voice calling my name. "Lindsey!"

The deck was dark, completely covered in steam.

When he walked from the shadows, I sighed when I realized who it was.

"Linds, come inside. Now." It was my father.

I got up, swaying and nauseated. "I think we've been in too long," I muttered and dragged myself from the tub. I lay on the concrete and stared up at the sky. It was beautiful. More stars than I had seen in ages, unless of course some of them were a result of me being in the hot tub too long.

Lainey came and lay beside me, sighing and then breathing shallowly. "You okay, Linds?" she asked softly, the way she did everything.

I shook my head, knowing we needed to go inside and face the music. My father wouldn't wait long for us before he would come out and drag us in.

"Me either," she whispered, her voice cracking again.

Sage started to cry, making whimpering noises as she sloshed to where we were and plunked down too. She turned her face to mine and whispered softly, "I don't know what happened, Linds. I don't remember anything. We got to the party and I saw Vince and Rachel, and then that's it. I don't remember anything else."

"Did someone hand you a drink, Sage?" Lainey asked, her voice a little high pitched. "Did you drink a glass of something someone handed you?"

"I don't know. I don't remember."

Lainey looked at me, her dark eyes glistening in the mist. It was a knowing look. "Someone tried to give us drinks. I bet they gave Sage a drink."

My insides sank but my heart lifted. The strangest sensation came over me. It was like a battle of good versus evil as I worked out the details.

Were we nearly drugged? It would appear so.

Sage could have been drugged. If she was she didn't murder Rachel.

But why would someone drug Sage?

Could they be separate incidents?

Why drug Sage, me, and Lainey and then murder Rachel?

None of it made sense.

I turned and saw Sierra flop onto the deck, face down and breathing weirdly. "Did someone try to give you a drink?" I asked.

She nodded. "Some girl. I didn't know her. She was blonde and slim and she had on a dress like mine. She called my name and handed me a red drink. She was like a blonde Barbie."

"Did you drink it?" Lainey asked softly.

"I didn't get the chance. Some guy fell and knocked it all over my left arm and leg. My shoe was sticky all night long because of it."

"Her shoes were sticky," Lainey whispered.

"Oh my God," I murmured and continued to work it out in my head.

"So someone tried to drug us and maybe drugged you, Sage. Unless you drank enough to pass out. But why were you with Rachel? We found you that way. I thought you were dead," Sierra mumbled from where she lay. None of us had the energy to be as worked up as we should have been.

"What if the same person who drugged us killed Rachel?" I asked, hating the possibilities that whispered.

Was Sage then made to look like she had killed Rachel?

And if so, that meant Lainey hadn't killed Rachel either.

What if none of us had and it was being made to look like we did?

That was a whole other ball of wax I wasn't certain I wanted to explore. That meant someone was trying to frame us. But at least my friends might not have killed her. I hadn't really believed they could have, even though I'd seen the evidence. My brain swirled in circles.

After a moment Lainey spoke, "What if the same person killed Rachel and drugged us to make it look like we did it?"

I was long past that assumption but I didn't say anything. I had nothing good to add to it.

"We better go inside. Your dad didn't sound happy."

"I bet he isn't." I chuckled a little, not on purpose. But

the whole thing was insane. We had just called my father to come and help us cover up a murder. I dragged myself up to my knees, wincing when I felt a stabbing pain. I stood and looked at the shard of wood in my knee. I pulled it out and staggered into the house looking intoxicated, but in reality I was overwhelmed, overcooked, and bleeding from the knee.

I grabbed a towel from the rack and wrapped it around my soaking wet body, not even bothering to dry off.

Inside the games room off the back of the house, I expected to find my father but what I got was much worse. Lainey's dad sat at the counter. My father poured drinks behind the bar, a job he rarely did. Someone was on speakerphone, talking to our dads at the bar. I listened for a second and realized quickly it was Sierra's dad.

Those all were explainable, but the strikingly gorgeous woman sitting by the fire in a slimming black dress was not. I didn't know her at all. And I couldn't place the girl sitting next to her who looked just like her. Clearly they were sisters, which around here meant they were mother and daughter. Both tall, slim, olive skinned, dark haired, and stunningly beautiful. The girl appeared to have had a rough night as well. Her gray eyes were haunted looking and her lip quivered every few seconds.

I stood in the doorway, completely confused by what I saw.

Had Dad called a gathering?

CHAPTER EIGHT
Excuses, explanations, and lies?

My dad offered us hot cocoa with some Baileys in it. I sipped mine, letting it attempt to warm me inside. It didn't succeed but the heat from it was nice.

We sat, huddled by the fire, each of us confused about the reason for the other two people being in the room. It hadn't been explained to us yet. My dad finished putting the bandage on my knee and stood up, looking at us all. "Girls, we need to hear exactly what happened. Sierra, your father is on speakerphone. He's in New York and driving here now, but he wants to know the details so he's ready in case there are accusations thrown about."

"Hi, Sierra. Girls." Her father spoke in a tone I knew too well. It was the one I got from my father when he was really angry. So angry he was quiet.

"Sage, your mom is on her way back. They managed to leave earlier than they had intended. She will be here in a few hours," my father offered, looking uncomfortably at Sage. My eyes darted to the girl on the couch opposite me. My father saw my stare and nodded. "This is Helen and her daughter Marguerite Lacroix. I'm sure I don't have to tell you that Mr. Lacroix is the mayor here. You all know of him, of course." He was not there though.

The girl's gray eyes darted to me. We stared at each other, and I realized in that moment she wasn't what I expected her to be.

She seemed vulnerable and frightened.

Seeing her mother in the flesh was something else as well. I had no idea she was as beautiful as she was. The pictures in their home didn't do her justice. I had only been there once for landscaping and was indoors for no more than a few moments. It was long enough to see the mayor lived very similarly to the rest of us.

"Louisa's sleeping pills will last a solid six hours. We have four left; let's make them count before she wakes up. We need an exact account of every moment from the time you left this house." My father gave me a look. "Lindsey, you go first."

I cleared my throat. "We drove to Sage's, met with Ashton in the driveway. We went inside and Sierra showed up. We drove to Rachel's in the limo. When we got there we danced and had a couple of drinks. I spoke to Vince at the waterfront and walked up the hill, leaving the party. I saw Sierra in the bushes and then she was by the pool house. She called to me and I went there, but she wasn't there. I found her a ways back, sobbing. She led me into the woods where Rachel was"—I shuddered and closed my eyes— "Rachel was on the ground. Sage was unconscious next to her. Lainey and Sierra had both seen this already and were crying. When Sage woke we stole Rachel's car and went to Sierra's and called you."

My dad shook his head and turned to Sierra. "You next."

She swallowed hard and pressed her lips together. Her brow furrowed and her eyes lowered, but she managed to get words out, "Like Lindsey said, we met at Sage's. We drove in my dad's car to Rachel's. When we got there we danced and drank. Someone gave me a drink but it spilled on my shoe. I went to wash it off and I heard something. Rachel was screaming at Ashton." Her eyes unfocused as the story started to become too real in her mind. "I laughed and went back to dance. I was with Lainey for a long time, dancing and having fun, but my shoe was still sticky." Her words trailed off again.

"You have to keep talking loud, Sierra." Her father sighed, starting to sound annoyed.

She twitched and looked down. "I was at the pool, dragging my shoe in the water and trying to rinse the booze off. The lights flicked off and everyone was screaming, but then someone behind me screamed and it sounded different.

The lights came back on so I turned and walked that way, thinking it was someone being drunk and stupid." Her voice trailed off so low I could hardly hear her. "I hoped it was Rachel, still getting mad about being dumped by Ashton."

"Sierra, I can't hear you," her father barked over the phone.

"I thought it was Rachel screaming. I walked there and it was Lainey. She was shaking Sage and Rachel and trying to wake them up. I tried to help her, but when we moved Rachel's head something was snapping under the skin—" Her words became sobs and she stopped, shaking her head. "I can't."

"YOU HAVE TO! GET IT TOGETHER! YOU ARE IN A LOT OF TROUBLE!" her father screamed.

I jumped, shaking and sweating but somehow still cold from it all.

"I-I-I-I went to fi-find help. I couldn't walk anymore because I s-saw the blood on my ha-hands. So I stopped and I froze and then Lindsey came. She was there and I tried to tell her but I couldn't. So I sh-showed her." She collapsed into her own hands and sobbed harder.

I realized then, Sierra's story didn't match mine. She hadn't been in the woods by the docks, and she hadn't called to me from beside the pool house. I'd seen her though, or had I? What if I was meant to see her? What if someone at the party had led me there?

My father didn't wait for her to get it together. He looked at Sage. "You tell us what you saw and did."

She shook her head. "I don't remember anything. I was at the party and then I woke up with Rachel there." Her face pinched and tears squeezed from her eyes. "And she was dead. And there was so much blood." She looked at her hands and I knew she still saw it. Her lip was fat and redder than normal, but she was clean of any blood to us—to herself she was never going to be clean.

My father nodded and glanced back at Lainey's dad. He took another drink before he spoke softly, like she did, "Lainey, honey, you have to tell us every detail now, okay? All of it." She blinked and shook her head, but he encouraged her, "I know, baby. But you have to. We need it all."

She shuddered and closed her eyes, letting the entire night fall back into an instant replay.

"We got in Lindsey's car from here, driving to Sage's. Her brother, Ashton, was leaving the house as we arrived. He and Sage fought about something stupid. She was mean to him. He left angry and we were all led to believe he would be breaking it off with Rachel at the party. When we got inside, Sage told us she believed Rachel was being unfaithful, something we all suspected or knew."

I nodded. We had.

She took a breath and continued, "Then Sierra arrived and we all rode to Rachel's in Mr. Casey's limo. The driver took us the long way, much longer than it needed to be. He said a tree was down so we had to take another route. We arrived and the party was in full swing—we were late. Rachel and Ashton were fighting and he left the party. She was screaming with rage. Right then, someone tried to give Lindsey and me a drink, but I remembered we had been drugged once so we dumped the drinks. We got our own drinks and danced with Sierra for about an hour and a half. I went to the bathroom, and on the way I saw Rachel, Vince, and Sage by the edge of the woods. Vincent tried to stop them from fighting, but eventually he threw his hands up in the air and left them where they were. Rachel was angry because Ashton had dumped her. Sage said something I didn't hear and Rachel slapped her hard. Sage was being weird. She didn't fight back; she just staggered away. I thought she was really drunk."

Her lips twisted and she tensed, looking like she didn't want to say the rest.

"What happened then?" her dad coaxed her.

"I went back to dance with Sierra and Lindsey. Then Lindsey went to the water to look at the sky. It was really hot in the crowd. Sierra said she couldn't take the stickiness in her shoe. She said she was going to rinse it again. So I left the dance floor to see where Lindsey had gone. I went looking for her, and when I found her, she was kissing Vince on the docks. I didn't know what to do. So I turned and ran away, heading up the yard behind the guesthouse," her voice cracked.

I lowered my face as my eyes filled with disgust. I didn't know anyone had seen that, but I wished she had seen the next few moments. I felt sick and couldn't look at Sage. I didn't want her to think anything. I hadn't done anything.

"Keep going, Lainey." Her dad sounded impatient.

"I got to the far side of the guesthouse and I heard a noise—whimpering. I thought it was Sage. It sounded like her. The lights flickered and then the power went out, but the sound in the woods happened again. So I ran to it, thinking it was Rachel and Sage again." She sniffled as tears started to roll down her cheeks. "They were there. Rach was dead. Sage was—I thought they were both dead. I started screaming." Her words came faster as her voice cracked more with the sobs. "I screamed for help and then Sierra was there. I told her to call 9-1-1, and she got up and left, and then Lindsey came back with her. I don't really remember the rest." She opened her eyes and looked at me, no doubt baffled that she was in so much shock she didn't see everything. "Until we came here and got into the hot tub. Everything else is a blur."

My father also turned to me, his eyes shining like he was relieved, or sad for me maybe. But it was Sierra's dad who spoke, "The story you will tell everyone is that you all found Sage drunk—very drunk. You worried she was truly sick. You brought her to my house and called Lindsey's father. He brought you to his house and now he is going to bring Sage to the hospital. She will be tested for drugging, which clearly she will fail and have drugs in her system. She will be your alibi. Did anyone else see you?"

My insides tightened. "Hailey, a local girl. She works at the Shack. She saw us in the hot tub here."

"Would she have seen Sage?"

I shook my head. "No. It was steaming. She wouldn't be able to say for sure it was Sage."

"Mark, take Sage now. Gerry, if you can stay with the

girls there that would be great. Girls, the police might want to talk to you. I will call back after I speak to the driver and make sure the story is solid. When I have it, I will tell it to you. You do not speak to anyone without a lawyer present. I am that lawyer." The phone turned off, letting us know he had hung up.

I lifted my gaze to Sage, desperate to explain, but her eyes narrowed into a glare. I slumped and shivered, still cold and unable to shake the death shroud I felt like I was wearing.

Helen sighed, rubbing her eyes. "And how does Rita's story fit into theirs then?"

I turned and looked at Marguerite who bit her lip and shook her head. "It doesn't." She clung to the blanket she was wrapped in and sighed. "I must have stumbled upon Rachel after they had left her. I didn't see them leave though. I drank too much and woke up in the bushes. I heard voices and crying and then nothing. I walked right to where Rachel was and fell, tripping and landing on her. Her blood was all over me. I screamed and ran, leaving her there. I don't know why I didn't try to help her or call the police. I got scared."

Lainey's red and puffy eyes squinted. "Maybe you were drugged too? Why you?"

Marguerite shrugged. "Wrong place, wrong time, I guess. Some pervert drugging girls isn't exactly a new thing at a party." She sounded completely Jersey.

Sierra wiped her face and dried her tears, sniffling and shaking her head. "How did you get home?"

Marguerite's eyes darted to her mother next to her. "I called my mom. She called your dad. He called Lindsey's dad. My mom came and got me from the road. I was hiding in the bushes." Her face was stricken. "We came here straightaway."

We were all stricken.

My father stood, offering his hand to Sage. "You should come too, Marguerite. I think you were both drugged." His eyes landed on me. "And I think you girls are all in some serious trouble, but we know none of you did this and that's the important part." He nodded at the door as

Marguerite stood with him and Sage. "The staff have been told to take tomorrow off and Louisa will sleep for another three and a half hours with no chance of waking. After that you need to be yourself again, do you understand?"

I shook my head. How would I ever be myself again?

"None of you know Rachel is dead. Not one of you knows this. You left the party because Sage and Marguerite were sick. That's it. So when they come and inform you that your friend has been murdered, you need to be overcome with grief. Louisa has to buy it—so does every one of your friends. And you need to make sure that girl who saw you in the hot tub suspects nothing." He wrapped an arm around Sage and led her from the room. Marguerite and her mother followed.

We sat there by the fire and let it all soak in.

We had three hours to be sad.

CHAPTER NINE

You kids today, with your GHB and coming out of the pantry

Apparently, three hours to be sad wasn't enough.

We hadn't really slept and we hadn't really eaten, so when lunch came to where we were camped out on the new lounge chairs, we were all emotional.

Sierra gave me a look and sighed, picking at her panini. "He kissed you, didn't he? Vincent."

I lifted my head, sniffled and nodded. "He grabbed me and kissed me. I fought him off but it was too late."

She rolled her bright-blue eyes. "He did the same thing to me. She isn't going to believe you."

I sighed. "I know."

"But I do."

Lainey lifted her red-rimmed eyes too, squinting and trying to see me without her glasses. "I do too. I know you wouldn't have kissed him. I'm sorry for saying that. I got caught up."

"It doesn't matter now."

"What doesn't matter now?" Louisa asked as she clicked out onto the huge deck and flopped into a chair. We all lowered our faces back into the chairs and tried to not look like we had been crying.

"Nothing, Louisa. We just feel bad that Sage and Marguerite got drugged. It was the worst party and they were so sick." Sierra lied like she was paid to do it. She was a lot like her dad.

Through the gap in the chair where my face was, I could tell Louisa didn't give a shit. She was messing with her phone and drinking her green shake. I blinked and in that space of time she dropped the glass, shattering it everywhere. A scream tore from her lips as she checked her phone, obviously seeing something terrible.

I hated that I knew what the terrible thing was.

I turned and faced Sierra and Lainey, giving them both the look. The one I used to express that it was showtime.

"OH MY GOD! OH MY GOD!" Louisa jumped up, clicking frantically and ran inside.

"Shit," Sierra whispered.

"Guess it's hit the local news," I muttered.

Louisa came running back out, her arms waving and her face covered in real tears. "Oh girls! Oh my God! Oh the worst thing—" She sobbed and covered her mouth.

"What?" I asked, trying my best not to understand. "Is Dad okay? Is it the boys?"

She shook her head. "Rachel Swanson!" She sobbed harder.

"What?" Lainey asked, squinting like a crazy person.

"What happened to Rachel?" Sierra sat up, her red eyes were so obvious. "What do you mean?"

Louisa bawled, barely making sense and tossed her phone at me. I looked down at it, reading the headline and letting my jaw drop. "Rachel was murdered last night." I dropped the phone, watching it fall and spin until it hit the concrete. My hands flew to my eyes just as I realized I was out—I had no more tears. Not a single drop fell from my squeezed-shut lids, but I made sobbing sounds. I had cried so hard that I had literally cried until there was nothing left.

The girls did better than I did, both were hysterically sobbing. I switched to soft cries and small whimpers, shaking my head and denying this was a possibility. "No. No. No. We were there. She was fine."

Louisa wrapped herself around me; her coconut sunscreen almost asphyxiated me. "I am so sorry, Linds. I am so sorry. I know she was your best friend."

Sobbing and heaving I nodded, wondering how the hell she had gotten that impression.

The pain and agony of the whole death was still fresh,

but the horrible idea that someone was trying to frame us was much worse for me. I honestly was stuck on the fact that someone wanted us to fry for the murder of our friend.

Someone knew we hated her when she was alive.

And this person wasn't playing around.

They were serious.

They had already killed one person to try to frame five.

My brain was too busy trying to sift through the possibilities to properly mourn my dead friend.

But Lainey and Sierra were doing it justice. They both sobbed and cried and wailed, joining Louisa in the dramatics. I stayed covered, taking breaths and making odd sounds, noises of denial and heartbreak.

When I surfaced, wiping my dry eyes, Louisa was drinking a huge glass of something. Lori, who was supposed to be on a day off, gave me a look. She offered a drink from the tray she had. "You want some lemonade?"

I nodded, taking one and praying there was a bunch of liquor in it. My head was spinning. She put down the tray and started cleaning up the green shake and broken glass.

"Miss Lindsey, some of your friends are here," Robert, the English butler, who was supposed to be on a day off as well, stood in the doorway speaking to me. I pulled my hand back from Lori and stood up, picking the eternal wedgie from my butt as Vincent, Jake, and Andrew walked in.

They seemed normal.

I wondered if they knew yet.

Andrew wore a random graphic tee, dressed down as always. He was the ultimate version of down-to-earth. Always in a tee shirt, cargo shorts, and some Chucks. I believed the lie his soft-brown eyes told me, that everything was going to be all right. "Hey, Linds," he mumbled, no different than the tone he would have used to tell me that he would rather be skateboarding or snowboarding at that moment.

Jake walked to me and wrapped his arms around me, muttering into my neck and encasing my body in his. "I'm so sorry, Linds. I know how much you guys loved Rach. We're gonna find whoever did this." He whispered the last part.

I didn't have a response to that. From the way it looked, we had done it. And if not us, it looked like it might be Ashton, Jake's best friend. They were so close we called them a bromance. They played football together. Jake was the wide receiver to Ashton being the quarterback.

He pulled back and it was obvious he had been crying. His red-rimmed blue eyes were a bit puffy as he sighed. "I saw her at like ten. She was so mad that Ash had left and broken up with her. I don't know what could have happened."

"Me either." I shook my head as he let go of me and ran his hands through his chestnut hair. It was true; I honestly didn't know what could have happened. *How did someone get so many broken bones?*

He draped one of his huge arms over me and turned to face the others.

In my peripheral I caught Vincent slipping me his weird smirk, the one I hated. The one he always gave that said he knew what was going on. Or he knew what you looked like naked, and he liked it. "You girls must be crushed." He said it like he was sincere, but I saw the gleam in his eyes. He knew how we felt about Rachel. Sage must have told him.

We never discussed it with anyone but the four of us. It had been a secret amongst us. Something we had sworn to take to the grave.

He winked at me. "You need a hug, princess?"

"No." I glared, wanting to ask him if his balls needed another whack, but this wasn't the time or place. "But Sage might. She got drugged last night," I offered, trying to make sure no one suspected us. "You should be at the hospital with her."

Jake looked down on me. "No way."

"Yeah. She and that new girl, Rita." I nodded.

He winced. "So someone drugged our girls and then killed one of them?" His arm tightened around me. "When I find out who it was, they're dead."

I shrugged out of the embrace. "Sage and Rita are

still in the hospital."

Louisa gave me a look from her phone where she was finding the news and social media feeds for more on the story. "Your father failed to mention that."

Sierra helped me out. "He took them in the middle of the night. We got back here around eleven, eleven thirty. He took them right away. They were both sick."

Lainey nodded, still squinting like a nerd. "It was scary. Sage was spacey and weird for like two hours after we got home."

"GHB? Did it wear off fast?" Vincent narrowed his gaze and cocked an eyebrow. His green eyes seemed to be focused on me, like I knew something about it.

I squeezed my lips tight, fighting the urge to admit aloud to the fact that he was the only one in our midst who might use date rape drugs. "I don't know."

Sierra nodded. "It did."

I turned back to the house. "Lainey, let me get your glasses. They're still in my room." I hurried into the house and up the stairs.

When I got to my room, I paused in the doorway. It looked different.

There were ghosts here now.

A vision of Rachel walked by my bed, berating me for kissing the German exchange student, Gunter. She smiled and laughed at me, shaking her head. I couldn't hear her. I didn't need to. I remembered how it all went.

"Lindsey, you are a six. Your personality would make you a five, but your wealth and connections bump you up to a seven at best. That exchange student is a nine for sure, just based on looks. His father, being who he is, makes Gunter a ten, maybe an eleven. That's out of your league." She dropped to her knees, lifting my chin. *"I just don't want to see you get hurt."*

I stood there, remembering exactly how bad she had made me feel. The bitterness still rotted away inside me.

She was a bitch. A horrible bitch. She had treated me like garbage my entire life. I dropped to my knees, crying out when my knee hit the ground. I sobbed, staring at the room, freeing myself of any guilt I might have over not mourning her death properly.

She was never a friend of mine, and she treated the people I loved the most even worse.

I sobbed, holding my face and letting the guilt slide down my cheeks in the form of tears. They were not for her. They were for me. I could finally grieve the terrible way she had treated me—no, bullied me. I was free of her and I was ashamed I felt that way.

Warmth surrounded me as arms wrapped themselves around my waist and back. I shook, letting the person holding me think I was crying for Rachel.

It didn't matter that I wasn't.

A hand brushed my hair and lips, and delicately placed soft kisses caressed my forehead. The breath was different but the rest of the feeling was too familiar.

I opened my eyes, immediately tensing and pushing Vincent away from me. But he was stronger than I was and held me to him. "Let me console you. I know you're sadder than you want anyone to know, my sweet princess Lindsey."

"No." I shook my head, sniffling and struggling to get away. "I don't want you to do this. Sage is one of my best friends. And you are a pig. And for the last damned time, I am *not* a princess."

He let out a slight chuckle and looked down, only smiling with one side of his mouth. "Sage and I aren't together, Linds. We haven't been for about three weeks. Maybe four. Maybe even five." His gaze narrowed like he was counting.

My jaw dropped. "What?"

"Yeah, five weeks." He nodded indifferently. "I broke up with her at the beginning of summer. She asked me not to tell anyone. She wanted me not to and I honestly didn't care." He said it so matter-of-factly that I had no response. He stood, brushing off his dark chinos and dress shirt. "If you require anything at all, I will do it for you with no questions asked. Whatever you need, come to me. I really need you to know that I mean it. I would do anything for you." He gave me a look, a weird one I didn't understand, and then he turned and walked away.

I might have said it was the weirdest two minutes I had ever spent with someone, but last night was always going to top that. Forever.

Or so I thought.

I grabbed Lainey's glasses from my dresser and carried them downstairs, still weirded out by the hug and strangely sincere words I'd gotten from Vincent. I took a breath, grateful for the swelling and random tears still sitting in my eyes, and walked out onto the patio. At least I seemed as though I was grieving my friend.

As soon as I got outside, I saw that my father was back. He was hugging Louisa because she relished in the drama. His eyes darted to me and he appeared drained. I lifted my hand in a stupid wave. He nodded and let go of Louisa, walking to me. He wrapped himself around me and whispered, "We need to talk."

I agreed. "Okay. Let me just give Lainey her glasses. She's blind as a bat." I pulled away from him and hurried to Lainey, handing her the thick black frames. She placed them on and blinked, shaking her head. "These aren't mine." She hauled them back off.

"What? Those are yours. They were the only glasses in my room."

She lifted her swollen eyes and squinted. "I think I know my own glasses, Linds. These aren't them."

I took them back and put them on, realizing they were clear glass. I turned and looked back up at my bedroom window, confused about why I had glasses that matched hers, but they had no prescription in them.

I took them off and clutched my hand around them, walking back to my father and leaving Lainey to talk more with Andrew, Sierra, Vincent, and Jake.

"I'm going to take a nap. I need to lie down before the gala." Louisa clicked inside with her ridiculous heels. She leaned in and kissed my father on the cheek before retiring for the afternoon.

Her words floated about in my empty head, but when I managed to make sense of them I peered up at my father in disgust. "Gala?"

He flashed a look, one suggesting we weren't negotiating on this.

"Dad, you guys can't seriously go ahead with the gala?" My voice raised, piquing the interest of my friends. They stopped talking and my dad sighed, more like seethed.

"Of course we will go ahead with the gala. The Swanson family wants us to. They want the diversion created by all of us and the gala."

"Dad, Rach—our friend just died! We can't be expected to party and smile politely."

His face didn't change. He wasn't negotiating. "And yet, you are." He grabbed me by the arm and dragged me inside, squeezing harder than he ever had. He pulled me through the games room and into the kitchen. He shoved me against the counter and shook me. "Do you have any idea what I have been through? Do any of you girls understand what has happened? You were reckless and careless, and one of your friends is dead because of it!"

I nodded in shock. "I know."

His face contorted and his eyes were on fire with fury. But it all died there in a seething ball of rage. Because a moment later, he collapsed into me, hugging and crying. I hugged him back, again weepy and sniffling. My arms burned where he had squeezed them and my chest hurt from all the crying.

I had to remind myself that he understood better than any of the other parents. He had seen us right afterward. He comprehended better than anyone that one of his best friends had lost his little girl, and we were very close to joining her.

He wiped his face and pulled back after a minute. "The family has asked that we carry on with the gala and take some of the focus off of them in their time of grieving. I think we can all do that. I think we can be a little selfless in this and do that for them. No matter how hurt we are, they are incomparably worse off." He stood and wiped my face. "We will all wear black and we will all mourn, but we will do it with class and grace because that is who we are. Do you understand me?"

"Yes, sir." I nodded, biting my lip and desperate to ask the real questions burning in my brain—my evil, overly focused brain. "How is Sage?"

"Sage and Rita were both drugged—GHB is what the doctor said. He said it was completely different than the normal GHB. It was intended to wear off quicker, giving the possible rapist only about a forty-minute window." He looked like he might gag when he said rapist.

I recoiled in horror. "Were they raped?" That hadn't even crossed my mind. Of course finding Sage next to Rachel's dead body was fairly distracting. But then standing there, it made sense that they might have been. Maybe Rachel had fought the rapist off but died as a result, and maybe all of that happened while Sage was unconscious. Which would have then given the killer a lot of free time with Sage. Why else did people drug girls at a party?

"No, of course not. Both girls were checked and neither had been assaulted." His dark-blue eyes, the ones that matched mine perfectly, narrowed. "I don't understand your generation. I don't understand drugging someone for sex. In my day you bought a girl a drink, and if she liked you, you got lucky. If she didn't, all you had wasted was a couple of bucks. We certainly didn't drug girls to have our way with them like you kids."

I scowled. "Dad, I don't drug girls to have sex with them—"

"Is this it then—is this the time you come out of the pantry and confess? You have to do it now?" His eyes widened as he cut me off.

"What? What pantry? No, I don't know." I was lost.

He slammed his fist on the counter. "Lindsey Marie, dammit, this is not the time nor the place to be so self—"

"Linds, princess?" Vincent called randomly from the hallway past the kitchen, like he had lost his puppy and she happened to have my name.

I squeezed my eyes shut and begged the gods of everything good that he would vanish, but he came up right behind my dad. "Oh hey, there you are. Sorry to interrupt,

Mr. Bueller, but I need to make sure Lindsey and I match for tonight."

My dad stopped his outburst with a mid-rant pause, as an unsatisfied look crested his face.

Vincent leaned in, kissed me on the cheek, and wrapped his arms around me. "You okay?"

I shook my head. I was still incredibly lost but the truth was, I was not okay. I might never be okay again.

He tilted my face and smiled down on me, offering something of a wicked grin but perhaps softer. "So both of us black then, maybe a red rose lapel?"

"White was her favorite." The words sort of slipped from me.

And then, without asking my permission, he brushed his lips softly on mine, hovering there long enough that I closed my eyes and let him kiss me. He stayed so long I forgot I hated him.

There was a smell that I liked. Deodorant, sweat, and cologne. There was a reaction in my stomach, a tightening that made my knees weak and my heart beat faster. I liked it all.

He pulled back and offered his hand to my father. "I will pick her up at seven and have her home by midnight, and not take my eyes off her once."

My father looked like he too might kiss Vincent. He took his hand and then ended up in a one-armed embrace. He winced like he might cry again.

I was lost. Very lost.

Vincent patted my father on the back and walked out, offering me a single wave and a sly grin.

My dad hugged me, kissing the side of my face. "Oh, thank God. I was so worried you were gay."

"What?" The whole thing hit then. The pantry was the closet, and I was the cast member of *Orange is the New Black*.

Vincent had been eavesdropping. My father had thought I was confessing my sexuality, and Vincent used it all as a great opportunity to save me from my dad so he could torture me all night long. I was officially in hell.

"The short hair and the not wanting to date and not caring how you looked. I assumed—"

"DAD! Gay people don't always have short hair, and they care about how they look. I'm just lazy and not interested in boys."

His eyes narrowed back to the evil look.

"Except Vince, obviously," I forced myself to say.

"That's good. Vince is a good guy." He nodded against the side of my face and sighed. "And this—this makes me happy. You and him. No wonder you've been so hush-hush about it. Sage is still madly in love with him. I honestly thought they were still an item. She was devastated when he didn't come to the hospital."

"Is she all right, Dad?" I didn't want to talk about me and Vince. I wanted to kill Vince, but he was the only thing saving me from a "Pray the Gay Away" bible retreat.

"No." He shook his head and pulled back, wiping away a rogue tear. "Sage is far from all right. She won't be coming tonight. Her family is with Rachel's. They are all going to be together tonight." He narrowed his gaze. "Have you seen Ashton?"

I bit my lip, not sure what to say. "No." I didn't know why I lied. I supposed it was the way he had asked, like there was a motive behind it or Ash was in trouble.

"He hasn't come home and no one has seen him since he left the party. Some are fearing he is either dead along with her or he killed her."

"He didn't." I shook my head with absolute certainty. "I'm sure he's just sad and wanting to be alone. He broke up with her that night." I swallowed hard. "He left the party long before any of us. He didn't kill her. He just wanted to be away from her. He dumped her and took her car, the Benz, and left the party. I saw him."

My dad's eyes narrowed. "Well, that's good then. The police *are* asking for him. I hope he turns himself in before they have to look for him."

"Are they at Rachel's right now?"

"Yes. They have the entire yard under scrutiny as we speak. The family is cooperating and they are certain they will have this all solved straightaway. When Dick Swanson phoned me this morning to find out what had happened to you all, he sounded strong. He was certain whoever had drugged the girls was just trying to get lucky with one of you and Rachel was the unlucky one."

I nodded like a zombie might, agreeing but not agreeing at all.

His eyes darkened a little as he furrowed his brow. "But I think you and I both know that's not what happened. I have a terrible suspicion this has nothing to do with rape and more to do with the fact Sage was put next to Rachel. Almost as if the killer wanted it to look like the two of them had fought and Sage had killed Rachel. Everyone at the party remembers seeing Rachel and Sage fight. They remember that Ashton broke it off with Rachel. We need to make certain no one finds out the truth that Sage's unconscious body was there with Rachel—ever."

He was handling all of this too well. And he had Hendricks on speed dial. That told me my father had cleaned up messes before.

"What about Sierra's guesthouse?"

"Cleaned, completely. Being refurnished as we speak." His eyes told me not to ask any more questions and for once I listened. "Our best hope is that Rachel's body comes back with some sort of rape evidence. I hate to say it, but it'll clear the rest of you."

I sighed and hugged him, needing to feel safe for just a moment.

CHAPTER TEN
Kick in the nuts and kiss on the cheek
kind of night

My black dress was a repeat I had worn to a celebration of life last year. It was fancy but not too fancy: a simple gown with an empire waist and off-the-shoulder sleeves that were a little too ruffled for my taste. But I hadn't bought the dress. I never bought dresses. Having a personal shopper meant never really shopping when it was decided you had no actual taste. When it was left up to me, I bought comfortable clothing. Louisa called them my grubbies and they were only permitted when I was working or bumming around the beach, but I snuck out with them on all the time.

My eyes darted to Sierra in the mirror. She moved like a robot, applying Erase Paste to her eyes and cheeks to try to hide the puffiness and the reddening. She reminded me of a dead princess in her black gown and her haunted stare. An Ophelia if she were floating in a pond maybe.

"Can you tell I've been bawling all day?" Lainey asked as she gave me a look, blinking and suffering through the contacts she was wearing. "These things are killing me. My eyes are so dry from crying." She blinked again, getting one eyelid a bit stuck for a second.

"You look lovely," I offered. She did. Her dress was short and poufy, showing off her slim legs and gorgeous black shoes. Her mother had shown up with the outfit. Her makeup was a bit much, but it always was when her mother did it.

"Sage isn't coming," I said before I recalled already having said it.

They both nodded, exactly as they had when I said it the first time.

"We should go see her after the party," I suggested as I turned around again, looking at the back of the dress.

Sierra glanced up at me. "You're going with Vincent. She isn't going to want to see you."

My jaw dropped, seeing the flash of something hateful in her eyes. But I bit my tongue, flustered by the fact he had just saved me from my father thinking I had come out of the closet, or pantry in his case.

Sierra winced, realizing she had been a bit harsh. "Sorry, you know what I meant."

Lainey walked to me, wrapping her arms around me. "We just wish you'd told us something was going on with you guys, instead of lying."

"I'm not lying. I swear to the gods of all that is unholy in this friggin' town. He dumped Sage at the beginning of the summer." I gave Sierra a look. "When he hit on you he was single. She is the one who has been lying to us."

Her jaw dropped. "What? No way."

I nodded, hating that it was easier to take the coward's path and out Sage for being dumped, than it was to confess that my father outright asked me if I was gay.

Sierra lifted a manicured finger to her lips. "He did say that, but I didn't believe him. I just assumed—it's Vincent."

I nodded. "Me too. But I don't think he's lying. He honestly doesn't care what she thinks of him, and I think coming on to us is his way of telling her that. He talked about me and him at the gala tonight in front of my dad. How could I argue?"

"You couldn't. Every father's dream is Vincent Banks. Poor Sage." Lainey's pale cheeks flushed. "I think we all knew that her parents told her outright she was to date Vincent, so at least she never loved him. I think she likes Jake. God, I hope she does. I do not want him trying to paw me all night. I will stab him."

Sierra and I both looked shocked. "What?"

"Which part?" Lainey jumped. "Oh shit. I wasn't supposed to know that, was I?" Her facts always got mixed up. Some things she was allowed to blab and other things she shouldn't let slip. "I must have heard it somewhere." She tried lying, but it didn't work when we knew she remembered every detail of where she'd heard it.

"From your mother," Sierra noted.

Lainey nodded, looking down. "She really is the worst of the worst. She was on the phone, telling whoever she was talking to that Sage's parents told her Vincent Banks would be the most successful of all the guys we knew. He was a guarantee of a bright future filled with financial growth and opportunity. She said her parents were mad because they had caught her with Jake a couple of times. And she confessed she wanted to be with him and not Vince at all. Her parents didn't care. Well, Tom didn't care."

"He forced her to date Vince?" I wrinkled my nose. "Gross."

Sierra shook her head. "My parents might be insane, but they would never force me to date someone."

I opened my mouth to agree but then closed it. They both laughed at my face. "We all know my parents would completely tell me who to date." I rolled my eyes. "Louisa can convince my dad of anything. I'm going to end up at the Crimson Cove debutante ball and they will be auctioning me off to the richest person." I mimicked a weird accent and closed one eye like I was a Caribbean pirate. "Hey, you. I got a good woman for you. Very cheap!" We all laughed but deep down we knew it was true. Arranged marriages weren't uncommon amongst the people our parents wanted us to be.

"Speaking of the richest people in the crowd, are you dating Vince?" Sierra asked.

"No." I slumped in the chair and covered my face, speaking through my fingers. "Honestly, he just saved me from my dad. He heard my dad getting mad at me, and he interrupted and made it seem like we were going out tonight. And of course Dad was ecstatic."

"Ewwwww, now you owe him." Lainey laughed again.

I nodded, hands on my face and all.

"Well, so long v-card," Sierra mocked and grabbed my arm, pulling me into her and stroking my head. "And Sage is never going to get over this, so you better start planning the path to redemption with her. Sucking up, phase one, commences the moment she is allowed out of the yard again."

I smiled weakly. "At least this gets you off the hook. She will be so busy hating me, she won't remember to hate you."

"True story."

The three of us hugged, and I wondered if they were as confused as I was.

We wiped and powdered once more before leaving my bedroom, looking like we were going to the Goth prom.

When we got downstairs my dad smiled wide, but the hurt and fear still lingered in his eyes—Louisa, not so much. She beamed and nodded. "You girls look lovely. Very elegant."

"Let's get this over with," I muttered just low enough that the stepmonster didn't hear it.

"Yup." Lainey sighed and Sierra stalked to where her father was in a tux and talking on the phone. I followed her, wanting to know what he was saying and if he had heard anything from Sage.

"I will be in touch." He hung up and smiled at us all, his stare also filled with emotion. "You girls look beautiful." He kissed Sierra on the cheek.

"How's Sage?" Lainey asked, without even trying to contain her worry.

"She's been discharged from the hospital. Her family is terribly upset, naturally. Ra—the Swansons are at the Millers' place trying to cope as the police search their property and clear away the remains. They left the bod—her there a long time to process the site, apparently. Had to call in someone from New York." He struggled with that, which was out of character. He was a big-time New York lawyer. He didn't struggle to speak about anything. He nodded and glanced at Sierra. "But we will all put on brave faces for our friends and show the world no one can bring Crimson Cove down. This will be solved before dinner tomorrow night, I'm sure of it." His left eye twitched a bit.

"Why don't we get a picture of you three looking so lovely before your dates arrive?" Louisa pulled out the camera as Lainey's mom jumped up and forced lip gloss on Lainey who didn't even struggle.

They positioned us at the fireplace and stepped back, all looking too excited and far too normal.

"Smile, girls." Lainey's mom lifted her cheeks, reminding us how one smiled.

I lifted my cheeks as Lainey's hand sought out mine. I reached and grabbed for Sierra's, and we held to one another, still rocked from the events of the past twenty-four hours.

"Cheers." Louisa laughed and took the photo. "Now that is a great photo of solidarity and friendship."

I swallowed hard; I hadn't realized just how tough this would be. Our friendship and our secrets were a heavy burden to bear.

We gripped one another, not moving, maybe not knowing where we should go next.

The doorbell rang, making me jump and the grip on our hands tighten. Jake and Andrew strolled in, smiling wide and looking the way they should, both in tuxes with their hair slicked back and their perfectly straight teeth gleaming white. They were freshly shaven and dressed like gentlemen. There was something in their eyes though—something that lingered there from the news none of us could shake.

Jake walked to Sierra and Andrew to Lainey, offering the girls white rose corsages to match their lapels. They let go of me and joined their dates so we could finish getting ready. We knew the group photos would come next.

Vincent came in after them, holding a white rose bracelet and wearing his cheeky grin. I contemplated telling him I didn't want an escort, but the look on my dad's face was too much to bear. I couldn't break his heart, not on the night of the gala and the night after Rachel had been murdered. Dad was barely holding it together.

Vincent walked to me, looking down on me with appreciation or perversion; it was tough to tell with him sometimes. "You look beautiful." He said it so low I almost didn't hear him, and he was close enough I could taste his delicious cologne. He slipped the stunning bracelet over my hand and tightened it so the rose sat perfectly. He bit his lip and stared at the sight of our hands together. "I have to talk to you." Again he whispered.

I nodded, realizing I had been right and this had been a ploy of some sort. "Not here. Whatever game this is, let it play for the night so my poor dad doesn't think I dumped you for one of the cocktail waitresses."

"You mean when you come out of the pantry and go on a crazed hot-waitress safari?" He smiled wryly.

"I will kill you if you ever bring that up again." I couldn't help but laugh. "Anyway, I'll break the sad news to him tomorrow that we just didn't work out."

He chuckled and lifted his gaze to mine. "We aren't breaking up, Linds. That's not what I want to talk to you about."

"What?" My stomach landed in my lower belly with a thud. Those devilish green eyes, and the way his stare bored into me as if he might devour me any second, had me on pins and needles. But the fact we were suddenly an item, and it was his idea, freaked me out completely. "Do you need me to hide some drugs or smuggle a girl into the country or something? Did you kill Rachel?"

"No. None of the above. I just want to spend time with you. Jesus, you look beautiful. That's it."

"You said that already." I swallowed hard, wishing he wasn't staring down on me so intently.

"I just wanted to say it again, in case you doubted my sincerity."

"That's fair. I usually do."

His lips twisted into that grin, the one I hated. The one I had to remind myself I hated. "I know you do." He lifted my hand and kissed the back of it, squeezing gently.

"More pictures—one of all of you, then one of the gentlemen, and then one of the couples," Louisa started barking her orders and waving her hands.

Lainey's mom and Louisa positioned us into one long row, girls standing just in front of their prospective guys.

Vincent slid his left hand, the one my dad couldn't see, around the front of me and pulled me into him with a subtle jerk. His breath hit my ear and I stood there, completely confused sexually and insanely uncomfortable for all five photos she took of the six of us.

The initial discomfort didn't go anywhere, and it worsened when it was time for the couples photos.

"You guys are such a pair," Louisa squealed as we positioned, just the two of us in front of my massive fireplace.

"Yes, we are," Vincent whispered in my ear.

"Stop," I muttered back using Sage's stawwwwwp.

"We both know I don't have to and you can't make me." He chuckled, tickling the side of my face with his laugh. "Your dad wants you to marry me, we both know it. So play nice or I will propose in front of everyone."

"You wouldn't dare."

He scoffed. "Hands down, I would. In a heartbeat." His eyes sparkled.

"I am going to knee you in the balls again, before this night is out."

"I look forward to it."

That made me smile for real.

CHAPTER ELEVEN
King Poop of Turd Island

When I walked out of the house after eight hundred photos were taken and retaken, I groaned, stretching my neck and back.

"And this shit just started." Lainey grumbled with me.

"We are never going to make the night. I am already exhausted. I think I slept for an hour this morning, maybe two."

"I think I had three." Sierra yawned and climbed into the back of Vincent's limo.

"I have something in the back I think we can all use," Vincent said with a laugh as he climbed in after me. He sat next to me, placing his hand on my knee. I glared at it until he moved it. "We need to look the part. I have never seen your dad this happy. Honeymoon in Monaco maybe?"

I brushed my dress where he had touched and spoke through my teeth, "Stop."

He leaned in with a grin. "Never."

Sierra wrinkled her nose. "Oh my God, you all actually like each other. Look at the sexual tension coming off you both."

Vincent gave her a harsh look while I gasped, shaking my head in protest and pleading with my eyes, but she just laughed cruelly.

Jake chuckled and nudged Vincent as he climbed in. "Vince has always liked you, Linds. Don't you remember the photos we had taken when we were little? It was always Sage staring at Vince who was staring at Linds who was staring at Ra—never mind." He stopped short and laughed uncomfortably. I glared at him, wondering if he was going to say Rachel? I was probably always staring at her, but my eyes would have been filled with daggers. I had hated her my entire life.

"Who wants some?" Jake cleared his throat as he grabbed the bottle of champagne from the holder, popping it out the door so it fizzed onto my driveway.

I remembered those photos. Who the hell had I been staring at? It had to be Rachel. No one else's name started with a Ra—"

My cheeks were bright red, and I couldn't lift my eyes above the knees of the people in front of me. When I did, Lainey was still giggling and nodding. "I remember that."

"You're embarrassing Lindsey and of course myself." Vincent's voice was its usual blend of insincerity and mockery.

"Nothing embarrasses you, Vince." Jake scoffed.

"Okay, you're embarrassing yourselves."

I sighed, avoiding Vincent's stare. I knew it was on me. Normally, I could feel his eyes from across a crowd. I had thought it was because he was fond of tormenting me or judging me. I used to imagine he was thinking of all the things that were wrong with me. The list was fairly huge in my mind.

Andrew held up the glasses for Vincent and Jake to pour. "We getting hammered or what?" he asked in his typical chilled-out tone.

My flaming cheeks and pressed lips made it impossible for me to answer, but I nodded my head uncomfortably as I took my drink.

"Hell, yes we are. We are getting drunk and acting like crazy teenagers because it's what we do. It's what the media expects from us, and it's what Rachel would give them." Vincent lifted his glass. "To Rach, may she be at peace in a beautiful place filled with designer clothes and hot guys and drama enough to appease even her."

I shuddered, remembering the last time we had toasted Rachel, and lifted my glass, clinking it against his with everyone else. A pasted and forced smile rested on my face as we all downed the first glass. Sierra grabbed the bottle and drank from it. "And may she find friends twice as loyal as we ever were." She laughed and chugged from the bottle.

My forced smile fell from my face, as did Lainey's.

Jake pulled the bottle from her hands. "Sierra, why don't we hold off on getting sloppy drunk until closer to midnight?"

"Why don't you stop telling me what to do?" She held her glass out at Andrew who poured her another, all the while looking uncertain about his choice.

Lainey gave me a look. I had to assume she was worried Sierra would spill the beans on what had happened the night Rachel had died and get us all in trouble. Sierra was the most reckless of us all, and we all knew too well how loose lips sank ships.

Vince leaned in, speaking softly, "You want some ephedrine?"

I shook my head.

"I do." Sierra held her hand out. He placed three small pills in her palm and gave three to Jake. Lainey, Andrew, and I didn't take any.

"How much longer till we're there?" Sierra sighed, looking restless.

"It's a ten-minute drive from my place," I offered, trying not to sound as pissed with her as I was. I was done giving her leeway. She was being an asshole. She had gone from tired to cranky addict in a matter of moments.

She flashed her sexy smirk. "We should blow this off and go skinny-dipping."

Jake nodded but Lainey and I both shook our heads. "We can't. You know we can't. We have to at least make an appearance." I turned to Vincent. "You know we have to go."

He shrugged. "I'm down with skinny-dipping. My place is empty. My pool is clean. We can just go there."

"Drop us off at the gala first." I glared at him, grateful he was up to his usual asshole antics. It was easier to be mean to him when he was being a douche.

"An hour at the gala and then we go skinny-dipping?" Jake threw it out there, obviously trying to be helpful with a compromise.

"Fine," I said, knowing I wouldn't be going anywhere with any of them. I would suffer through the stupid gala before I went skinny-dipping the day after Rachel died.

The ride got awkward as Sierra stopped talking, maybe getting the sense that Lainey and I were annoyed with her. The guys joked but we didn't talk.

When we got to the clubhouse even I was impressed with the decorations. There were twice as many as last year, covering the beautiful seaside golf resort.

It was lit up so as the sun was setting, the clubhouse became brighter. There were paths lit by torches and the patios had tiny white lights everywhere. The sky was calm and dark blue, with just the hint of pale blue at the horizon.

There was a red carpet where the car stopped, and when the valet got the door I noticed the way he kept his eyes low. I didn't like this trend of drivers and valets not looking you in the eyes. It was unnerving.

I climbed out behind everyone else, letting Vincent take my hand in his and squeeze it as he lifted me from the car. He held me tightly, leading me away from the cameras and the flash. I kept my face down, but I could hear the words being spoken by the reporters lining the strip.

"This is Vincent Banks' limo. Over here! Vincent, over here!"

"Smile. Vincent, over here!"

"Friends of the deceased girl, Rachel Swanson, are just arriving. Each is in black with a white rose, signifying the loss this quaint town has suffered."

"Vincent Banks, the son of the shipping tycoon and oil billionaire Grant Banks, is here tonight. He has with him a girl I believe is the daughter of one of the initial Crimson Cove investors, Mark Bueller. But where is Sage Miller, the girl we are so accustomed to seeing on his arm?"

"You are right, that is Mark Bueller's daughter. I think her name is Louisa Bueller. She's probably a fill-in for the lovely Sage Miller, who we reported earlier was taken to hospital after finding out her friend had died. She hasn't taken the news well."

"Poor girl. Of course she hasn't."

"Good on Vincent for coming out and showing his support of the town and his father."

I tried not to notice they had called me Louisa. I tried not to have hurt feelings when they called me a fill-in girl. I tried not to take it personally that they didn't really know me that well.

Anonymity was not something most of us had. But Lainey, Andrew, and I usually managed to scrape by with some. People recalled us but not in the way they remembered Vincent, Rachel, Sage, Sierra, Ashton, or Jake.

Vincent apparently took it personally enough for us both. He stopped walking and turned, waving slightly while sliding an arm into my waist and pulling me to him, too tightly to be a fill-in girl. "Thanks for coming everyone! As you know, we have suffered a terrible loss here in Crimson Cove. The death of one of our dear friends has been unbearable. Our hearts are with the Swanson family. I am grateful to you who all still managed to come out and get shots of the dresses and tuxes when a much more important story is here—just up the shore." He managed to sound sincere in it all as he mocked them.

He waved and then glanced down at me. "Thank them, Lindsey!" He said my name loud enough that I winced.

"Thank you!" I waved as well, flinching when the cameras' flashes hit me. I hated the stupid rags and our town being part of the gossip. I liked my bit of obscurity, and I suspected I had just watched it die.

Vincent leaned down and pressed his lips again my cheek while whispering, "I am going to have that man fired for calling you a fill-in girl."

I forced a laugh. "Please don't. I don't actually care." I didn't jerk away from him but I turned, dragging him with me this time.

When we got inside I sighed. The room was beautiful and there were only the photographers who were polite enough to ask before they shot you. "That was insane. Why are there so many here? Why aren't they at Rachel's?" I glanced at Vincent, giving him a scowl. "Sage's going to see the news and see the kiss, and she's going to hate me."

He shrugged. "She isn't going to hate you. She's just going to be pissed her little lies are over."

I jerked my hand free from his. "I get it—you think I'm the least likely to be offended that you are using me to make Sierra get over you. You want your freedom from her, and you think pretending to be into me will help that along. But I'm not actually as cool with this as you think. I actually have feelings, you ass. And I actually like the way you smell and look. And—ugh!" I turned and walked to the bar, hoping they weren't going to try the whole "must be twenty-one to drink" thing now that the cameras were rolling because I needed a stiff one.

I leaned against the huge mahogany bar and waved. The bartender, the one from the party the night before, strutted over. "Hey, I know you." He gave me one of those smiles boys give when they think they have a chance with you.

"I know. I threw up a lot and you helped me. I remember."

He wrinkled his nose. "No, last night."

I paused. "Right, and last night."

"You want that same thing with the cranberry juice and vodka?" He looked confused all of a sudden.

"No. Just a scotch on the rocks, please. Make it a double."

"Yes, ma'am." He cocked an eyebrow. He turned and poured, looking baffled. He was obviously rifling through his memories, trying to find the puking story while I was wishing I had kept it to myself. He passed me the drink as the lightbulb turned on in his head. "The yacht!" He laughed and shook his head. "I forgot all about that. You had the wicked stepmom who yelled at you for drinking too much, but you were seasick." He grinned wider, still chuckling. "How have you been?"

I sighed, not sure where to go with that. "Great."

His gaze narrowed. "You aren't friends with that girl, who just got uhm—were you?"

"I was," I answered quickly, looking around. I wasn't

fast enough to escape before Vincent was there, leaning against the counter, blocking the bartender and grinning. "You got my favorite. Thanks, princess."

I rolled my eyes and let him drink my scotch. I lifted my fingers at the bartender to tell him I needed another two. Vincent would tear through this drink like it was his first one.

"Tell me why you hate being called princess." He sipped and watched my eyes like he was studying them. When I didn't speak he did, "Because as far as I can tell, you are. Your family is rich, you live in a palace, your dad acts like he's King Shit of Turd Island, and you have a wicked stepmother."

I snorted at the King Shit comment.

He lifted a finger. "And when you flash your beautiful smile I can't help but wonder if maybe woodland creatures are on their way to assist you in whatever deviant behavior you have planned for the evening."

I stopped smiling. "You are the deviant. And you watch way too much Disney." I shuddered, remembering the pictures in his drawer.

He shrugged. "It's all part of being a teenaged boy. A little Disney and a little deviancy. Keeps the blood flowing."

That arrogance made me angry. "Those girls didn't look like it was a typical day for them, Vince. They could have been human trafficking victims." I turned and stalked off, completely annoyed.

His hand bit in, spinning me around. The fun look on his face was gone as he lowered his stare to mine. "What did you see?"

I shoved him, tearing my arm from him. "Screw you!"

"What?" His tone made me jump. "What did you see?"

I swallowed and confessed, hating that I wasn't nearly as sneaky as I thought. "Your drawer. I saw the photos in the false bottom."

His jaw fell and his eyes closed. He released me, shaking his head.

"I don't even know why the hell I am here, but I definitely know I shouldn't be with you. You're an ass and a pervert." I turned and walked into the crowd, not waiting around to hear his lies about how they weren't his or he was holding them for someone. I couldn't believe I'd let him kiss me, or that I'd liked it.

I walked to where Sierra was slamming booze and tapped her on the shoulder. "You ready to go?"

She smiled wide, putting her drink down on the counter. "Let's do this."

I linked my arm in hers and nodded at Lainey who fled from her mother's side and joined us on the way out.

"Where are we going?"

"I need to see Sage. This was a terrible idea. This is morbid, dancing and drinking as if there isn't a storm pouring down on us."

CHAPTER TWELVE
Kidnapper font?

Sage's night guard gave me a look. "The Miller family isn't seeing anyone."

Sierra leaned across me and fluttered her eyelashes. "Tell Sage that Sierra wants to see her."

He sighed and walked back to his desk. Seconds later the gate opened, but he didn't look impressed. I glanced at Sierra. "I hope my car is still here."

"I'm sure their driver took it home for you after that kiss."

I winced. "I don't like people driving my car."

She rolled her eyes as the car parked in front of the house. "You are such a diva."

Lainey, who had been sitting quietly, climbed out first and walked calmly. She seemed really uncomfortable.

We followed her to the door, smiling at Hennessey, the butler. I walked in behind Sierra and Lainey, noting the weird look he gave me. "You having a good night, Miss Lindsey?"

I shrugged and glanced past him, realizing he had motioned for me to wait a moment. I sighed. "How bad is it?"

"You don't want to be here. I shouldn't be doing this; we both know that. But she is quite unsettled. Her father just had his driver take your car home before Sage lit it on fire." His British accent was thicker than my butler Robert's.

"Oh God. Did she touch it at all?"

He shook his head.

"Thanks. Maybe I'll wait in her room and talk to her alone." I slipped past him and headed for the stairs. I didn't have to walk near the room where everyone else was to get upstairs, thankfully.

Taking each stair slowly, I had the funniest feeling. It was the first time in my life I had ever experienced it so the sensation took me a second to recognize.

It started low in my belly and prickled my skin, making me anxious and worried.

I was scared to be alone.

I exhaled and glanced around nervously, certain I was being watched from all sides. Every shadow became a person lurking. Every corner had a body around it. And in each room I couldn't see I knew there was someone following my every step.

It was the most miserable sensation I had ever had. My eyes ached from staring and my head hurt. It was like I had to strain to see everything, and yet the walls felt as if they were closing in.

At the top of the stairs, I did the thing the old me would have done: I walked to Ashton's room and lifted my hand to the knob. When I turned it I exhaled and reminded myself I liked the dark, I could hide in the dark. It was the light that showed too much.

When I cracked open his door my mouth went dry.

The large room, easily the size of mine if not bigger, was completely dark except where the light of the silver moon shone in the huge windows, casting shadows everywhere. I shuddered and entered, closing the door and pressing my back against it.

My palms were sweaty and I could hear my heart beating as I gazed about the dark space as if it were a blank canvas or this was my first time snooping in someone's room.

But it wasn't.

I was seasoned at snooping, as well as sniffing out the best hiding places.

But there in the dark I was alone, as in *on my own,* and I felt it.

Pushing myself away from the door, I stumbled out into the room, unsure of which way to go. The stillness of the room and the silence in the air haunted me. I turned to the right, opening the door to his bathroom. I closed it again, feeling a bit weird about going in there. Ashton didn't seem like the type who would hide anything but if he did, it wouldn't be in a bathroom.

And I hated bathrooms anyway. If I was going to be murdered, out of all rooms, I feared it being in the bathroom the most. I had made the mistake of watching *Psycho* too many times. Combining that with the movie *It,* and I was not going in there.

I glanced at the door next to me. I stepped lightly, opening the closet and flicking on the light. I exhaled, liking the light being on.

His closet overwhelmed me. I didn't even know where to start. But the empty hangers on the floor seemed like a good place. I took a step in farther, noting the way the clothes seemed pulled forward on the shelves, like Ashton or someone had grabbed clothes and not noticed these had been pulled forward too. It was too disheveled to be any one of our closets.

Empty hangers were still hung up, randomly spaced. All the clothes that were moved and hangers that were bare seemed to be in the comfortable clothing section of the closet. None of his tuxes, suits, or dress shirts seemed to be missing.

It was weird, to say the least. But it was weirder still that I didn't suspect him of killing Rachel. He clearly knew she was dead. When I told him, he hadn't even flinched. And he knew Sage had been hurt. But how and why? And his clothing was missing and the police were looking for him.

Why would he run if he were innocent?

I left the closet, realizing he would not have hidden anything in there. Someone else came in daily to put his clothes away.

I stepped back into the dark room, leaving the light on in the closet to brighten the bedroom just enough. His bed was made but there was an imprint in the bedding, like someone had lain on top of it. The shadows from the light created mountains and valleys where the person's outline was.

His desk was empty and his bedside tables were clean and without false bottoms. I checked under the bed and in the laundry, and even in the walls, pushing and tapping lightly. I was about to lose hope in my mad skills, which had returned tenfold while I had been snooping, when I caught a glimpse of something.

It was a crumpled piece of paper in the wastebasket.

His maid was just like ours; she cleaned the garbage every day, just like she put away the clothes and straightened everything up.

Only I knew Ashton had fled in Rachel's car or that he was aware of what had happened when we arrived at Sierra's. I hadn't told a single person Ashton had taken Rachel's car. I hadn't told anyone he was missing. And I certainly hadn't shared the fact he knew what had happened at the party.

So the maid would have definitely cleaned this room today. The mess in here was new.

Ashton had come home today and taken things. I wondered if Sage and her family knew and just hadn't filled the rest of us in on it. But mostly I wondered why he had left in the first place.

Something about the garbage called to me. I bent down and picked up the basket, lifting the one single piece of paper from it.

When I lowered the basket my nerves started to twinge with anxiety. I smoothed the paper and opened it, gasping.

In kidnapper's-ransom-note style it read, "Leave town or your sister is next!"

I swallowed hard, realizing suddenly I had my answer. Ashton had come home, but I would bet he hadn't told anyone. I would bet he had left town in a hurry.

Completely terrified and still convinced I was being watched, I looked up from the paper and glanced around. Through the window I saw a figure on the grass below staring up at me.

I jumped, leaping behind the drapes so I could hide and peek. My hands shook as I tried to get a glimpse through the side of the curtain, but the person was gone. I exhaled, though I hadn't realized I was holding my breath.

If that was the killer, then he or she knew I had seen the note.

Did that mean I was next?

I closed his door and ran toward Sage's room. When I got inside Sage, Sierra, and Lainey were already there.

Sage rolled her eyes, sighing loudly. "No one invited you, Lindsey. Leave." She pointed at the door.

I tried to catch my breath and twitched my head in a no. I didn't want to go outside and I needed to explain. More than anything, my brain screamed, *what if the killer is still there? What if they are coming in here?* "No, Sage. Stop being an ass." I sighed and lifted a hand.

"I'm the ass? You made out with my boyfriend on national television and I'm the ass?"

"He isn't your boyfriend. You need to stop lying to us all." I rolled my eyes, in no mood for her dramatics over petty shit, not while her brother had run off and the killer was threatening her.

She gasped but I silenced her with a fierce look. "You have been lying to us for months about him and you. You made Sierra feel like shit for HIM kissing HER, when in reality you had been broken up for a month. I don't even understand why you want to date him—he's a pig. But I never made out with him, and I never came on to him. Believe it or not, I have zero interest in him. Now stop being a little bitch and tell us what the hell is going on here." I flashed the ransom-looking note at her, still trying catch my breath.

She looked cruel for half a second and then it melted away to confusion. "What is that?" Her eyes widened, as did everyone else's.

"I found this in Ashton's wastebasket and there's someone in a dark hoodie on the lawn." I wiped the cold sweat from my brow.

Sage's eyes filled with tears as she sniffled. "That was in Ash's room?"

"Yeah. I assume it means you are next." I pointed at

her window. "Let's not forget about the person on the lawn who might be here to kill you," I repeated and pointed at her closed curtains. "I saw someone."

Lainey's mouth dropped open.

Sierra, who had been sporting a bit of a cocky look when Sage and I were squabbling, swallowed hard after taking a sip of her Pepsi. That look had since washed away.

Sage shook her head. "I don't know what you mean. Why would that be in Ashton's room? Where is he? That's a joke. That's not real. Where is he?"

"Well, I think he must have come here after his room was cleaned this morning. His closet's a mess, and it looks like he rifled through things in his room." It was my turn to swallow hard and confess. "And this was in his wastebasket, crumpled up."

"But why?" Sage still seemed suspicious.

I sighed and let it all out. "He was at Sierra's last night, just before I called my dad. But my dad never took care of Rachel's car—Ash did. He showed up moments after we arrived, maybe guessing we would go to Sierra's or maybe following us, and he took her car. He told me to clean us all up and left. I haven't seen him since. I assumed he would clean the car or get rid of it altogether because he thought you killed Rachel."

Sierra snapped. "You kept this from us?"

"You were all freaking out and I was freaking out, and honestly, I didn't think it would do him any good to be named as part of this. He and Rachel had been fighting; I didn't want him to get in trouble. Especially, since I believed it was you who killed Rachel, and he was cleaning up your mess, like the rest of us."

Lainey nodded but Sage shoved me, hard too. "You always want to be the only one who knows shit, Linds. You are such a liar—how do we know you didn't plant that in Ash's room? And no one but you saw him at Sierra's—you probably made that up. You probably killed Rachel!"

Sierra nodded but Lainey looked torn.

"That doesn't even make sense." I shoved back, knocking Sage onto her bed.

"Rachel hated you and loved to torment you. It makes perfect sense."

I lost it then, pointing at her and screaming, "You were the one fighting with Rachel, and you are the one we found covered in her blood and injured like she'd knocked you out. How do we know that you didn't kill her and then take the GHB so you would suddenly have an alibi? How do we know you didn't write this stupid note to make it look like you're innocent and next on the killer's list?" I stepped back, disgusted. "And I am not a liar. I'm not the one who's been lying about her relationship all summer!"

"Least I have had a relationship and am not currently pining after the emo coffeehouse whore!"

My insides tightened and I might have let out a small whimper. "Screw you, Sage. And get rid of the disgusting naked selfies you have in your journal before someone sees them and they end up on the net!" I turned and stormed from the room, leaving Sage crying, the note on the floor, and the other two stunned silent. It was such an offside way of threatening her with the naked photos. I wasn't sure she would even get that it meant I had snooped through her room and knew her dirty little secrets.

I didn't even care that there was a hoodie weirdo on the lawn. I just wanted out. If he messed with me I would kill him myself.

Stomping down the stairs, I pulled out my earrings and stalked for the front door. I was outside and across the driveway before I realized I was alone with the maybe killer and far less skilled in hand-to-hand combat than I had anticipated being. I knew in my heart Sage hadn't done any of it. I knew that. In spite of the drama she was still the nicest girl in the world. I knew that. She was just angry.

And knowing that meant I was alone with a killer or, at the very least, a stalker.

My steps quickened but my heels were killing my feet. I stepped out of them, tucking my earrings in the toes, and then holding them like the heel was a weapon.

A sound broke the silence behind me. I didn't look back, I ran for the gatehouse, imagining the killer was chasing me. My brain was super helpful by offering up all the imagery I had stored in there from the night Rachel died.

Images of the way her body had been lying in the leaves and dirt flashed behind my eyes as I sprinted for the guard.

CHAPTER THIRTEEN
Blackmail's a B

My feet padded along the driveway, making the only noise I could hear. When I turned the corner and saw the guardhouse, I sighed and slowed down, breathing like I might have done a marathon.

The guard gave me a slight wave from his booth, but I hurried to him, pointing behind me. "I saw someone, back on the lawn when I was leaving. You should check it out."

He cocked an eyebrow. "No one got past here."

"No, but you can climb the walls and fences or come up from the beach. How do you think we have snuck past you so many times?" I shook my head and walked to the road, hoping he would at least check.

I pulled my cell phone from my clutch, about to dial my dad for a ride when a limo pulled up next to me. My own reflection gave me a chill. The wild look in my dark-blue eyes and the sweat on my brow gave me the appearance of a stranger. My short brown hair was wild from the running.

Before I had the chance to walk away, the window came down and a smug-looking Vincent nodded his head at me. "Get in, princess. I called your dad already and told him we were headed back to the house."

My nose wrinkled and my upper lip lifted in disgust. "I am going nowhere with you."

"Let me explain." He sounded desperate. I turned on a heel and started up the road. The driver kept pace with me as Vincent begged, "Please, Linds. Don't do this now. I finally have the chance, and I'm blowing it by trying to win you over like a normal girl, and you aren't normal at all. I should have just been honest with you from the start."

"Night, Vince." I continued ignoring him and walked,

hating the fact my bare feet were on the street and he had called me not normal. *Asshole.*

"Hugo, close the window but keep pace," Vincent shouted as he jumped out from the slow-moving car and walked next to me, still talking. He wasn't wearing his suit anymore. "I was sent those pictures. They were sent to me with a weird note done like it was written by a kidnapper. It honestly looked like a ransom note. Like kidnapper font?" He sounded confused.

I paused when I realized that was exactly the same as the letter to Ashton, making Vincent and the car stop dead in their tracks. "What?"

"Yeah." He nodded, looking sincere and worried even. "Someone sent a few of them to me, told me I had to put the pictures in my bedside drawer or more would come every week and they would get worse. At first they were normal pictures. I threw them out, thinking it was a joke. But sure enough, more came, some even addressed to my dad. I managed to get them before he saw them. The handwriting on the envelopes is always the same. They come from random addresses around the world, no consistency. No rhyme or reason, just disgusting pictures of girls in weird poses. Nothing worse than I have seen online but owning them makes me feel weird."

"You are an idiot. Why didn't you pretend to keep them there and then burn them at night?" I tilted my head back, noting the swirling skies and dark clouds.

He nodded again, looking unsettled. "I *did* try that."

My stomach landed with a thud. "The person sending them knew you had burned them?"

"They knew. I got worse and worse pictures. So I did the false bottom on the drawer, pretending the handle needed to be fixed, but really I had that done. I usually leave the more harmless ones in the top part of the drawer and the bad ones below when I leave the house. When I'm home I have them all in the false part. So long as the stupid photos are in that part of my room, more don't come in the mail. The moment I move them, worse ones come."

"How do they know if the pictures have been moved?"

He shook his head. "I don't know."

"They must be watching us all the time." I swallowed hard as my eyes trailed off back toward the Miller residence. "Someone was in the yard watching me when I was in Ashton's room."

His lips twitched into a smile. "Hoodie? That was me." He flinched when he saw my face and pointed sheepishly at the sky. "It seemed like it was going to rain and my jacket's expensive. I didn't want to get it wet."

"Why were you spying on me?" My insides tightened again. I glanced at the car and then his shoes, wondering if I could outrun him.

"I had to make sure you were safe. I told your—"

I shoved him. "What were you thinking? You almost gave me a heart attack. I thought you were the killer." I stepped back, realizing he could still be the killer. He could be lying.

"I told your father I wouldn't take my eyes off you. I meant it. Especially since Rachel—" His voice trailed off.

"This person has been in your house?" I changed the subject, suddenly realizing the person who had sent the letters to Ashton and Vincent killed Rachel.

He shrugged. "Had to have been. I assume everything is bugged now or I am being watched. I have sensors that check for recording devices." He pursed his lips with a troubled look upon his face. I had never seen this side of him before this week. It made me think he wasn't the killer, but it didn't make me trust that thought, not one-hundred percent. Reasonably anyone could be the killer.

"Ashton had one too." I said it to see his reaction.

He looked genuinely confused. "What? Security cameras and sensors?"

"No." I shook my head as the wind started to pick up, rustling the leaves all around us and cooling the air. "Ashton had a note in his room—a note made to look like a kidnapper's ransom note. At first the letters appeared to have been glued on, but it was a font."

His eyes widened as he appeared to not breathe for several moments before he spoke in a hushed tone, "What did it say?"

"Leave town or your sister is next."

He closed his eyes, no doubt worried about Sage even though they had broken up. He had spent the last three years dating her. "Oh no." He shook his head. "No, this is bad. This is connected. Rachel getting murdered and me and the weird pictures, and now Ash. Someone is screwing with us all, and it went too far with Rach. What if she was getting the letters too? What if she had figured out who it was?"

"That's a theory." I stared down at the concrete, the words getting stuck in my throat and making my voice husky when I spoke, "I think the killer wants the police to believe Ashton is guilty of killing her."

"He would never."

I nodded. "I know. He was done being with her, but he was truly the kindest guy in the world and would never harm a hair on her head."

"He left town then?"

"I think so." I shrugged as the wind picked up. "I think it's going to rain. We better hurry." A raindrop splatted on my nose, making me wince. A coastal storm was just what we needed to add to the creepiness of the night.

"What if the person screwing with us is a psychopath?" He sounded lost in his thoughts.

I glanced up at him, noting the weird expression on his face. "What are we going to do? We should go to the police with what we know. I don't know anything about psychopaths beyond the stuff Lainey and I have read." I said it before I remembered exactly what I knew and how badly it incriminated my friends and even my family.

"No." Thankfully, he shook his head. "That's not a good idea. We don't know who is doing this, but we do know the circle of people it's affecting is growing. They might have ways of making it appear like one of us did it."

I sighed, so tired of the whole thing already and wishing I could just tell him what I had seen that night. "We don't even know if it's connected. We're assuming."

"The letter in Ashton's room seems pretty specific,

making it likely that the person sending the weird letters is also the killer."

I shivered as I hugged myself and confessed something I didn't mean to, "I'm scared."

"Me too, princess. But not for the same reason." Vincent stepped closer to me, his eyes wide and showing an emotion I didn't really trust until he spoke, "I don't sleep. I don't go out anymore, not unless you're going too. I can't eat and I can't stop worrying about you. If something were to happen to you, I would die." He stepped closer again as the sky opened up on us, making noise as the heavy rain hammered the road and car. "I'm not scared by the idea that someone is watching me and wants to hurt me. But if they are watching you, I will kill them."

I considered pointing out that if I wasn't being watched, his being around me added me to the list of people the killer was stalking. But I didn't. Partly because I assumed I was on that list already, and not because of Vincent. But mostly I didn't stop him because I found myself wanting to believe the words he spoke. I wanted to believe he—the almighty Vincent Banks—liked me. I was a five and he was a fourteen, until he opened his mouth and then he slunk back to a ten. But it didn't even matter; he was Vincent Banks.

I got a bit lost staring up at him as he looked down on me with droplets of water hanging from his nose and lips. "There is a reason I was always looking at you in pictures. The photographer just caught me in my natural state. I *was* always looking at you. I still am."

With the way the week had been going, it might have been a creepy confession, but it wasn't. I let him step a little closer. I didn't flinch or move away. I didn't sneer or say something that was only half true. I stayed still as his hand came up to my cold, wet cheek and brushed it so softly. I didn't have a reason to let him be nice to me but I liked it.

"I have had feelings for you my whole life, I can't remember a time I didn't wish you were my girl."

I shook my head in little twitches. "That's impossible. You always make fun of me."

"I don't know how to be with someone like you. I know I'm not good enough for you."

I had officially lost my mind. I was standing in the rain, swooning over Vincent Banks.

I thought he might kiss me, but he hovered over me, staring into my eyes for a moment. I wanted him to kiss me. I even parted my lips a little and tilted my head back, but he pulled back, lowering his hand to mine and taking my shoes for me. "I won't try to kiss you again without your permission." I was almost scared of what had happened to him, if he had lost his mind from the fearful state we had both been in, but then his grin popped up. "I'll just wait for you to beg me to do it, princess."

I rolled my eyes and climbed into the back of the limo, grateful he wasn't being too sweet. There was a small worry in my mind that *I* might kiss *him* if he was.

I was soaked and cold and ready for bed, but the idea of being home alone was scary. So I turned and said the last thing I ever imagined I might say, "Can you stay at my house with me?"

He smiled, losing his cocky asshole grin and replacing it with an incredibly sweet one. "I was going to sleep there anyway."

I scowled, sort of put off by it but sort of flattered that he had my safety at heart.

CHAPTER FOURTEEN
Slumber party confessions

I stared at the stars on my ceiling, the perfect replicas of the summer sky over the Northeast.

In the dark his hand crept across my king-sized bed and wrapped around mine. I sighed and smiled, grateful he couldn't see me. I knew I had a ridiculously goofy look on my face.

"What are these constellations?"

I lifted a hand, even though it was lost in the dark room and whispered as I pointed, "Lyra, Corona Australis, Sagittarius, Scutum, Draco, Hercules, Scorpius, and Telescopium."

He turned his head. His breath brushed my cheek. "You are the weirdest girl in the world."

I nodded. "I know. My mom gave me the telescope when I was five. We had a few years with it before she died. Our plan had been to map all the skies—summer, winter, fall, and spring. But she became too sick so I just left the one we got done—summer. And now I like it too much to change it. I feel like she's watching me from the stars in the sky, even in here."

He squeezed my hand. "Your mom was the nicest lady I ever met. I remember the way she always smelled like cookies."

Tears filled my eyes, blurring the stars above me. "Vanilla. She wore Madagascar vanilla." I turned toward him in the dark, just making out the outline of his head against the white wall behind him. "When you go back to being you, can you not make fun of me for any of this? I don't care about the gay jokes or the other jokes, but this is sacred to me."

He moved too quickly, scooting across the bed and hovering his face close to mine. His lips brushed my cheek before I could remind him of his promise. "I have never made fun of you for being sexually confused. I adore that you think you're gay. And besides, I don't want to ever go back. I'm sorry Rachel is dead and Ashton and Sage are being threatened, but I don't want to go back. No matter what."

I leaned into his face and closed my eyes. "I feel exactly the opposite. I wish this week had never happened."

He laughed weakly. "I won't ever wish that," he whispered and held me. Somehow in the dark of the summer night he had managed to transform into a different person. A person I had never met. A person I couldn't consider as a possible killer.

I closed my eyes and fell asleep, feeling completely safe with the last soul on earth I would have envisioned myself ever trusting.

When I woke, it was with a start. I sat up, brushing my hair out of my face and blinking, trying to make my eyes clear.

I was alone and instantly aware of it. Vulnerability crept up on me as I recalled everything that had happened. Vincent walked out of my ensuite wearing nothing but a pair of my baggiest shorts, which were way too short for him. I turned my face away in horror. "What are you wearing?"

He looked down. "I needed a shower. I smelled bad. These were the largest pair of anything you owned." He hopped onto the bed as I flung blankets at him, forcing him to cover his tanned body and six pack. He laughed. "Sorry, jeesh. This is the first time I've ever had a complaint."

"While wearing women's shorts?"

He laughed harder. "No. I rarely wear women's shorts." He stretched out, pulling the covers to his belly, leaving his chest and arms out. I stared up at the ceiling, avoiding him altogether. I imagined this was what a one-night stand would feel like. Waking up awkward and uncomfortable and wishing you were either alone or at ease with each other's bodies.

"When did your letter show up?" I asked, trying to piece the puzzles together and desperately needing a new subject.

"About three weeks ago. I got home and there was a letter on my bed. But the staff never put my mail there. I thought it was strange. Then I opened it and confirmed it was indeed weird."

I turned, covering my mouth with the blankets but still trying to talk. "I think Ashton got his in his room too. He had crumpled it and put it in the garbage, packed clothes and left, by the looks of things. I can't believe this person goes right in your bedrooms."

"Must have. I don't think there is a single other explanation than that."

"Too creepy."

He stared at me, giving me his stupid grin. "Wanna kiss yet?"

I laughed. "I have morning breath, I will use it if I have to."

"You don't scare me." He challenged with his dark-green eyes.

"I have to get up—"

"LINDS!" Lainey called from the hall, cutting me off. My eyes widened, and I was about to shove him from my bed when the door opened. Lainey stopped in the frame with Sierra hovering behind her. Both of their jaws dropped.

Vincent waved, offering a smile. "Morning."

I shook my head immediately. "It's not what it looks like." I waved my hand, motioning for them to come in. "Just come in and close the door."

Vincent fixed the covers so he wasn't as exposed.

"He has shorts on. I have full pajamas on."

Sierra started laughing but Lainey looked horrified. Her expressive face hid nothing.

I pulled the covers over my face. "I swear to God, nothing at all even close. We haven't even kissed!"

"Scouts honor." He mocked me or the situation or both.

I opened my eyes to see Vincent with his right hand in the air. I shoved him and got up, flinging back the covers to prove I was fully dressed.

Lainey stepped in, but I think Sierra pushed her. They

119

walked to my small sofa and sat in the window, both red faced and silent.

"I was scared. The whole thing is freaking me out, and I didn't know when my dad would be home. I asked Vince to stay. He did. He was in boxers, but he showered and all I had were those shorts." I nattered and seemed awfully guilty because of it.

Sierra shrugged. "I feel like we've all woken up next to Vince." She winked at him. The act bothered me but Vincent shook his head. "You wish." He lay back, clearly not moving from the bed anytime soon.

Lainey gave me a look like she wanted to talk. I sighed, adding him to the party. "Vincent got some of those letters too. The ransom ones. He and Ashton both got them."

Sierra looked dubious. "He's pulling your legs to get them apart."

"No. He really got them." I laughed but shook my head as Lainey choked on a laugh.

Sierra's eyes drifted to where he was. "What did it say?"

He didn't look impressed, but I suspected he knew he would have to trust them if they would ever trust him. "That I had to keep some damaging photos in my room at all times. If they weren't in my drawer, I would continue to get much worse ones."

"And you tested the boundaries of that?" Lainey asked quickly.

"I did." He nodded, looking at Lainey like he didn't know how to take her.

She wrinkled her nose. "And you—wanna date Linds?"

He nodded again, looking even more pained.

"Maybe the pictures were meant to be there so Linds would find them and think you're disgusting."

I winced, realizing she had outed me for the snooping. Something I had outed myself for already, but I hated that we might all talk about it.

"Because she snoops in my room every time she comes and does the lawn and gardens?" Vincent asked nonchalantly.

Lainey shrugged. "It's possible. Who else would snoop in your stuff?"

"You do snoop in everyone's shit." Sierra nodded.

Vincent appeared lost and then bit his lip, thinking or already daydreaming. "Yeah. That does make sense. Who else would snoop enough to find the false bottom of my drawer?"

My cheeks flamed but I admitted it. "I did find it."

I hated myself and my weird flaw in that moment, but he smiled wide, taunting me further, "I like to solicit dirty photos and talk from Sasha in hopes you will be shocked when you read my email."

My jaw dropped. "That's terrible."

Lainey wore a horrified expression but Sierra laughed. "Gross. Your computer probably got something from that. She is nasty. She makes me look like a saint."

Vincent cocked an eyebrow doubtfully. "Well, maybe don't go too far."

She tossed a throw pillow at him and it started to feel like a slumber party.

Until the door opened and my dad strolled in, giving us smiles until his eyes met with Vincent. Then his cheeks flushed and his jaw dropped. "Morning."

"Morning, Mr. Bueller." Vincent nodded politely.

"Morning," I muttered. My dad smiled wide, his panicked eyes meeting mine. "I will tell Lori we need a big breakfast served. Ready in thirty minutes?" He didn't wait for our answer and hurried from the room.

I grabbed a throw pillow and covered my face. "OH MY GOD!" I screamed into it. When I lowered it, Sierra gave me a confused look, but Lainey was also embarrassed. "Your dad thinks—"

"Did he see you guys come into the house?" I asked.

Lainey shook her head blankly.

I nodded. "I think he thinks we all slept in here."

Vincent grinned wide. "Yeah, he does." He winked at us, earning the same look from Lainey and me, but a twinkle in Sierra's eyes told me she didn't think it was gross at all.

It dawned on me then that she might have a thing for him.

My jealousy at her twinkling her eyes at him made me think I had a thing for him too.

I had to change the subject fast, "Anyway, the path I think we all need to be on is complete honesty with each other." I glanced at Lainey and Sierra, and they both nodded, so I turned to Vincent and said the thing I had wished I could have before, "The night Rachel died, Sage was with her."

"I know." He nodded.

I shook my head. "No, I mean Sage was unconscious next to Rachel and her blood was all over Sage. Lainey and Sierra found them. When I got there they were all covered in blood from trying to save Rachel. Sage woke up and we ran for Sierra's. I called my dad and he came and cleaned it all up."

Vincent's eyes grew. "You were all there?"

"Yeah."

He winced. "Oh shit. Linds, that's a thing. You ran from a murder scene and left Sage's blood behind?" He made the same face my dad had. "I might know someone who can take care of that with the police."

I grimaced as Sierra shook her head. "No. Sage didn't have a single injury on her. It was all Rachel's blood." That wasn't completely true; she did have a huge fat lip.

He processed for a moment before leaning forward and looking confused. "So she was covered in the blood but had been drugged?"

"Yeah," Lainey offered.

"How did she get there?"

"We think she was posed."

He gave me a panicked look. "Seriously?"

I nodded. "Let's get ready for breakfast and we'll fill you in."

He looked like he might bolt for the door. He didn't. His mind was too busy, processing it all.

CHAPTER FIFTEEN
We are never getting back together

I sat, staring out at the sea, wrapped in a blanket and lost in thought.

"So it's official then?"

I turned to see Sage, a rather distraught-looking version of her, standing on the patio staring at me.

I shook my head. "Go away." There was not enough fight in me to even bother.

"Just tell me if it's official," she demanded.

My head snapped to the right as a fierce look crossed my face. "Is this really the most important thing in your world, Sage? Our friend is dead and someone is blackmailing your brother and Vince, and all you care about is whether Vince and me are official? I don't give two shits about a guy or a possible relationship right now. I care that I had to let someone I have disliked for a very long time sleep next to me because my friends kicked me out to be killed next. Then my father caught us all in the bedroom together. Vince was in my friggin' bed, even though nothing happened. My father thinks Vince slept with us all. I tried telling him it was just safety in numbers, but he didn't look like he believed me." It was meaner than I had intended to go, but I couldn't stop myself. "I am distraught over the fact someone I have known my entire life is dead. I am broken up inside that I hated her until the moment she died, and we toasted her rotting in hell at the likely moment the killer was stalking her. I am scared because some crazy person killed her and they are still out there, sending us hate mail and watching what we do. And for the life of me, I cannot imagine why anyone would hate us all this much. Rachel maybe, but Ashton? Or Lainey? No. Marguerite isn't even from here—why her?"

Tears flooded her eyes as she stumbled over to the large chair I was on and slumped into the seat next to me.

She sobbed and leaned against me, not coherent at all, and yet I knew what she was saying. She was repeating everything I had just said.

Someone had killed our friend.

Someone was tormenting her brother and Vince.

That someone wanted us to know they had savagely murdered Rachel and made it look like Sage had done it.

Everything she blubbered made sense to me.

We were all clearly still in shock, and I didn't see an end to it anytime soon. Not unless we got some much needed closure or answers.

I wrapped an arm around her and snuggled her into me, stroking her sweaty blonde hair from her face and letting her soak my blanket in tears.

Eventually, she started making sense. She sniffled and stuttered, "I just d-d-don't want any of this to be real. It's not possible. It's actually not."

"Before we get too far ahead of ourselves, we need to finish the other discussion. We can't have this hanging between us." Desperate to block it all out, I lifted her face, giving her a hard stare. "Tell me the truth—the real truth. Do you really love Vincent? Did you always love him?"

That for me would seal the deal on if I ever asked Vincent to kiss me.

She closed her eyes and shook her head, completely defeated. It was everything I imagined it would be. "Tom said I had to do my part. I-I had to keep Vince happy so our families could do business together. I had to be the perfect girlfriend and I wasn't. And Tom said it was all I was good for and I had failed."

I winced, hating Tom just a little bit more.

"When I told my mom Vince broke up with me, she told me I should try to get him back before Tom ever found out. I told her I didn't want to. I said I had someone I had been sort of seeing and she flipped out on me. I tried so hard to get Vince back after that, but he doesn't love me—he doesn't love me." Her bright-blue eyes filled with hate. "He has always loved you."

"That's awkward for me," I confessed quickly.

She laughed, losing the hate in her eyes. "I don't even get it. You're you and I'm me and he's Vince. He should want to be with me."

I laughed. "You will get no arguments there from me." We hugged and cried and watched the sea until she finally spoke again, but she didn't look at me, "I don't think I killed her. I have been thinking about it a lot, and I don't think I could do it." Her voice cracked, "I mean, maybe if I was really drunk and she made me crazy angry, but I can't see myself, my hands"—she lifted them in the air and stared at them—"I can't see me breaking her bones like that." She started to sniffle again.

I shook my head against her. "I can't either. I have known you longer than I knew Rachel, and even she couldn't do something so horrible. And she was officially the worst person we know—knew."

"And even if she was evil and we wished we were rid of her most days, she didn't deserve to die that way. Not one of us really wished this on her." Sage sounded like she was trying to convince me.

I nodded, letting tears just fall from my eyes.

"What's that?" Sage asked as she traced the bandage on my knee.

I scowled. "I got it the other night in the woods."

"Where?"

"In the woods." I didn't want to say where.

She lifted her head quickly. "You got that in the woods at Rachel's?" Her eyes were wide. I immediately went where she was going with it and closed my eyes, sighing. "Linds, that means you left your blood at the scene."

I nodded. I hadn't been thinking about that fact. I had sort of been ignoring it completely, hoping the stick in my leg had stopped blood from coming out. "Maybe we trampled it so much they won't find it."

She sighed. "Maybe. Lord knows my blood is there too. My lip is still fat."

"We can't let anyone take our DNA as a sample. If they match it we won't have a story. We have no witnesses except the four of us." I rubbed my hand over the bandage.

She got up, pushing off of me and stretched. "I need to go home. The funeral is tomorrow. I just wanted to make sure we were cool."

"We are always cool."

She gave me a defeated look. "And if you want to date Vincent, I'm cool with it. At least one of us will have him."

I was disturbed by the way she saw boys as possessions. I always knew she was materialistic, but this was ridiculous. "Hos before bros. I won't date him, Sage. He's your ex and he isn't my type." I winked at her.

She rolled her eyes and backed up. "You can date the coffeehouse girl without telling anyone, and let Vincent be in love with you to satisfy your parents, Linds. That's the world we live in. Someone should snatch him up." She waved and walked away slowly, leaving me to think about the coffeehouse girl.

Her words were food for thought.

I got up after about ten minutes of contemplating and hurried to my room, throwing on some shorts and a tank top and pulling my baseball cap on. It was my incognito outfit. No one ever recognized me like this. I ran down the stairs and hurried to the car, driving politely so my dad wouldn't lock the gate.

It was good to be on the open road and driving my car again, even if Sage's dad's driver had brought it back for me against my wishes. I hated it when other people drove my car. The skies remained gray from the storm that still seemed to be hanging on the coastline. When I got to the Shack, I hurried to the door, sighing when I saw she wasn't working.

"Lindsey?"

I turned around to see her at the picnic bench in the garden off to the right of the coffeehouse, looking confused. "Hey," I offered weakly.

She raised one eyebrow. "Hey." She was pissed, that much was obvious.

"I'm sorry about the other night. My friend was sort of sick and then we found out some really bad news." I frowned at myself. *My friend was brutally murdered and I was going with bad news?*

She paused, maybe also thinking the same thing. "It's cool. You want a coffee?"

"Sure, why don't I grab them? What do you want?"

"Iced chai latte."

I wrinkled my nose. "Spicy tea needs to be hot. Dude." I shook my head and walked inside, getting us coffees from the quiet barista guy who never ever said a word to me. As I carried the coffees outside, someone walked in and held the door open for me. The moment I saw him my stomach sank.

Winter hat, beard, skinny jeans, extra long white wife-beater shirt, and a vest. He was so hipster he probably peed sriracha and rooibos tea.

He winked at me as I walked by, unable to stop staring at him.

He had to be the guy Rachel had been making out with. There was no doubt in my mind.

I put the coffees down when I got to the picnic table, and winced at the foam on my hand. "I have to grab napkins." I hurried back inside, staring at him as he ordered his coffee. His body was slim but he was muscled. His dark hair had a sandy highlight to it, maybe from the sun. His skin was tanned and his hands were rough, like he did manual labor. I knew the look of a laborer well enough.

I couldn't shake the fact he gave off an incredibly mellow vibe. He didn't come across as violent or angry. But apparently neither did Ted Bundy.

I watched him from the corner of my eye as I grabbed napkins and slipped my phone from my pocket. I lifted it out and snapped a quick photo before turning and leaving.

When I got back outside I sent the photo to Sage with a quick text: *Him?*

She texted back right away: *Yes. Could he be the one who did it?*

"So did you manage to see the stars and the northern lights?" Hailey asked as I sat down.

"No." I shook my head, jumping a little when the door

opened and the hipster strolled out. I angled my phone a little, taking a picture of his car but pretending it was a selfie with duck lips. "God, I hate Snapchat. I am so tired of seeing pictures of myself. Aren't you?"

"Snapchat?" She furrowed her brow. "I don't take selfies."

"Smart girl." I lifted my head, staring intently into her azure eyes, and suddenly realized I was less sexually confused. In fact, I wasn't confused at all.

Being close to her, I noted it wasn't the same as being close to Vincent. She didn't smell like sweat and deodorant or cologne. She smelled like flowers and the wind, and for some crazy reason I swore I smelled tobacco. Like pipe tobacco. The smell reminded me of something, but I couldn't place it. "Do you smoke?" I asked randomly.

She shook her head. "No selfies, no smoking, no drinking, and no drama. Those are my actual life rules." She made me smile because I finally saw it.

The answer was so obvious. I didn't love her or lust after her. I just really wanted to be her. I wanted to be that confident and easygoing and not care what anyone thought about me.

I wanted to be free.

She lived in a car and no one had her tied down. She had no expectations and no rules. No personal shoppers or debutante balls. She was free and I wished I were too.

As I was stuck mid thought, she leaned in and whispered, "Are you ever going to ask me out?" She offered a cocky grin and sipped her cold tea.

Surprising both of us, I shook my head, answering us both. I truly hadn't known until this moment.

I blamed Vincent and his smell and the way he made my stomach ache. But deep down I think I always knew I wasn't actually gay. I liked the idea it might make me different from the others, it might free me from this society. It might make me unique and cool. But, no different than the douche in the winter hat in the middle of summer, it would be an act, fake and sad.

"I'm not gay," I answered her and a thousand others

simultaneously.

She winced. "Oh shit. I am so sorry. I super thought this was going somewhere else—obviously. Clearly, it's not. Oh my God."

I reached across the table, touching her cool arm. "It's fine. I honestly don't think I knew until this moment."

Her smile flashed wide. "Me either. You're the first girl I think I ever imagined kissing. I think you might have bewitched me, Lindsey."

I nodded, agreeing and seeing it completely. We had bewitched each other.

"Should we kiss, just in case we're wrong?" she asked, leaning in more. "In case it's more than being bewitched?"

Leaning in and tilting my head, I let her come the rest of the way. I didn't need to answer her question; my movement did it for me.

She came so close I could smell the berries on her lips and the chai on her breath as she brushed her glossy lips against mine. They slithered against my lips for a second, gently grazing and caressing. My insides didn't tighten the way I wanted them to. My heart raced but mostly because I was doing something forbidden.

That was what she was—forbidden. She was never going to be my father's choice and that had made her very appealing to me. I lifted my hand into her hair, noting just how silky it was.

The smell and the feel and the taste were all wrong, but it was still the best kiss I had ever had. We stopped kissing, just hovering above each other's mouths. I felt her smile as she whispered, "I think I like kissing you."

I nodded, not smiling back. "Me too." I pulled back, sitting back down and staring at my coffee.

She got up, giving me a cool wave. "See ya 'round, Lindsey." She sauntered to her piece-of-crap cobalt blue car and drove off, leaving me there to process what it all meant.

A disappointed sigh left my lips, becoming part of the breeze coming off the ocean. "I'm definitely not gay," I muttered, still sort of confused.

CHAPTER SIXTEEN
Can I play too?

I scrutinized my reflection, seeing some things I didn't want to.

Somehow in the past four days I had lost track of things—traits that had made me, me. There was freedom in liking kissing Hailey, but my lack of actual attraction was disappointing. It was akin to being denied a university I had always dreamed of. I sensed my planned future slipping away from me.

I would never vex my father with a lesbian lover and a Harley. I would never stand in the middle of the Senate protesting my rights to marry whomever I chose, protesting my father's friends at the same time.

I could protest but it wouldn't feel the same anymore.

There was something lackluster about protesting when it wasn't your actual cause. I believed in equal rights and equal rights to marry, and that would have to be enough. I wouldn't ever be with the downtrodden.

Becoming a journalist with a Brown's education would have to do. My father was a Princeton boy, at least I could still crush his lineage there.

But in the reflection I wondered if the girl staring back at me had the brass balls she once thought she had.

There was a serious amount of doubt playing in my mind, being that my world was falling apart, that I would ever be able to snoop or investigate.

I still had the key from Vincent's, but my desire to discover its origins lacked drive, motivation, and true curiosity.

What I saw in the mirror was too basic to be me. It

was just a girl with dark-blue eyes, light-brown hair, and too much makeup. I saw a weak-spirited girl who was wearing the dress she was told to wear with the matching earrings and necklace, thank you very much. I saw a girl who was being bent to the will of her family because she was suddenly afraid to stand alone and be different.

I wanted to fit in suddenly.

It was unsettling and disheartening.

I got up and turned around, noting the white rose bracelet I had worn to the gala was on the dresser. I picked it up and slipped it on my wrist. It was still fairly fresh, only slightly wilted. Lori must have found it for me. I smiled when I saw it, running my fingers over the pale petals.

White was the color of retreat and surrender and truce. It was weird that it was Rachel's favorite.

When I glanced back up, I saw a replay in the mirror, or maybe in my mind, of the times Rachel had treated me cruelly.

They didn't make me sad anymore.

I felt okay.

Okay?

What a weak and blunt word but it was my feeling.

I wasn't great, I wasn't happy, and I wasn't sad.

I was okay.

Rachel might have been mean, and she might have been cruel, but she was my friend. It was okay to hate how she had treated me, but I didn't have to believe the things she had told me. I didn't have to see them as her only trait either.

It was okay to know there was more to her and forgive the small bits when she had acted like an insecure bitch.

Her telling me I was gay might have been where my confusion began. Her telling everyone else was how it had become a rumor. But it wasn't a fact.

The weird fact of the matter was that I wasn't gay; randomly I was into sweaty boys, abs and pecs, cologne, and whatever the hell that smirk was that Vincent wore. Remembering the way he looked in the rain, conflicted and desirous of me—that was what made my knees weak and my breath hitch.

I couldn't even try to deny how I felt about that. I got the same rush from him that I did from snooping. If I stepped back and analyzed it all. My feelings for him explained why I liked snooping in his things so much and why I had hated him so easily. Why I was so vexed when he had pictures of Sasha or other girls. And as much as I hated that he'd put them there to make me jealous, I hated it even more that I was.

A slow smile spread across my face as it dawned on me that I enjoyed knowing he liked me.

He, Vincent Banks—the one and only Vincent Banks—liked me.

So what if I felt the same about him? It didn't matter; he liked me.

In a small, petty corner of my brain, it made me grin that his liking me would have made Rachel insane, but my mother's voice reminded me it too didn't matter anymore.

Rachel was dead and that was sad. It would be the biggest thing in my world for some time, bigger than anything else and it would remain bigger. Apart from the killer still being on the loose.

I walked from the room, ready for the funeral. As ready as I could be. I hated funerals.

When I got to the kitchen my dad hugged me. He held me tighter these days. Louisa interrupted the hug with an annoyed sigh. "We are late. Move it." She clicked in and out, adjusting earrings and muttering to herself. I lifted my head, about to ask him how he did it, but decided maybe that was a conversation for another time.

The ride over to the church was uncomfortable.

Louisa nattered about nothing while my dad and I looked out the window of our limo. My dad's reflection pointed out to me that we had more in common than I ever gave us credit for having. We both sat in quiet reflection, blocking out her annoying voice.

The driver dropped us at the front stairs to the church our parents all pretended to be a part of. A valet got the door. His eyes met mine and he smiled, winking and making me feel funny.

It took a second to realize he was the hipster. His beard was gone. That part of his face was much paler than the rest of his skin, and his winter hat had been replaced with a valet's cap. He wore a black suit with a white shirt beneath it.

New clothes and no beard, but he was the guy.

I climbed out and started up the stairs, stopping when I saw the boy with the grin leaning against the outer wall of the church like he was waiting just for me. He smiled, but it didn't change the dirty look on his face. I imagined he was thinking something vile, even at a funeral.

I walked up the steps to him, letting him offer me his arm. I leaned into him and murmured, "The valet behind me is the guy Sage saw Rachel with the night before she was murdered. He's the hipster Rach brought to Andrew's house."

He coughed and glanced back, giving me a look. "You sure?"

"Yeah. He was super hipster yesterday with a beard and skinny jeans and a winter hat."

"Men in skinny jeans confuse me sexually," he whispered, not even cracking a smile.

I pulled back. "Dude. Creepy jokes at the funeral are not awesome."

"Can we leave then?"

"No." I rolled my eyes.

"I hate funerals," he whispered, escorting me to my seat in the fourth row, the friends' row. I sat next to Andrew as Vincent walked off, leaving me there.

"Hey, Linds," he offered solemnly.

"Hey, Andrew," I said as I watched Vincent walk to the side door and exit slowly.

"Pretty crazy, huh?"

I nodded, watching Rachel's parents sit at the front, both silent and still when they got settled. My insides ached for them and my heart felt like it couldn't fit another emotion in it.

Rachel had no siblings so her parents were suddenly

childless. I didn't know how that would feel, but I imagined it was worse than anything else on earth. They sat there looking like a world was nestled between them.

It made me glance over my shoulder at my own father who had sat back a row. He smiled weakly, but I saw the toll this had taken on him—him and all our parents. They all looked weak and exhausted. Sierra's dad hadn't even shaved. He sat there texting, looking as rough as I had ever seen him.

I hated funerals. I hated them more than anything and my dad knew it. He sighed. In my peripheral I saw Dad's chest rise and fall heavily. I smiled back at him as he offered me a wink. Louisa dabbed her eyes, sniffling and pressing her lips together.

That almost made me smile wider. She was such a diva.

Dad started texting too, bringing a scowl to my lips as I turned my head back around. Lainey caught my eyes, lifting a hand and waving awkwardly. It was a pathetic wave, but one didn't get exuberant in a church at a funeral. I offered back the same wave, noting her eyes narrowed when she saw my hand. I couldn't help but notice then that there was a white rose on her wrist too.

I scowled, just a little and nodded my head at the rose. She shook hers, biting her lip. I glanced down my row to the left, seeing Sage. She waved slightly, also lifting a white rose.

She hadn't even been there at the gala to get a white rose bracelet from one of the guys. I pulled out my phone and texted Sierra: *You wearing your white rose?*

She texted back: *Yeah, why?*

I am too. So is Lainey.

Cool.

I sighed, texting Sierra again: *Sage has a rose too, and she wasn't at the gala!!!* Sierra leaned forward and shrugged at me.

Why are we all wearing white roses? I texted in the group chat, turning my phone completely to silent mode.

Sierra sent her text first: *Because they were Rachel's*

favorite!

I sighed, annoyed that Sierra was entirely missing the point. Lainey leaned forward, inspecting mine again. She shook her head and texted furiously. *Yours isn't the same, Linds. It's not the same one. Yours at the gala had a green tie around the wrist that sat alongside the pearls and made a bow.*

I glanced down, dread filling me. *You're right. Who left these for us?*

My fingers moving quickly as I texted Vincent: *Did you send me another wrist corsage for today?*

He popped back out of the door he had gone in, his eyes instantly finding mine. He checked his phone once more and then lifted his gaze back to me as he shook his head subtly.

I sent him another message: *Please ask Jake if he dropped them off for the four of us.*

He nodded and texted at the same time, lifting his eyes a moment later and shaking his head again.

I panicked a little bit. *Vince, someone left this rose for me at my house, in my room. I think the girls all got them the same way.*

His eyes narrowed as he read my text and then sent me a weird one in return: *How very vexing.*

Vexing? I gave him a look and then turned, glancing back as Marguerite walked in with her family. She lifted her Pucci scarf to her face, like she was smelling it or something. My jaw dropped when I noticed she too had a white rose on her wrist.

I turned and looked at Lainey, nodding my head. Her face paled as Marguerite walked by, swinging the white rose. She walked around the top and came in the left-hand side to settle next to Sage, both looking solemn.

I texted in the group chat again: *Ask Marguerite where she got that rose, Sage.*

Sage's head turned. Her face was moving. They both lifted their roses and shrugged their shoulders. Sage glanced back at me, worry filling her blue eyes. She shook her head and sent a quick text: *She doesn't know where it came from.*

I don't know either. I added her to the chat.

That felt weird—someone I hadn't even said two words to being added to our private chat. We had terrible things in that chat. Rachel had said the worst things imaginable in there.

Hi girls, I found the rose on my dressing table. It had a note saying it was Rachel's favorite color rose, Marguerite messaged us all.

I added her number to my phone as Rita; Marguerite was too huge. I agreed with her being Rita completely. Then I texted back: *Hi, Rita. This is Lindsey, if you want to add me to your phone.*

Hi, Lindsey. I will. She leaned forward and smiled wide, mesmerizing me with her beauty.

The conversation blew up as everyone introduced themselves and added her to their phones. It was too weird. Not that we were doing it, just that we were doing it at a funeral.

I watched as Vincent strolled casually across the room, nodding at people who greeted him. He always looked like he owned the room. He came and sat next to me, earning me a look from Tom, Sage's stepdad.

I scowled back at him. I had always hated that man.

"The valet was gone by the time I got back to the front. I talked with my dad in the wings. Once he was privy to the information, he messaged all the other dads. No one recalls hiring a valet for the church," Vincent leaned in, whispering into my neck. I shuddered from both his breath and his words.

"You sure?"

He nodded, brushing his face against mine. "Very. Since Sierra's dad found out the driver who took you girls to Rachel's party that night wasn't his driver, he's been pretty vigilant about who's who."

My head turned sharply, my face almost hitting his. I had to back up because we were so close my eyes couldn't focus. "What?"

He nodded, licking his upper lip like it was a tick or a tell. "His driver was sick, terribly sick. He didn't read the text from Sierra that he was driving you girls. His phone was on his dresser in his apartment. He lives above the garage at her place."

"I know."

"He was passed out up there. He's still not fully better. The doctor said it's food poisoning. The driver who drove Sierra around wasn't her dad's driver. No one knows who took you to the party that night. And your dad checked—no tree was downed on the road to Rachel's. For whatever reason, that driver wanted you girls there then."

I swallowed hard, sitting back in my chair as the music started and the people were all seated. No wonder our dads all looked like they hadn't slept in a week. I lowered my hands, sending one more text: *We need to meet up after this. Group meeting. Rita, you are part of this group now too.*

Then an unexpected text came through.

Can I come too, bitches?

I blinked, staring at it, my mind disbelieving the sight my eyes saw. There was no way Rachel had just sent us all a text. Her coffin was literally fifteen feet from my face, and yet the text had her name on it.

I lifted my gaze, noting my friends were all doing the exact same thing, looking about the room with fear in their eyes.

Instead of turning the phone off, I tilted it so Vincent could read it as well.

"Oh shit," he whispered as I clicked it off and pretended to sing a hymn for the dead girl who was still sending me messages.

CHAPTER SEVENTEEN
I can hit her if you hold her down

The hug Rachel's mother offered me on the stairs outside at the end of the service was weak, but I assumed it was all the strength she had left. She sniffled and nodded. "Thank you for coming, dear."

"I'm so sorry." I squeezed her and closed my eyes. "I am going to miss her so much." It was a lie, but it was the sort you told the grieving parent of the mean girl in school. It was the sort of lie you told yourself you had to believe.

"Me too," she whispered.

I gave her one last pat on the back and pulled away, letting Sierra get in there next. She hugged and sobbed far better than I did.

Lainey nudged herself against me, leaning and sighing. Mr. Swanson walked to where we stood and pulled me into his arms with a thump. He shook, trembled maybe. He wasn't weak or feeble the way his wife was. His hug seemed angry and exhausted. He gripped me, squeezing and shaking his head. He didn't say anything. He just let go as suddenly as he had grabbed me and moved on to Lainey, flopping himself on her the way he had done to me. It was weird and in any other setting it would have been creepy.

Sierra was next as Sage comforted Mrs. Swanson.

There just wasn't anything to say to either of them.

Louisa rescued us all. She worked her way in, grabbing Mrs. Swanson and sobbing. They cried together and eventually Mr. Swanson was wrapped around them both.

Our parents didn't do this. Especially not when the cameras were on us. They didn't hug or kiss or snuggle.

They certainly didn't cry.

But today, even with the cameras rolling in the park across the road, the stairs of the church were covered in embracing and sobbing people.

No one here expected something like this. No one.

We walked down the stairs, the four of us, until Rita joined us. I slipped my white rose corsage off and placed it in the trash bin at the bottom of the steps as my eyes scanned the park. "Do you think whoever sent the message is watching us right now?" I asked.

We walked to the side of the church where no one else was. "Do you think they watch us all the time?"

"Yes. Psychopaths always watch under normal circumstances. They always come to the funeral. Always," Lainey added.

I folded my arms across my chest, noticing the wind more than I should. It was colder than any August wind I had ever felt.

"What are we going to do?" Sage asked softly, rubbing her wrist where the bracelet had been.

"We need to go to the police." Lainey nodded, still looking out across the town square. "We need to ping Rachel's phone and find out where the killer is."

"We can't," I almost snapped but held back just a little. "You're forgetting all the illegal shit we've done. We fled a murder scene. Sage was at the murder scene, covered in the blood. I lied about Ashton and have still not told anyone that I saw him. We never told anyone about the kidnapper notes. We stole her car and burned all the evidence. We brought our parents into this."

They all gulped but Rita. She nodded. "She's right. We can't go to the police until we know what is going on. We don't even know if the killer has evidence on us. They might have taken pictures of Sage and Rachel in the woods. They might have been watching you all there getting Sage."

Lainey sighed, looking defeated. "But we aren't dealing with something small. We're dealing with a blackmailing psychopath who has already killed one person. We need the police."

I glanced down, hating that I was about to scare them all more. "Sierra, your dad's driver isn't who took us to the party. Your dad knows this and hasn't told you yet. Your driver was sick. And there was no fallen tree. A stranger dropped us off and the timing was somehow important to them."

"The drinks," Lainey blurted before she even processed what it all meant. "They wanted us there late so it was congested and they could slip us the drinks. It would be too crowded and no one would even realize we were drugged or missing after the drugs kicked in. I didn't even see the face of the person who gave us the drinks. I saw a hand and a white dress and that's it."

I nodded, realizing we had likely confirmed our worst fears. "There's more than one of them, and they were trying to drug us all on purpose."

Sierra, Sage, and Rita gave us both a look. Rita's look was more awe than anything though. I nodded at her. "Lainey has an eidetic memory. She can't forget anything once she has seen it or heard it."

Rita cocked an eyebrow. "Damn, girl. That must be heavy."

Lainey nodded, smiling almost. Rita was the first person to get it. Everyone else always said how lucky she was. But Lainey never saw it as luck.

"And the valet when I walked in here was the hipster guy. He has shaved off his beard. His face is crazy pale where the beard was."

Sage lifted her gaze. "You sure?"

I nodded. "I saw him at the coffeehouse yesterday when I sent you that pic. He had the beard then. I can't forget his face even if I wanted to. It was him both times."

Rita sighed. "The hipster moron who wore the winter hat at that guy Andrew's?"

We all gaped at her. "You saw him too? He was at the party?"

"I don't know if he was at the party, but I saw him making out with Rachel a few days before that, and she brought him when we went to that Andrew guy's house. She called him Skip. He said it was his sailing name. He had come into town on a boat and was waiting on it to leave before he skipped town. He wore skinny jeans and smelled weird." Rita wrinkled her nose. "Rachel had invited him and a bunch of town kids from the Northside to the party, but I never saw him. I think I assumed he was waiting to show his face once Rachel dumped Ashton. She had said she was going to. Then she started fighting with Ashton and I lost track of them."

We all stood, stunned and silent. Rachel had been planning to dump Ashton for the Skip guy?

"What if he showed up late because he was our driver and you were already drugged so you didn't notice him?" Lainey offered, clearly searching her brain for answers.

Sage nodded. "That makes sense. And if he killed Rachel and he was stalking us, being our driver makes the most sense. He showed up as we got there, signaling his partner to send the drinks to us."

"But why? Why kill Rachel and drug us? To what end? Who is he? What could any one of us have done to him to deserve this?" I scowled, not one-hundred-percent convinced of the killer inside the hipster.

Those were questions none of us could answer. We all took turns opening our mouths to say something but then closing them.

Lainey shook her head. "The timing wouldn't work. If you were unconscious at the same time as Sage, it would mean you were drugged at the same time. And if Skip had driven us you wouldn't have noticed him anyway. The party was crowded and you never notice the driver."

We all nodded as Vincent, Andrew, and Jake walked over to us. Sage instantly got a hateful look on her face. "What?" she snarled at Vincent.

"Oh, how I miss your random emotional outbursts." He chuckled and shook his head. "Your dads want you all home now. Sierra, your driver is to take each of you home. Andrew and Jake will ride with you girls. Linds, you can come with me."

I frowned. "Why?"

"Because you live near my house and the rest of them live farther down the cove. I told your dad I would get you home."

I rolled my eyes. "No, why do they want us to go home now?"

Vincent swallowed hard, glancing at Andrew and Jake. Even they looked worried. "The parents are going for a little meeting with the police. The FBI has been brought in so they will also be there."

My stomach tightened. "The FBI? Because of our parents' connections?"

"I don't know." He shook his head. "I do know I have been instructed to tell all of you it is time to go home. Your parents will tell you whatever they want you to know or are allowed to tell you. I don't know anything; I'm not invited to the party either." He slipped his hand into my arm and tugged me gently from the girls and led me toward the limo he had parked three cars down.

We were steps away from the girls when he leaned in and whispered, "Those roses were each delivered to the houses by a false company, No Name Deliveries. Robert answered the door at your house when the deliveryman showed up. He signed for the parcel, but he says he left it on the counter for you. Louisa, your father, and Lori all say they never even saw the package. You say it was in your room?"

I nodded.

"Then the person screwing with us put it there. I don't want you home alone."

I glanced back at my friends as Andrew and Jake ushered them into the limo. "But what about them? They'll be alone. We have to tell them."

"No. And they won't be alone, their mothers are all home. Each household has been put on alert with security added. Lainey and Sage have their sisters to help take care of."

I stopped, jerking my arm free. "We need to stay together. Forget our parents and their plans. I want to know the truth."

He stepped closer, wrapping his arms around me,

again with the PDA. I moaned and wriggled free, hurrying to the car before someone took our picture. "Can you not do that in front of cameras?" When his driver opened the door I eyed him up nervously. He was a beast of a man, like Lurch on *The Addams Family.*

Vincent nodded. "Thanks, Hugo." I looked back at Vincent and then climbed in, hating the fact I wasn't in my car or with my friends.

We sat there in silence as Hugo started the car and drove off.

Finally, he gave me a look. "I just want to be sure you're safe."

"What about my friends—?"

Vincent's phone made a weird sound, cutting me off. He pulled it out, seething suddenly. "Son of a bitch. If that fuc—"

"What?" It was my turn to cut him off as I leaned over, gasping at the sight. "You can see the cameras from your phone?" His cell phone had a video of his room. It seemed to be coming from an angle, above the room. Suddenly a person walked across in a hoodie. I jumped. "Oh my God!"

"I am going to mess that bastard up," he snarled, not sounding scared but angry.

The person glanced about, clearly wearing something so their face was completely black, like there was nothing inside the hoodie.

The stream switched to a different camera, giving us another angle as the dark figure crept around the room, going right for the bedside table.

"Holy shit, Vince. That's the killer," I whispered, light-headed and a little dry in the mouth.

"I know. Looks like a guy, right? Those shoulders? I'm going to kill him."

I shook my head. "I don't know. Could be a girl with layers on."

"In this heat? It better not be a girl. I don't know that I could hit a girl."

"I can," I murmured. "But you have to hold her down for me."

"Deal," he muttered as we both watched the killer open the drawer, pushing down on the false bottom and lifting it out. The dark face looked right back at the camera, as if to brag. Then he or she turned their face back to the drawer.

Vincent slammed his hand down on the seat and pressed the button, shouting into it, "Hugo, home before Miss Bueller's!" I continued to watch as the killer ripped apart the dresser, like they didn't seem to find what they were looking for.

"What's in there, Vince?"

"My dad's spare key to the vault."

I winced. "Oh." How did I say what I knew without looking insane? There was no way. So I leaned across him and pressed the button. "Just take us to my house, please, Hugo." I sat back, hating myself and closed my eyes. "I have your key at my house. I stole it. You should call the police about the intruder."

He growled. "Why do you have my key?"

"I was in your bedside table, snooping, and I saw it and wondered what it was. That's when I saw the pictures of the girls." I shook my head and tried not to sound crazy. "I like solving little things. I was going to put it back after I figured it out. I swear." Tears leaked from my eyes. I was a little scared and a little ashamed and a lot worried. "You should call the cops about the intruder, Vince."

His breathing leveled off as he sat back and sighed. "I already knew you spied on me, obviously the pictures gave you away, but I knew long before then. I caught you once. Let's just say you are the least talented spy I have ever met. Hence the reason I got girls to send me pictures."

I turned and gave him a tearful scowl. "So couldn't you tell I took the key when I was there?"

He shook his head. "I didn't have the cameras on that day. The wiring was being weird. I was out getting a new part for it when you asked if I was home and I asked you to have dinner with me. I didn't want the electrician at the house again because I didn't want my dad to find out I had wired the house." He smiled, sighing and calming down a little. "I can't even tell you how relieved I am that you steal my shit randomly."

"You need to call the police," I whispered as his words jumped about in my head, coming to one distinct conclusion. "Your father doesn't know you have a key to the safe, does he?"

He shook his head.

"But the killer must know. Look at that bedside table." I pointed at the image of the ripped up wood. "Was that the only thing they might be after that is missing?"

"I assume so." He nodded, again licking his top lip. It was clearly a stress-induced tick. "Those burner phones were for someone else. They weren't mine."

"Do I want to know what's in your dad's safe, Vince?"

He swallowed hard, shaking his head. "But we should be worried that someone besides my father knows what's in there. My father doesn't ever tell anyone anything about anything. My mother left for a reason."

The car came to a halt and then drove again. We were at the four-way stop just before my turnoff. I lifted Vincent's phone from his fingers. "You need to call the police."

He sighed and dialed, lifting the phone to the front of his face.

"Vince, what's going on?" His dad's voice was loud.

"There's someone in the house. My computer monitor was on, linked to my phone. I was accessing something and the camera was on, and I caught a glimpse of someone in my room. Then the computer cut out."

"Did you call the police?"

"No."

"Good." His dad hung up.

Vincent sat back in the chair, tapping on the phone, checking the other cameras in the house but nothing else was disturbed.

"Why didn't you call the cops?" I asked, truly curious about what was in their house.

He lifted his face, pressing his lips together and taking a long breath. "I just can't. My dad is particular about the house and the police. That's all I have, okay?"

I nodded, dissatisfied and more intrigued than before. I had been in their house snooping a lot, but I was a close family friend. I was in the inner circle. Mr. Banks wouldn't even bat an eyelash at me lurking about the house. I had never found anything except that Mr. Banks kept his office locked up tight with special drawers, safes, and locks on everything.

The car stopped and Hugo opened the door, giving me the creepy Lurch look. I shuddered and stepped out.

"Thanks, Hugo. Take a nap or see if Lori will make you something to eat." Vincent slapped the massive man on the arm.

I walked up to the front entrance, ready to strip from my clothes, throw on a bathing suit, and go for a swim. Lori met me at the door with two men who looked like they might be secret service. I jumped, seeing them.

Lori held a hand up. "These are the men who are going to be on the grounds, watching the house. I just wanted you to be aware before you went anywhere."

I sneered, not at her or the men but the situation. "Okay."

Robert strolled in, smiling when he saw me. "Miss Lindsey, your father has asked that you stay in the house until he returns home."

"Of course he has." I sighed, nodding as I walked past them all, heading for the stairs. I realized Vincent was right behind me when I heard him on the steps. I stopped and turned, jumping again when I saw how close he was. "What are you doing? I'm going to change."

"You can change in the bathroom. I want to check your room first."

I rolled my eyes. "I'm sure the stiffs in the monkey suits did that."

He cocked an eyebrow. "This person has gotten past all of my dad's security, every time."

"Fine, whatever," I moaned and climbed the stairs. I was suddenly very tired and very cranky. "I feel like shit."

"That's the adrenaline. You need something to pick

you back up. Some sugary foods are usually good for that. I get it when I rock climb sometimes." He turned on the stairs and spoke loudly, "Lori?"

I turned and watched as she came around the corner, looking indignant. She hated being bossed around by kids, but Vincent wasn't a regular kid. "Be a dear and fix us something sweet, please. Some cinnamon buns or some Danish or something."

Her lip twitched but she nodded. "Of course." She turned and stalked off.

"She's going to spit in our food."

He turned back at me, making a face and laughing loudly. "She wouldn't dare spit in my food. I would have her replaced before she could even breathe her next breath. They better be the best pastries I have ever eaten." He winked and walked past me on the stairs.

I knew she had heard him but I didn't care. I went into all my meals assuming she had spit in them.

When I got to my room, he had the door open and his face was pinched. He lifted a hand and shook his head. "Don't come in here. You don't want to see this."

"What?"

He winced, holding his arms out for me. I walked toward him but peered past him to see inside the room.

I gasped when I saw it. I cringed and held back the scream that was lodged in my throat, blocking off the air. He wrapped himself around me as my phone started going nuts.

I pulled it from my pocket to see the girls had started a new group chat, one without Rachel. It had the same image that was in my room. Each of them had posted it with comments. I dialed immediately.

"Linds. Did you see?" Lainey cried into the phone with a soft voice. I nodded and stared at the picture of the five of us in the woods, all of them covered in blood and me staring at Sage and Rachel who were on the ground.

"Linds, you there?"

I handed the phone to Vincent as I dropped to my knees, again wincing in pain as I hurt my knee with the landing.

"Hi, Lainey. She's here. She's got the same photo the rest of you have," Vincent whispered. "I am sending Hugo to pick you up right now. Bring your little sister." He hung up and called the rest of them.

I closed my eyes and shook my head, forcing myself not to see or believe.

CHAPTER EIGHTEEN
More of me

I glanced at the clock and tipped over the queen, sighing and sitting up. "I don't want to play anymore. I'm tired and I just want to know what the hell is going on."

Sage snuggled into me, sighing the same way I just had. "Me too. I'm hungry again too. I think stress makes me hungry. We better solve this, or I'm going to be two hundred pounds." She glanced over at Lainey. "Did you check and make sure the girls were asleep?"

Lainey nodded. "They both are." Sage and Lainey had both brought their little sisters to the house with them.

I moaned. "This whole thing sucks." I still shuddered when I thought about it all.

"Super sucks." Sage pouted.

Vincent gave us both a look. "Sitting here babysitting you isn't my idea of fun either." He rearranged the chessboard so the pieces were back where they should be.

I opened my mouth to complain again, but Sierra beat me to it, "I have an idea. Why don't we do some shots and come up with an idea board. Between all of us, someone for sure knows the killer."

Jake gave Sierra a look. "Shots, yes. Hot tub—hell yes. Decorating a board about death, hard pass."

Sage nodded. "Drinking and hot tub sounds good. We are all about to die anyway—who cares who the killer is?" She stood and lifted her shirt off. She glanced back at Vincent as she walked to the bar, grabbed my dad's bottle of scotch, and headed out the back door to the pool. Her laugh sounded like she was the evil queen or something.

Rita got up and pulled off her shirt too. "I'm down for whatever." She followed Sage outside. She hadn't really said much to us, considering she was from New York. But what a first weekend at your new home—a girl invites you over and then gets brutally murdered. I wouldn't have too much to say either. In fact, I didn't.

Vincent gave me a look. "This is a colossally bad idea. I think we should decorate that board of death."

Lainey nodded aggressively. "I agree. I don't think drinking in a hot tub is a good idea."

Andrew shrugged and pulled off his hoodie. "Last one in is a rotten tomato."

"It's egg, moron." Sierra scoffed and dragged off her shirt and pants, slipping through my games room in her bra and underwear.

Screams filled the air. The three of us jumped up and ran for the door, stopping to see that Jake had tossed Sierra, Rita, and Sage into the pool. Sage swam to the side and splashed Jake who jumped in, cannonballing them. Rita was swimming and wiping her eyes, cussing at Jake.

Lainey huddled into herself. "I don't want to swim."

"Let's just go in the hot tub. I can grab some girlier drinks than scotch. Sage is just trying to taunt Vincent into getting naked with her again."

"I'm right here!" He gave me a look.

"Duh." I nodded. "I know that. I just mean, we all know what she's doing. She doesn't like to admit defeat. She's all about being proactive. Being fun and jumping into the pool in her skimpiest French lingerie is bound to get you back, right?"

"You really just said duh? Seriously? I think I had more respect for you than a duh-spouting girl." He shook his head. "And while I agree about her motives, I don't want to talk about it. I broke up with her for a reason. These sort of antics are the icing on the crazy cake." He sighed and walked through the door, leaving me and Lainey staring at each other.

"You getting the idea we don't really know her as well as we think we do?" Lainey asked.

"I don't know what to think." I gulped and turned back for the bar fridge. "This is stupid, but we don't have to drink. Help me carry some of these out there." She slumped and sighed again in defeat and followed me to the bar fridge.

We hauled out cans of Palm Bay and a couple of San Pellegrinos for Lainey and I. We both hated drinking in hot tubs—too hot and too drunk, too fast.

I pulled off my shorts and tee shirt, flashing my Spiderman underwear and black sports bra.

Jake made a face. "Why did I always know that is exactly what was lurking under there?" I tossed a drink at his head but he caught it fast.

"Because she always has sports-bra boobs. It's like a loaf of boob." Sage laughed and winked at me.

I lifted my middle finger up at her.

Lainey pulled her pants off and laughed quietly so no one could hear her except me. "Twinsies." She had on Batman underwear and a white sports bra.

We both giggled; we were alone in that. Even Rita gave us a horrified stare.

"Girls in superhero underwear are so hot." Andrew laughed and nodded at Lainey. She blushed and scrambled to get in on the other side.

I sat down and stuck my feet in the pool and cracked my clementine sparkling water. Vincent waded over to me, giving me that look. The one that always made my insides tighten. I used to mistake it for disgust.

I shivered, not from the cold, and slipped down into the water. I wasn't trying to get closer. I was trying to cover myself up. He took my drink and sipped some of it and handed it back. I wrinkled my nose and put it on the patio, making him laugh.

Lainey snuggled up next to me, third wheeling in all the best ways. "Dude, I don't like being in my underwear in front of people." She was covering her breasts fiercely. Not that it mattered—she was wearing a completely see-through white sports bra.

Vincent's jaw dropped as his stare glanced her way and his eyes bugged out of his head. He snapped his jaw shut and pressed his lips together.

I kicked him under the water, knowing exactly what he was looking at.

Lainey was the queen of wearing super tight bras with tape around her chest if she had to, to avoid being chesty for a skinny girl.

On a normal body, she wouldn't even be chesty, but on a skinny girl a nice pair of C boobs made her look a little plastic. She had no ass, none whatsoever, so the chest really was noticeable if unleashed.

Her bathing suits were always the ones competitive swimmers wore. They sucked every ounce of shape from your chest. She was curveless everywhere else. She was like a kid with boobs, like a really small kid. We bugged her constantly that she only gained her weight there. But all that aside, in a white sports bra her boobs were pretty obvious.

I leaned over. "Hey, you know how you're smart in a lot of things, but every now and then we come across that one thing where you aren't?"

She nodded. I lowered my eyes to her see-through sports bra. "Grab a tee shirt or a bra or bathing suit top from the pool house."

She looked down and gasped, turning and jumping from the pool and running to the pool house.

I turned back to Sierra who laughed and made a face. She shook her fiery red mop of wet locks and shrugged. "She kicks our asses on every test and every common sense thing, so whatever. One wet tee shirt contest won't kill her."

Sage burst out laughing. "Like we all haven't done one."

Andrew laughed too but Vincent rolled his eyes. "You haven't ever been in a wet tee shirt contest."

She growled. "You don't know." He nodded calmly. "And yet I feel like I do."

I didn't know exactly when the whole discomfort thing would end with Vincent and her, but it was awkward as ass for the rest of us. Or as Sierra would say, awkward as balls. I still didn't understand the balls and ass thing. Or why Vincent and Sage couldn't just be those people who had once dated and no longer felt the same way but got along.

Lainey came back out in a black bathing suit top. It wasn't her usual competitive swimsuit so she was flashing cleavage, but it was better than being naked.

We moved from the pool to the hot tub and sat in the steam, them getting sillier and sillier, and Lainey and I getting less and less comfortable.

Sierra was trying to touch her elbows behind her back, acting like she wasn't clever enough to know not to. Sage copied her, obviously vying for Vincent's attention. I had started to get a bit insecure about the whole thing; mousy brunettes just couldn't compete with tall blondes. And to top it all off, that just wasn't me. I didn't do competitions.

Rita twirled her hair and laughed as she leaned into Jake and spoke with a very sudden Southern accent.

I didn't know what to make of it all and eventually I was so drained of moisture and ready for bed that I crawled for the stairs. I got out, giving Lainey a look. She followed me inside.

I wrapped myself in my towel and sat on the barstool, sipping a Perrier and staring at the door to outside.

"Sage is acting weird."

"I know." I looked at Lainey as she grabbed a Perrier too. "But she did wake up next to a dead girl, so maybe we should give her a bit more time before we ride her about it."

Lainey nodded. "Are you and Vince a thing?"

I shook my head. "It's going to sound selfish, but I like the fact he likes me. I like the fact he watches me, studying me. I've spent my entire life watching other people, and I always wondered if someone watched me as closely as I watched everyone else."

"That's totally happened to you already. Don't forget the stalker killer who is watching us all the time."

I laughed, bitterly but hard. She had a point. Of course it would be her who had made the point. She couldn't even fight saying it.

"But back to you and him." She sighed and leaned back against the bar. "Vince has always watched you. I really thought you knew and just hated the attention."

I shook my head. "I saw him watching, but what I'd imagined he was thinking was completely different from what it turns out he was thinking."

"That's the problem with seeing things and hearing things. We always take our personality and our experiences and add them to everything. Our perspective changes everything. We all see things through a filter that carries all the bad things inside us, and we make assumptions based on that filter. No one ever sees the truth. They see their version of it. Even me. I will remember my version of it forever, tainted by the bad things that have happened to me."

I turned and shook my head, taking a sip. "You are so smart, Lainey. So very smart."

"I know." She nodded. "It's what comes of never forgetting anything." She twitched a tiny bit when she said it, and I knew exactly the moment she was remembering. She chuckled softly. "I have heard that heroin takes away memories."

"What?"

"Yeah. That's why people who have been abused or hurt take it, or do it rather. They can forget for as long as the high lasts." Her voice trailed off. "But I bet it never lasts long enough."

"Don't forget about the other bad parts like the picking of the sores and losing all your friends and living on the streets and being a drugged-out hooker and getting ugly."

She laughed. She didn't scare me. She never did drugs, no matter what. But she seemed distant, distracted. Until she turned and gave me a look. "You like him too, don't you?"

I opened my mouth as my eyes dropped to the floor, but I shook my head. It was a lie. I knew it in my heart. "I don't. He's not my type." It was the worst lie I had ever told.

"I'm in love with Ash." She blurted it and I lifted my head, nodding. "I have been for so long I don't even know when I wasn't."

"I know." My eyes teared, I didn't even know why. Maybe her honesty and fearlessness inspired me, but I blurted it back at her, "I think I'm falling in something I don't understand with Vince."

She smiled. "I can tell."

I reached over and squeezed her hand. "I'm so glad you know me and you are part of my life. I don't think I could make it through any of this without you."

She sighed and glanced at the doorway, straightening her back. I snapped my head around, flinching when I saw Vincent standing there. He seemed confused.

I didn't understand why he was staring at us or why he looked so weird, hurt maybe or scared. I turned and glanced behind me, afraid the killer was there, but it was just the bar.

Lainey got up and walked toward him, exiting through the door and leaving us alone.

He had wrapped his lower body in a towel, and it was hard not to notice that the other half was still very naked.

I clung to my towel and prayed for strength of virtue and morality.

Neither of those things seemed to be readily on hand. I had admitted aloud that I was falling into something with him. Nothing else mattered.

My eyes focused on the V-shaped thing on his hips that blended into the abs, pronouncing the cut of his six-pack. I swallowed and tried to make my brain switch from staring at the V things. I honestly couldn't have named it if my life was dependent upon it, but I did know it had me flustered.

I lifted my gaze, realizing my mistake the moment our eyes touched. His dark-green eyes were framed by thick, clumpy wet black lashes. I think I might have made a sound like a moan or a swoony sigh when our eyes met.

I had a scowl on my face. I fought the good fight, internally. But those eyes and those long lashes, and the way the water dropped down his chest had me.

It was akin to mind control the CIA might have used. Or watching *Magic Mike* with the sound muted.

I would have easily fallen for the subliminal messaging. I *was* falling for it. He walked to me, nestling himself in between my thighs and lifting my towel up them like a skirt. His cold skin burned a little against mine. He trailed his hands up my legs, making me gulp so loudly it echoed throughout the games room.

He lifted his hands, cupping my face, and stared at me, blinking those green eyes with that stare.

The smugness was gone from his gaze.

The grin he taunted me with—nowhere to be found.

In his eyes I saw my reflection and maybe the way he saw me. I blinked too, confused on where this was going until he lowered his face on mine, delicately grazing my lips with his. The kiss pulled at me, dragging me into it. My head swirled, and I didn't recall lifting my hands that were suddenly moving up into his hair.

I didn't know when it was I offered him my tongue, but it was suddenly in his grasp, sliding and massaging against his. His soft lips and the way they coaxed mine open, took away all my air. I think I volunteered it for sacrifice.

His hands slipped back around me, pulling me into him and crushing me against his bare chest. My towel fell but I didn't care if my nearly naked body touched his. I didn't care about anything.

I needed more of this. More of his kisses and his touch. More of the way my entire body was rushing about, bouncing like a Ping-Pong ball. My nerves were on fire but I didn't care.

I sucked his lip the way he had done to mine. After a moment he pulled back, tearing our faces apart. He breathed heavily, gasping almost with a heaving chest.

I was gasping completely.

That smile crested his lips as he stepped back, leaving me cold. He paused and then stepped back once more, lifting a hand to point but said nothing. He just grinned and nodded, like the conversation in his head was something we both were hearing. He turned and walked out of the room, leaving me there cold and baffled.

I didn't know what had just happened, except that I had finally been kissed. I understood why people kissed so much. It wasn't just the butterflies or the tingling sensations. It was so much more. With him I felt like I was more.

CHAPTER NINETEEN
Dirty emails and midnight confessions

I brushed my fingers along my lips once more, remembering how it had felt. In the dark no one could see me doing it. The girls were all sleeping and it was pitch-black so I knew they didn't see. The guys were in the guesthouse and the girls in my room.

My eyes drew to the ceiling, and I wished for the millionth time she was here. If a teenaged girl ever needed her mother, it was the moment she found something desirable that she didn't understand in another person. Something that felt like it completed her.

Did I plan on dating him—no. He was my friend's ex so he wouldn't ever be mine. At least not until she had absolutely moved on with another person. And even then it might be in secret. I didn't want to lose the firm deniability I had, even if we were caught on camera. We were not dating.

But even though they were exes, it didn't change the fact that I wanted more of him. I wanted more kisses and more touching. I wanted to feel him against me and see where it led.

I knew where it led.

But with him I wanted to feel what going there was like.

I got up, slipping from my bed and stepping in between the beds on the floor where my friends were sleeping. Sage was snoring, as per the usual, so she masked the sound of me walking.

I tiptoed in the dark to my door, moving entirely from memorization, and opened it a crack. The hallway was dimly lit so I had to open the door fast and step out and close it quickly. I didn't want to wake anyone.

Hurrying down the hall to the stairs, I stopped short, hearing my dad talking. I held my breath, leaning against the wall and peeking down the stairs. He stood at the bottom of the stairs with Vincent.

"The police have a few theories. She was either assaulted right before she died or she had sex there, in the forest with the killer. Or the killer killed her after she had been with someone else. Her death might have even been accidental." My dad shuddered.

My insides tightened and my heart immediately went out to Rachel's parents who would have also received that news. It made me sick to know that detail. I prayed for them silently.

Vincent's eyes drew up to where I was. I sensed them on me and pulled back behind the wall. Vincent sighed. "Well, we can all talk about it tomorrow. I know my father wants to know exactly what has happened and what the facts are. The girls all got those roses in their bedrooms. That's creepy."

"The meeting is all scheduled for tomorrow. If you can get your dad to show up that would be amazing." My dad yawned. "Sleep tight, son. And thanks again for taking care of the girls."

"My pleasure, sir," he answered as I glanced around the corner again, seeing my father walking down the hall, away from Vincent whose eyes were firmly fixed on me.

He narrowed his gaze, shaking his head. I smiled with amusement, hoping my excuse to come and find him would be enough. I nodded my head at the guest room next to mine and slipped into the door quietly, leaving it open for him.

I waited behind the door in the dark for him to come to me. But he didn't, not at first. My insides tingled and my heart raced as a small lump of disappointment nestled in my throat. I was just about to admit my defeat at luring him into the room to kiss me, when the door pushed open a little and then closed again. Hands reached for me in the dark, pulling me into him.

Instead of the kiss I imagined we would share, he held my face and whispered harshly, "Why are you out of your room?"

I scowled. "I wanted to see—" I paused. I couldn't tell him I wanted to see him. That was an icky confession for me. I knew he felt the same, but I didn't want to say it. "I heard the voices and wanted to see," I lied.

"I was trying to come to see you when your dad finally got home. He just finished talking with everyone and assumed I wanted the details of the meeting. They were there nine hours, listening to the particulars of the murder and the evidence that was found and trying to come up with a list of suspects. The police keep some of it back, so if anyone knows those specifics, it's likely they have spoken with the killer or are the killer. So we don't know everything."

I pulled back a bit. "I don't want to talk about this, especially not in the dark."

He leaned in, pressing his face against mine and kissed my cheek. "You have to go back to bed. You have had a hard day, Linds. You need some sleep."

"I know." I slipped my hand into his and turned, pulling him to the bed in the large room. I pulled back the covers and sat on the cold sheets. I pulled him into the bed with me as I scooted over, resting my face next to his.

"We shouldn't be in here. It's not a good idea." He nestled into me, as if his body disagreed with his words.

"I know. But we don't have to stay here long. Just long enough for you to tell me what is going on with you." I nodded as he kissed my neck and slid his hands over my back, lifting my shirt a bit.

"What do you mean?" he asked as he trailed his breath along my jawline, pressing soft kisses every quarter inch.

I pushed him back. "That kiss, Vince—what was that? Why did you kiss me and then leave? You said you weren't going to kiss me until I asked you to."

"I know, but—" His breath on my face stopped as he obviously thought about his answer for several seconds. "I had to."

"Why were you looking so weird when you came in the room."

He paused again. "I heard you and Lainey talking. I heard you say you had fallen into something with me."

My stomach clenched.

"And I never imagined in all my twisted fantasies that you would ever say those words."

I wrinkled my nose. "Wrong week for twisted fantasies."

"Right. Sorry." He leaned in again but the mood was gone for me.

I had confessed my feelings to my dearest friend and he had heard them. I wasn't comfortable with that, at all. I pulled back again.

"What just happened?" he asked.

Reality hit me in the face. It wasn't innocent kissing or having fun if he knew how I felt about him. That made it real, and he was still my friend's ex. "I don't know. I just need to process a lot of things. We can't even be anything right now. I didn't mean for you to hear that."

He moved forward quickly, cupping my cheeks and pressing his lips against mine. He kissed and whispered, "I told you how I feel about you. I know you better than anyone. Why are you making this harder than it needs to be?"

I leaned into the kiss and breathed him in. "Hos before bros. And I still don't trust you."

"You will trust me, one day." He sighed. "And hos before bros and bros before hos is for when the people loved each other. Tom pushed Sage on me every chance he got. I didn't see it at the time, but it was more like an arranged marriage than a date. I agreed in the beginning—she was pretty and I was drunk and horny and it was fun. And secretly it meant I could be near you, which was never easy. I never cared about her that way. She's a nice enough girl. She was fun for a while and then she wasn't fun anymore. She got more how I imagined a wife might be. The honeymoon was over and she was demanding."

I shook my head, remembering what he had said. "Why did you say she was a crazy—whatever you called her—crazy cake?"

He paused again, obviously not willing to say what he knew. I hated secrets. When he did speak he sounded hesitant, "She is not the most stable of girls. When you told me she was found next to Rachel, I assumed she had killed Rachel. It was fleeting, but it went through my mind at least once. She is the nicest girl on earth, but she isn't the most sound-minded one. She can go from sweet and kind to downright insane in a notably short span of time. Like seconds. I don't want to talk about this, at all."

"And you liked me the entire time you were dating her?" The question came out prickly. Suddenly, I became fairly touchy about the whole thing.

"I did."

My gaze narrowed, even though he couldn't see me. "Then why did you agree to date her? Why didn't you try to tell me how you felt, instead of eyeing me up all the time? You spent like two years dating her and sleeping with random people behind her back. But you liked me?" I actually laughed at that part.

"You weren't a reality for me. I never imagined we might date, ever."

"Why?"

He lifted his hand and brushed it along my cheek before he sighed and rolled onto his back. I saw the silhouette of his face against the slight gap in the curtains and the moonlight. "You aren't an easy girl to talk to. You're sarcastic and rude, a lot. You are walled off like you don't care what people think about you, but I see you do care. It's taken years and years for me to chisel my way into your heart. I started with joking and making fun of little things. Then I moved it to actual conversations. Finally, I got your email address and I sent you jokes. I asked you out all the time but you never agreed. You have some serious low self-esteem and it gets in the way of your happiness."

I parted my lips to argue but there was no point. He had clearly been watching.

"You are uncomfortable a lot, which for you translates into defensive or irritable. If I could pick a girl to be infatuated with, it wouldn't be you. You're a lot of work. You don't put out on the first date. You don't drink so I can't ply your pants off with alcohol. And you never willingly have fun so I have a hard time convincing you I'm a fun guy. You hate fun."

My jaw dropped. "You are an asshole. Ply my pants with liquor?" Had he been listening?

"I'm kidding." He laughed after a second. "But you know you have said it a time or two."

"Yeah, to Lainey."

He turned and faced me again. "I listen better than you will ever know."

I rolled onto my back too. "I hate this bed."

"It is rather uncomfortable."

I turned and faced him, already dreading the lie I was about to tell, "I think we should be friends and nothing more."

"Friends who kiss and maybe have some sex, but only like every now and then?"

"No." I laughed. I couldn't stop myself. "I won't ever be a notch on your belt, Vincent Banks."

"Friends it is then." He sounded sad and I knew I was. But I couldn't break the one cardinal rule of friends, and Sage and I were already having a rough week. And I was still very stuck on his playboy behavior.

"Can I ask you a serious question about this though?"

"Yeah?"

He sighed heavily. "Can I still send you funny emails? I put a lot of thought into those. It takes me hours sometimes to find the right one."

That put a smile on my lips. I threw caution to the wind and rolled back to where he was. I hovered over his face, resting my hand on his tee shirt. Lowering my face to his, I whispered, "I want you to kiss me, Vincent." I kissed him softly.

But it didn't last that way. He rolled me onto my back, encasing me with his hands as he pulled me into him and his body squished me into the bed.

It was the second best kiss I had ever had.

Nothing would ever top the one we had in the games room.

I pushed him off me after a few minutes of hands roaming in places I wasn't ready for, regardless of what my brain said. "Sorry."

He snuggled into me, holding me tightly. "You are the best kind of friend a guy could ever have."

I laughed and closed my eyes. "Promise not to touch me while I sleep?"

"Absolutely not. Sleep at your own risk." His voice had a strong dose of sarcasm and a smile I returned before letting myself drift off to sleep.

CHAPTER TWENTY
A cold shower and a hot drink

When I woke he was still there. I winced and regretted all of my decisions all at once. I cracked one eye, letting my typical mood of the morning hit me. He was still asleep. His face wasn't turned toward me. It faced the ceiling. All the regret washed away as I inspected him, maybe closer than ever.

His skin was always golden, but not always tanned like it was then. His chestnut-brown hair had hints of summer in it, the way his bronzed skin did. His lips were a little big but not weirdly big. They made me think about how soft they were when we kissed. He had perfect skin; boys were so lucky. No makeup and not a pore in sight. He had dark, expressive eyebrows and thick wavy hair. He could rock trucker hat hair and be a grungy surfer, or he could slick it all back and look like he was refined.

His neck was thick to match his strong shoulders and arms. He had the perfect body, not as perfect as Ashton's or Jake's, but somehow to me it was better. He was leaner than both of them, the ideal body type for clothing with a European cut.

It made me smile, thinking about him playing football. He wasn't the type, and I knew he liked soccer better, but he played because he had to. He was absolutely the guy who got upset about going in the woods in Gucci shoes and spoke perfect French from being in the South of France for so much of his childhood.

His lips twitched, making me pull back as he cracked a grin. "It's a little unnerving waking with eyes on you." He turned his face, blinking and laughing. He had clearly been awake a lot longer than he was going to admit to. He wasn't bleary eyed or light sensitive at all.

"You were awake before me, weren't you?" I asked, knowing the answer.

His smile widened. "Maybe. But I'm not going to confess to watching you sleep until you woke up and then pretended to sleep so you didn't know I was watching you, only to end up as the watched and not the watcher."

He was also far more intellectual than he liked to admit, and he spoke like an adult all the time. A trait I enjoyed.

"Do you think anyone knows we're in here?"

He shook his head. "Not if we get up now, they won't."

I sat up and jumped out of the bed, smoothing the covers on my side. He didn't have the same sense of urgency I did so I hurried over to his side and pulled back the covers, recoiling in horror to see only underwear. I had assumed he'd just taken his shirt off, not his pants too.

He lowered his gaze to his legs and cocked an eyebrow. "What?"

"You took your pants off?"

"I can't sleep fully clothed. I'm not like you. I need freedom. You're lucky I kept my boxers on. I sleep naked at home."

"What if there was a fire?" I blurted, not even sure if he had the same thoughts or paranoias I did.

"Then I run outside naked?" He said it as more of a question. "I'm pretty confident about my nakedness, Linds, I can't lie." He winked but lifted his hands when he saw the horror on my face. "It was a joke, sort of. You do realize that someone seeing you naked isn't the end of the world, right?"

I gulped and backed away slowly, nodding. "Of course." I turned and walked from the room. "See ya downstairs." I hurried into the hallway and down the stairs to the kitchen. The gorgeous naked boy in my room was hard to leave.

The house was silent.

When I got into the kitchen, Lori cocked an eyebrow

at me from her steaming cup of coffee and newspaper. "Seriously?" I was never up before noon unless it was a workday, and even then I was not up and chipper. I usually stumbled and muttered bad things.

I nodded and sat, smiling. "I couldn't sleep. Too many girls in my room." I no sooner got the words out, and Vincent walked into the kitchen, smiling at Lori like he hadn't just threatened to have her fired the day before.

Lori gave me another look but this one was far more dubious. "Mmmhmmm." She got up and turned on the espresso maker.

Vincent sat next to me, nudging me and smiling. He wasn't being dirty to me anymore. It was weird to watch him switch it off. I nudged him back.

"Have dinner with me tonight," he muttered, dragging a thumb up the back of my arm with feathery lightness.

"Friends don't have dinner."

"They do, this is a thing." He grinned, but I saw the rejection was getting to him.

"Secret dinner in an incognito place?" I whispered.

He shrugged. "Or we could go somewhere nice. Whatever makes you happy."

It was a weird sentence to hear him say to me. I narrowed my gaze. "I have the worst feeling I'm going to wake up from this, and you're going to be calling me a virgin and making fun of me and my email will be full of dirty jokes."

"Your email is going to be full of dirty jokes, and I will probably be making fun of you later, but it's more like mocking in a loving way than it is being mean. If you recall I have never been mean to you." He leaned in, grazing his lips against the back of my arm. "And I have a serious amount of respect for the fact you are still a virgin. It might be one of my favorite things about you. Virgins are always respected. Except in certain cultures where they are considered a reward for bad behavior."

I cracked a smile. "You are a pervert."

His eyes darted to Lori who was foaming milk for our cappuccinos and nodded. "I am and have never pretended to be anything but." He blinked his thick lashes at me. "While we have a coffee we need to have a serious conversation about whether or not we are having dinner."

"No." I smiled wide, enjoying the view of his pout.

"I could beg."

I sighed. "Fine, God. I will have dinner with you. Stop asking." My eyes lifted as my dad walked into the kitchen. His eyes landed on Vincent and me making a slow smile cross his lips. "Good morning, children." He looked terrible.

I offered a weird wave, an awkward "I don't know how I feel about any of this" wave. "Morning."

Vincent sat up straight. "Good morning, Mr. Bueller."

Dad glanced at the coffees Lori was perfecting the foam art of and grinned. "Don't suppose those are for me?"

She shook her head. "The hearts are for the love birds. You are getting some kind of dog crap-shaped foam for letting all these teenagers sleep here."

He laughed but I scowled. She was such a grump.

She handed us our coffees and smiled wide. "And I even managed not to spit in the foam."

My cheeks blushed but Vincent laughed. She grinned at him, and I realized they liked each other. He seemed to get the crabby-lady thing.

I took my coffee, almost bowing as I backed away from the kitchen. "Thank you." She nodded but didn't give me a grin or a smile. I turned to Dad. "We're going to drink outside."

"Be out in a minute."

I walked out to the games room with Vincent following me. When I got outside I complained, "Why does she like you and not me? She's hated me since she got here."

"I have yet to meet a woman who can't be charmed. You just have to know your audience. She doesn't like sucking up, something you do nonstop while assuming you will win more flies with honey than with vinegar. That woman likes vinegar. She has a sick sense of humor."

I sat in one of the new chairs and nodded. "Makes sense." I sipped my coffee, moaning at the robust flavor. "She does make a mean coffee, hateful or not."

Dad came strolling out with his coffee and the same

tense look on his face. He sat and sighed, giving me the dad look. "We need to talk."

My stomach sank. He knew we had shared a bed. "Okay." I glanced nervously at Vincent, not sure if I wanted him here for my dad to lecture me about sharing beds with boys. It was a valid complaint even if nothing had happened.

"Rachel was possibly assaulted right before she died. Either that or she knew her killer and died after they had been active in the woods."

I winced, not needing this story a second time. The first had been horrifying enough.

"That was my response as well. I don't even want to be talking about this, but I can't stand the thought that maybe the killer is someone you all know."

My throat tightened as the threat of being sick lingered, causing my cheeks to sour.

"The police report says she had been dead for almost three hours when they found her body. A guy from the party went to take a bathroom break in the trees and saw her. He called 9-1-1 immediately and that was around two. They are saying her time of death was 11 p.m."

I nodded again. I didn't have words, just sour cheeks and discomfort. We had found her right after she was killed. She was still warm.

My dad sipped his coffee before speaking again, "It was strangulation." He shuddered and forced himself to speak, "The wounds didn't bleed like they would have if her heart had been beating. And she had no defensive wounds. No skin under her nails or anything. They had assumed there was GHB in her system but in reality there wasn't. Marguerite and Sage were the only ones who had any in their systems. Cups were found at the scene with fingerprints and traces of GHB in the residue, but they have no leads at all."

That confused me. "She wasn't drugged?"

He shook his head. "No. She had drugs in her system, but it was Ecstasy I believe."

Vincent sat back, taking it all in. He clearly knew it all from his talk with my father in the hallway the night before.

Hearing it again didn't make him look less uncomfortable. In fact, he looked like he was more so.

I blurted, "So she had sex, someone strangled her, and then they cut her dead body and formed her body into that weird position?" My dad seemed like he might say something but the words flew from my lips. "And afterward they took the trouble to bring Sage up there and leave her covered in blood and unconscious and then put Rita in the woods behind them? That doesn't even make sense. Why didn't she fight back when they were strangling her if she wasn't drugged."

My dad's eyes widened and Vincent licked his lips. They looked like I had them both in the hot seat. Finally, Dad swallowed hard, but it was Vincent who spoke softly, "You aren't a sexually active teenager"—his eyes darted to my dad—"so you might not know that sometimes when people are engaging in the activity they enjoy a bit of choking." He flushed and forced his gaze to stay on me as my dad turned his face to Vince. I wasn't sure if Dad was grateful Vince had said it or if Dad was flipping out because Vince had said it.

I was flipping out. "So the police think maybe she wanted a bit of choking, and then maybe she died accidentally, and then maybe the person who had sex with her cut her and broke her bones?" I gagged a little bit and shuddered from the taste.

Dad shot up from his chair. "Another coffee?" He hurried inside, leaving Vincent to finish the conversation.

Vincent gave me a really conflicted stare for seconds before talking, "Since it was made known to them that Rachel liked a bit of choking, the police think it's possible maybe someone was watching Rachel and her friend have sex. Her friend might have killed her by accident, which happens all the time with the kids and strangulation. It also explains why there were no defensive wounds. The guy was obviously upset and fled the forest, leaving behind the body for the psychopath to do disgusting things with. And I think that the psycho is the person sending us the letters and watching us all the time."

I scoffed. "That's the worst theory I have ever heard. I

knew Rachel. There's no way she was into that."

His eyes widened and he coughed a little. Guilt smothered his face.

"Oh my God. Are you kids high? You're having unprotected sex and choking each other, and yet half of you can't even finish high school?"

Vincent cocked an eyebrow, sighing. "I am a straight-A student and don't call me a kid—I'm a year older than you."

I shot up. "I have to go. I need a shower."

He got up and ran after me, spinning me around. "I never choked her. I never even kissed Rachel. I just know Ashton refused to do it. It was why she cheated on him all the time. He really liked her but he couldn't do it."

My jaw dropped. "You knew that she cheated, and you let him date her?"

He backed up. "How is any of this my fault? I am not responsible for Ash or his happiness. If he wanted to date a crazy slut like Rachel while she banged every townie she could find, that was his problem."

"Oh my God." I turned about to leave but paused, seeing my friends and my dad standing in the doorway to the games room. Sage cocked an eyebrow.

I shook my head. "If anyone tries to tell you what the police know, don't listen." I stormed past them all and headed for my room. I needed a shower.

CHAPTER TWENTY-ONE
The Little Lying Mermaid

I floated on my back with my limbs stretched out around me, gazing at the sun that was high in the sky.

"Are you ever going back to work?" My dad interrupted my peace. I shook my head, not answering him verbally. I couldn't talk to him or anyone. Lainey had stayed after the fiasco in the morning, but she hadn't asked any questions. She knew better. She floated in the water with me, silent and relaxing to be around.

Visions of Rachel doing bad things in the woods with someone wrapping their hands around her throat haunted me. I guessed it was how Lainey felt, not being able to forget anything they had said. Even if I begged God to take it away, that memory would stay with me for the rest of my life.

"So you quit then?" my dad asked again from the chairs on the patio. I lifted my head, sending my body down into the water. "Dad, seriously? How can I even landscape now? What if Rachel's parents' house was my next job? What if the killer's house was my next job?"

He clenched his jaw. "Yeah, you're done. Good thinking."

Lainey stood up in the shallow end and gave me a look. "So the killer could be a girl or a boy?"

I nodded. "They think she was getting it on in the woods right before she was killed. She got strangled and died and then the rest happened." I left out the parts that made me want to vomit.

Lainey winced. "Rachel always did like a good choking."

"What?" My jaw dropped. "You knew?"

"Everyone knew. I mean, like everyone but you and Sage. Sierra for sure knew. She's the one who accidentally let it slip to me."

"I can't believe you didn't tell me."

"Your generation is screwed up," my dad grumbled and got up, heading inside and away from the conversation.

Lainey cringed. "I didn't want to know. I assumed you didn't either."

"I don't but it almost makes sense. Vincent's idea is actually sound. He thinks the crazy person was watching Rachel in the woods, and when they realized she was dead from strangulation, then they did the rest of the other stuff."

Lainey started floating again. "That does make sense. We know someone is watching us all. They could be watching us right now. It's alarming." She sounded calm, eerily.

That lifted the hairs on the back of my neck and made me spin around. I didn't see a dark hooded figure or anything else, just the ocean and the downward sloping yard with a long boardwalk to the sea and tall grass along the sides of it.

I lay back in the water and tried to process it all. Nothing made sense except what Vincent had said. That made perfectly horrible sense.

Voices caught my attention and I lifted myself upright again, treading water and scowling as two men in suits came out onto the patio with my father. He was on the phone, seeming a little panicked. His eyes met mine and he nodded at the towels on the chairs. I swam to the edge and hopped out, grabbing my towel and wrapping it around myself and then carrying Lainey's to her.

Her squinting eyes widened when she saw them and she swam to me. When she climbed out I could read her expression like a book. She was scared and I knew exactly why. Even without her glasses she could see what they were.

I gave my dad a look as he hung up and walked to me. He stood between me and the men. "Lindsey and Lainey, these are special agents Ford and Burnett. They are with the FBI." He smiled at them, turning his back on us completely. "As soon as our attorney gets here, we will begin."

My entire body was pins and needles. I swallowed hard, sensing the two men's eyes on me in an uncomfortable way. "Can we get changed?"

My dad nodded and held his hand out. "Please." Lainey and I scooted past them and hurried inside. Lori went by us with a tray of drinks for the men. She offered a sympathetic look as she hurried outside.

"We are so screwed," I whispered as we climbed the stairs to my room.

"We didn't do anything, Linds. We really didn't."

"I know but I feel so guilty." I pulled on a terry-cloth beach shirt Louisa hated more than life itself and a pair of thick shorts.

Lainey hauled on some capri pants and a tee shirt. We bunched our wet hair into headbands, and she did a ponytail with her long tresses.

She threw on her glasses and sighed. "We need to wear extra deodorant and some of that pheromone perfume I have. It's made for people who get nervous. We don't want to smell like we are anxious." She rooted in her bag, brought it out, and slid some on her wrist. I finished putting on deodorant and held out my wrists.

We both turned and walked out the door. Halfway down the hall, I grabbed her arm. "Do you think the other girls have been interviewed?"

"Uhm, I don't know. Maybe. They would have sent us a text I think. I have nothing."

I pulled out my phone and texted Sage, Sierra, and Rita: *FBI is at my house. Lainey and me are about to be interviewed.*

Sage sent a scared emoticon and Sierra messaged back: *My dad and me are coming to your house now. They want to talk to us about that night. We all need the same story. They don't have anything on us, I don't think.*

Rita sent a sad emoticon.

I looked at Lainey. "What was the story again?"

She texted the story into the chat: *We got there late, meeting Rita at the party. She was there early to help Rachel. Rachel and Ashton broke up as we arrived. He left the party as Sage and Rach started fighting about it. Rita, you were with Sage the entire night. Rachel was being a dick as usual. Me, Sierra, and Lindsey ignored it and all partied together. We noticed later on that Sage and Rita weren't feeling well. We brought them to Sierra's house, but her dad wasn't home so we went to Lindsey's house and her dad took them to the hospital while the rest of us went in the hot tub. We left the party around eleven. We saw Ashton leave before us. Vincent was there, still at the docks around eleven, and he was trashed. We didn't see anyone else we remember. Sage, you and Rita remember nothing, exactly the way you actually are.*

I read her text and nodded. "Right. It's essentially what happened except the part in the woods." I lifted my gaze. "The one part someone took a lovely photo of."

Her eyes told me she was worried too. "We got this." She pushed her glasses up nervously and turned and walked down the stairs. Sierra and her dad walked in as we got to the bottom of the stairs.

He gave us a fierce look and lifted his long finger in our faces. "Say nothing. Let me do the talking. When they question you, let Sierra do the talking." He stormed through the house, leaving the three of us behind.

I gulped as Sierra leaned into Lainey and me. "I wish this week was over already."

I nodded, not even certain what day of the week it was. I couldn't be sure, but I had an idea it had been six days since Rachel had died.

The three of us walked back out onto the patio, hanging back and no doubt looking guilty as hell.

Sierra's dad was talking, shaking his head and looking confident. He was a master of this stuff.

He waved us over. "You can ask them questions all together. They have nothing to hide, but they are traumatized and you *are* strangers with no warrants. So don't push your luck."

We sat at the patio breakfast table as the two older-looking men sat across from us. They both smiled and tucked their matching sunglasses away. They reminded me of the *Men in Black,* only they were both white and one was sort of out of shape for an agent. He was sweaty and uncomfortable looking in his monkey suit.

"Hello, ladies. I am Special Agent Ford. This is my partner, Special Agent Burnett. We are here because of your friend who was killed. We're investigating it because it's a very violent crime for such a sleepy town."

I nodded as Sierra sighed and spoke like she was broken up about it, "Very violent. We heard from friends how bad it was."

His gaze narrowed. "You didn't see anything then?"

I hesitated answering because a no was a lie and a yes was a place I didn't want to go. Sierra shook her head, shrugging like a pro. "We were dancing together the whole night. We didn't see anything. We wish we had. We could have saved her maybe." There was a serious amount of truth in that statement.

I nodded along, not even looking at Lainey. I was sure her face told them all sorts of truths.

"What time did you arrive?"

"Late. Like nine maybe. I didn't look at the clock, but the party was in full swing and we were late," Sierra continued, answering for us all. "Rachel let us know that. She went at me and Sage as soon as we got there. We were supposed to be there for seven to help set up and only Rita showed up early to help out."

I had missed that, but Lainey and I had been on our own in the beginning.

Ford's eyes darted to me. "You all arrived together?"

I nodded as Lainey answered, "Me, Sage, Sierra, and Lindsey did."

Sierra blurted, "We met up with Rita there. She and Sage were sort of doing their thing all night." She lifted her hand and made a signal for drinking. Her dad scowled and twitched his head in a no.

"And then what happened?" Ford pressed me, leaning

in a bit.

"We found Sage and Rita and they seemed really trashed, like scary drunk. So we took them to Sierra's house but her dad wasn't there so we came to my house." I shook my head like I had given up everything.

Lainey shrugged, sounding nothing like herself. "And the party was a bit brutal anyway. Ashton, Sage's brother, had broken up with Rachel and he had left, really pissed off. And Rachel was being a tyrant, shouting and bitching. It was intense. She'd been in rough shape all night from the fighting. I don't think anyone really spent much time with her."

Agent Ford nodded, looking like he completely ate up her story. Which was true. She hadn't lied. That had all happened.

"So you went where after the party?" The man's eyes hit me. He was asking me directly again.

I opened my mouth and sighed my answer, "Well, we went to Sierra's and then came back here, but Sage and Rita were sick. They were too drunk, we thought. But after a while they weren't getting better so Dad took them to the hospital. He was pretty mad at us all. And we went in the hot tub to try to relax before we went to bed."

"When did you find out that Rachel had died?" His eyes stayed with me. I was clearly the weakest link.

"Facebook and the news the next day. My stepmom saw it and told us. She started screaming, and when I saw it I dropped the phone." I relived the image and shuddered.

"Did you see anyone who was suspicious or new to the party scene that night?"

I nodded before I could stop myself, still lost in the moment I had, remembering seeing the Facebook post.

"Who?" he asked, suddenly looking annoyed.

"There was a guy with a beard. It's summer. We don't really hang with guys who have beards in the summer. It was weird." Again it was the truth.

He cocked an eyebrow. "That's it?"

The three of us looked at each other, shrugging. "I guess so," Sierra offered.

Her dad winked at us. My dad still looked like he might poop his pants, but he was the one who had been on cleanup duty.

Agent Ford glanced over at the silent and creepy Burnett and shrugged. "Satisfied?"

Of course the silent one was the boss; he was the one analyzing us. Burnett shook his head. "I just have one question. Did you see Vincent Banks at all that night?"

I nodded. "I did. Twice. He was talking to Sage and Rachel, I think trying to get them to stop fighting, but Rachel was being a dick and Sage was drunk so he left them alone. I watched him stumble back into the crowd. Then about an hour later, the second time I saw him, he seemed pretty trashed. He was on the docks, from around ten thirty to just about eleven with me. We left just before eleven, and he was the last person I was with. I had gotten sweaty dancing and needed to cool off. So I went to the docks and Vince was there, chatting with me. Then I found Sage and Lainey again and we left with Sage and Rita and Sierra." It was almost the truth.

He nodded. "Andrew Henning has an alibi for the time period and so does Jackson Van der Wall."

I pursed my lips, hating the name Jackson, almost as much as Jake did, hence the reason he went by Jake. "Yeah, I saw Jake a lot, dancing and goofing around. I don't remember seeing Andrew much, but he was probably getting high." I said it and then winced. The men both laughed but neither of our fathers did.

"We aren't too worried about some pot, more so the other stuff. The cops can worry about what you kids do at your parties." Ford laughed but Burnett smiled and turned back to our fathers. "I would imagine the police around here know which kids to bother and which not to."

My dad took offence to that but Sierra's spoke cockily to them both, "I think this is done. These girls want to mourn their friend and move on. I'm sure you can understand why they don't want to keep rehashing the details. None of the five of them were anywhere near the Swanson house when the terrible acts occurred."

Both men stood and offered their hands to our fathers. "Thank you for your time, gentlemen. If we should have any follow-up questions we will be in touch. So far, all the kids are saying the same thing. Jacks—Jake, as you call him, recalls seeing you, Miss Bueller, and Vincent Banks on the docks at about ten thirty. And he recollected you two dancing around then as well." He nodded at Sierra and Lainey. "And he and several other youths remember you girls arriving late and Miss Swanson making a fuss over it. It's remarkable two hundred kids all remember the same things." His eyes darted to Sierra's dad.

Mr. Casey's eyes widened but he laughed. "If they all saw it that way, it must be true."

"We will see." Agent Burnett nodded. "Have a nice day, ladies."

They excused themselves and my father walked them out.

When the men were gone Sierra's dad nodded. "Nice work, girls. You appeared nervous and scared but adding the bit about the drinking will definitely make them understand why. Minors drinking and partying and doing drugs where a girl died, has scandal written all over it." His pleased demeanor lasted seconds. He sighed and gave us a hard look. "Whoever did this to Rachel knows you—we are almost certain of that fact. They were at the party and no one noticed someone who shouldn't have been there, except the bearded kid. Rachel didn't fight back." He sighed. "The reason I am telling you this is we all want you to take it seriously and please be careful. No drinking or drugs and no acting crazy. Sierra is on a curfew, and I am telling your parents to put you all on one as well. We need to take this very seriously until this person is caught." He looked at Sierra. "You coming home now or shall I send a car in a while?"

"Send a car."

He leaned in and kissed her on the cheek. "Behave and don't bother Mark. He's got a lot on his plate right now."

Lainey seemed to understand. He waved and walked away, heading for the games room.

I glanced at Lainey. "What did he mean?"

"Dude, shit hit the fan after the funeral. It's all real estate crap. The Van Harkers have pulled out and are no longer buying the lots."

"What?" I gasped.

"Yeah, I guess the Blacks went to see the Van Harkers and told them that my dad promised them the best lot in the parcel. The Van Harkers got pissed and said fine, we don't want any lots from you and are investing in South Carolina now. The Blacks have sold their house privately to an investor for no profit, making it look like the houses out here don't garner any revenues when they sell, which is bad for business and real estate values obviously. People are already worrying that Crimson Cove Inc. isn't the investment our fathers said it was because of Rachel being savagely murdered out here."

"Oh my God. Our dads must all be flipping out."

"They are. To make matters worse, the Blacks are still buying a new house, but it's in South Carolina where the Van Harkers are building. They have sold them the best lot for a discounted rate, essentially sticking it to our fathers."

Sierra looked like she might be asleep while standing but I winced. "Oh snap. My dad must be pissed. Who told the friggin' Blacks that the Van Harkers were buying the land?"

She shook her head. "No one knows yet. Our dads are working right now to find out who betrayed them. The deal was supposed to go through yesterday. Our dads had it all planned out. They would have sold the last piece of the Crimson Cove investment properties, saving them the taxes for the fall and winter when they wouldn't be building anyway. The Blacks would have had the land they wanted and the house they wanted. And the Van Harkers would have eaten the cost of the final subdivision to be built and made money off the sales as they built the homes. The Blacks wouldn't have cared who they were buying their house from. But when they discovered the land had been sold out from under them, they wouldn't listen to reason and they soured the Van Harkers too."

Sierra gave us both a look. "Why do you care so much?"

I parted my lips, but no explanation was there. Why did I care so much about gossip, real estate, and scandals? I shrugged. "I don't know. I just like it I guess."

Lainey nodded. "Me too. I love real estate, and I love the behind-the-scenes action no one sees."

"I couldn't possibly care less than I do about all of my dad's shit." Sierra yawned and pulled off her sundress, walking across the patio to the pool, diving in, and bobbing. "You guys coming in?"

Lainey cocked her head. "You look like Ariel. Only you lie better than any Disney princess I have ever seen."

"I never lied. I fixed the truth to make sure we weren't in trouble." Sierra lifted both her middle fingers up. "You look like Barbie's dark-haired friend."

Lainey pulled off her shirt and capris and ran for the pool, water bombing the Little Lying Mermaid. I dragged off my clothes and jumped in too.

Before I knew it, Sage and Rita showed up with Jake and Andrew, and we were having us a pool party by the time Vincent arrived, obviously dressed for dinner.

He seemed disappointed when he saw everyone. I hopped out of the pool, feeling weird about forgetting dinner and forgetting to tell him it was off. "Hey."

He stared down at my bikini and tilted his head. "You wearing that to dinner?"

"No." I laughed. "I can't go. I'm on curfew and my dad isn't in the mood to talk."

"You didn't text me all day. I was sending you messages." Vincent bit his lip, looking past me at the pool frothing with our friends.

"I was busy. The FBI came and interviewed me and Lainey and Sierra."

He didn't look surprised at all. "Can we talk inside for a second?"

I shook my head. "Let's talk down at the beach." I turned and grabbed my shorts and tee shirt from the chair, looking at the water and shouting at Lainey. "Be right back."

She nodded and screamed as Andrew dunked her.

I hurried to the beach, following Vince down the path through the grass to the water. He paused on the long boardwalk, leaning against the railing. He was too good to be true in his pale lavender dress shirt with sand-colored dress pants. His hair was slightly styled but mostly shaggy, exactly the way I liked it. But he didn't look happy.

I hugged myself, nervous about the stormy glare on his face. It matched the clouds that were hanging around out on the sea.

"What are we doing?" he asked loudly.

I shook my head as I got closer. "I don't know."

"Do you like me?"

My instinct was to lie. I hated the idea of sharing that with him in the daylight after I had said it already in the dark. "Yes." I fought my instinct on it.

"Do you love me?"

I clenched and froze on that question. My mother's voice even silenced for a second. I scowled and shook my head. "Don't ask me that."

He sighed. "I love you, Linds. I love you." Everything inside me tightened. He stepped toward me. "You are the first thing I think of in the morning, the very first thought I have. And you are the last thought when I fall asleep. To the point that I dream about you almost every night."

"Vince, you can't love me already—" I snapped my lips shut when I saw his face. I pressed them together, forbidding myself to speak further. I wanted to stop him. I wanted to go back to joking and laughing and pretending this wasn't ever going to be as serious as it was for him, even though it hadn't really started for me.

"I get it. I'm way ahead of you in everything. But it's only because I have spent my entire life watching you and thinking about you and driving myself insane around you. Believe me, I understand I am acting irrationally and I am not this guy. According to the magazines and the gossip mills and society's standards, I am the coolest guy we all know. I know that. I am the guy who doesn't do attachment. I am the guy who doesn't love girls. I have never been monogamous, and I don't know how many girls I have had sex with. I shit you not."

I grimaced, stepping back, wishing I had stopped him. I knew what he was, but I didn't need him to say it aloud. Andrew's mom floated about in my head, making me cringe.

He laughed. "But that face, even that scowl, makes me crazy. You make me crazy. I ache thinking about you— actual aching in my heart." He sort of trailed off and choked out the last words.

I stepped back a little more. I wanted to tell him so many things but a dark fear riled up inside me. I shook my head. "Just friends."

He sank. I watched him go down. "Don't say that."

"I have to. You know yourself what kind of person you are. We all know the things you've done. I don't know if I can ever look past that, but I do know if I did and you broke my heart I would never recover. We aren't the same." I closed my eyes for a second and begged my tears to stay back. "You and I are so different. You have loose morals and I am almost a nun, and will be a spinster."

"But we can meet in the middle."

"No, we can't." I nearly laughed. "I am terrified of your side."

"Then I can come over to your side."

I laughed. "What? With—with the choking and the drugs and the flagrant lack of care for STDs. Vincent, you won't go back, you've gone too far forward."

He shook his head. "I would go anywhere you asked and be anything."

"When I was little, my mom wrote me a letter for my dad to give to me when I became a teenager. He gave it to me when I turned fourteen. It was her list of things she wanted to tell me and she knew she wouldn't be able to." I lost control of my tears and they flowed down my cheeks in a steady stream. I had never told anyone about the letter, not even Lainey. "In it she said that she'd had relationships before she met my dad and she regretted them her whole life. She hated that she had let someone who wasn't worthy use her up. She had loved boys that were wrong for her and she knew it, and when they hurt her, which she had predicted would happen, she was damaged for a long time. She told me to be careful who I give my love and my heart to because most people will end up breaking it."

"That is the most fearful advice I have ever heard. You can't be serious. You have to live, Linds." He mocked me.

I spun and ran back up to the house with him shouting after me. I turned left at the pool house and sprinted up the side yard. I stopped when I was completely out of breath, but I was grabbed and whirled around.

I shoved and fought but Vincent's hands were stronger. He just pulled me into his chest and held me, letting me cry. He dropped to his knees, pulling me with him and cradled me to him. "This was the wrong week for all of this, and for that I am so sorry. I saw my chance and I took it. I wanted you to be mine so badly, I didn't care that everything else was going wrong. I am so sorry, Linds."

I sobbed, needing the release desperately. I hadn't realized how much I had been holding in until I finally snapped. After a while, I closed my eyes and listened to his heartbeat mixed in with my sniffles.

He didn't say anything else.

CHAPTER TWENTY-TWO
BOOM *goes the dynamite*

His hand had sought out mine in the dark again as we lay under the stars, the real ones. Everyone had left but him, and we had decided to camp out in the solarium with the windows open so the wind could get through the huge screens. We had nest-styled sun chairs that were giant. We each lay in one, holding hands over the edge.

"Can I read the letter?" he asked.

"What?"

"The letter your mom gave you, can I read it?"

It was a weird request but I nodded. "I guess. I'll go get it." I should have said no but I didn't. I wanted to share her with someone. I had never done that.

I got up and walked to my room and grabbed it, wanting him to see why I held virtue in such high regard. It had been an important matter to my mother.

I handed him the letter and he read it aloud using the light from his flashlight, but I heard it the way I always did, in my mother's voice.

Dearest Lindsey, I am writing this because there is a good chance I won't be able to tell you in person. If you are reading this, know I am watching over you. I made a special request to be a star that never leaves your skyline. I see that you are the beautiful, strong, proud, and smart girl I knew you would be. I am so proud of you. Believe it or not, I was once a teenaged girl like you are now. I had dreams and desires and a crazy head full of crazy ideas. I wanted to be a journalist and write tell-all's about bad companies for doing terrible things. I wanted to go to war-torn countries and tell their story. I wanted to see every nook and cranny in this world, especially the bad ones. But like all terrible ideas, that one was lost when I got old enough to have common sense. This is something you will get a little later on. It's essential to surviving your twenties. There are a few things I want you to know, things I wish I could be there right now telling you.

Firstly, do not give your heart away easily. I made this mistake a time or two. Some people are not worth the love you offer them. They will take it and use you up and leave you damaged. Now after being married to your father I regret ever having any of the relationships I had before him. But they are part of who I am now. Getting hurt and feeling destroyed is a natural part of life and you have to be prepared for that. I liked chocolate cake right from the pan, red wine, and my three favorite friends as a soother after a moment like that. Secondly, be safe. Be prudent and smart about the choices you make because some of them can last a lifetime. Pay attention in sexual health class, so you know what to avoid. Having a baby at sixteen can ruin a whole life. Thirdly, forgive people, baby. Forgive them and give them a second chance, but only one. Don't let people walk all over you. Be a leader but lead with compassion and kindness. Defend the weak. You never know when you might need the same kindness in return. But most of all, find your own way. If you lead with your heart you won't ever go wrong. It might feel wrong but it's just taking you the long way. And sometimes the long way has all the good stuff. I love you and I am always here, just whisper and I will hear you.

Love,
Mom

I gulped and sniffled a little. The letter always tore me up.

He lowered the letter and turned off the flashlight. "Lindsey, seriously?"

"I know, right? Imagine reading that at fourteen. It was intense. I haven't read it in a long time, maybe a year. At first I read it every day and then I slowed down." I wiped my eyes and smiled, missing her more than anything.

He lifted his gaze, shaking his head. "You read this letter all wrong. All kinds of wrong."

"What?" I sat up. "How would you know? You aren't even a teenaged girl."

He sighed. "No. I am far from a teenaged girl, which might be why I understand this letter better than you do. My common sense might have kicked in earlier."

"Asshole."

"Perhaps. Humor me. Your dad didn't talk to you at all about anything in this letter, did he?"

I cocked my head to the side. "Don't patronize me, Vince."

"Linds, I'm not." He chuckled. "I am trying so hard not to. You can't even imagine the self-control this is taking. Your mom was telling you to let your heart lead you and to be cautious, but not to get led around by your brain or by other people. She meant not to be a puppet, but not necessarily to be a virgin."

I lifted a finger but he lifted his hands innocently. "I'm not saying virginity is bad, at all. Your mom is right; I don't feel as awesome about the people I—anyway. It doesn't matter. What matters is she is saying, what's important to you and makes you happy, do that. What scares you and makes you uncomfortable, be cautious with that. How are you so dumb for a smart girl?" He laughed again and passed me back my letter.

"Shut up." I snatched it and folded it again. "I'm not dumb." But the thing Lainey had said about how people take their own perspective and read or see the world with it, based on all of their experiences, made sense suddenly. I didn't want to admit it to him but he was right. I might have taken my judgmental views on everything and assumed my mom had meant something she didn't mean at all.

I stuffed it in my pocket and lay back on the sun chair, not talking.

"Are you mad at me?"

"Yes," I snapped. "You called me stupid and laughed at me. I hate you."

"I'm sorry I laughed at you."

I turned his way. "No, you aren't. You love laughing at me."

"With you—I love laughing with you."

"Liar."

"We have known each other since we were very little. You know me, Linds." He sighed and climbed into my huge round sun chair, snuggling into me and kissing me on the cheek. "I am not a liar. I am a mincer of words. I am an exaggerator. And I am a withholder of the parts I don't want to share. But that doesn't make me a liar."

I turned my face sharply and his breath was on mine. "Yeah, it actually does."

"Your mom loved me, by the way. She always loved me. She would call me naughty little Vince and give me candy and wink. And she always smelled like cookies." He leaned in, pressing his lips against mine. "Stop fighting this so hard."

I shook my head. "No." But I did nestle my head into his chest and close my eyes again. Falling asleep on him was becoming a thing.

Waking up on him was also becoming a thing. I licked my lips and wiped the spit from my cheek. I blinked and realized I had slept the entire night curled into him. My legs and back were cramping as I stretched, waking him up.

"What time is it?"

I shook my head. "That looks like morning sun. It's early. I can feel it. I shouldn't be up yet."

He groaned and curled around me, kissing the top of my head. "I have to go home. I haven't been home in days, except to change."

"I have to go back to sleep so I can wake up and lie in the sun and maybe go and get a coffee later."

"Meet me for coffee."

I looked up, loving the color of his green eyes compared to the thick dark lashes. "Okay," I relented completely. "I will meet you and break bread with you in public and you can kiss me, but not in public and that will be our friendship for right now."

"Deal, but I mean this is a date. Look pretty and wash the chlorine out of your hair."

I stuck my tongue out.

He rolled his eyes and tried to stretch, wincing. "Oh my God, I'm too young for my back to hurt like this." His eyes popped open. "Oh shit."

"Did you dislocate something?"

"No, my back hurting reminded me of something." He shook his head. "I have football starting tomorrow. We have summer camp and warm-ups before tryouts." He didn't look excited.

"Why don't you stop playing if you don't love it?"

"Everyone loves football." He gave me a ridiculously judgmental look. "And I don't quit, anything. My dad expects me to play. Yale expects me to play. I will play. We dance for our dinners, Lindsey, you just haven't figured that out yet. You live like you have all the time in the world and you're a regular girl, but that's not the case. We have expectations. I slack off in every area I can. But when anyone is watching me or looking for something from me, I deliver." He puffed his chest, lifting me up a bit. "Banks men always deliver." He lowered his voice like his father's.

I laughed and rolled my eyes. "Oh my God, whatever. You are such the playboy, don't even."

He chuckled and squeezed me. "When no one but us kids are around, I am who I want to be, but when the adults are around, I am who I need to be. You need to learn how to be more flexible. Your family name depends on it." He winked all cocky and sassy and sounded just like my father.

"You are the worst person to be giving advice on protecting one's family name. I would bet my right arm that your dad hates the way you run around on your girlfriends and act like a dick."

"My dad knows when he needs me to be something or be somewhere or do anything, I'll do it." He turned and stretched his back.

I pulled away, sighing and struggling to get out of the huge nest chair. "I like being who I am all the time. I hate pretending."

"And I hate the idea that one day everyone will be looking at me to run the family fortune, but that day is going to come. It came for my dad and it'll come for me. It's who we are. Blue blood isn't such a bad thing when you know how and when to pretend to be a commoner."

"Commoner is a dirty word, Vince." I offered him my hand and pulled him from the crazy chair.

He weighed a ton, and when he came out, he wrapped himself around me. "The point I am making is that there will be people watching when we go for coffee and when we go anywhere. Can you try? I don't mean heels and a gown, but can you at least brush your hair and wear a clean tee shirt, and can it not be a graphic tee?"

My jaw dropped and I pulled back.

He shook his head. "We aren't doing the teenaged drama thing this early. Close that mouth and show me the way to coffee. I promise I will put aside time later for you to take the things I mean the wrong way and everything I say out of context." He took my hand in his and laughed like he was daring me to get upset. I pulled my hand from his and walked to the kitchen.

Again Lori gave me a look. "Can we stop meeting like this? I like my morning coffee Lindsey-free."

"Agreed." I nodded. "I'm going back to bed. Can you just make this thing here some coffee?" I pointed at Vincent before I turned and walked for the stairs, leaving them both in the kitchen. I staggered up to my room and crawled into my bed.

My head was spinning with thousands of things, but I shut them all down and closed my eyes, letting myself drift off into a slumber.

When I woke my phone was going crazy. It was worse than an alarm.

I reached for it blindly, stunned it was one o'clock in the afternoon. I had slept for five hours since Vincent had left, but I was way more tired.

There were messages galore in the group chat but it was in two places. And there were a bunch of messages from Vincent. I opened his first and read.

Linds, what time for coffee?

We could do high tea. Want to go to that place down the shore by Stamford?

Linds, are you still sleeping?

I'm coming over.

I'm watching you sleep, Lindsey. That message had just come in.

I cringed and looked up, seeing the crack in my door where it was partially open. I jumped, seeing his green eye in the space.

He laughed and walked in. "I did call and text."

I tossed a pillow at him. "That's not funny."

"It was funny. You were scared." He sat on the edge of my bed.

"That's because I was scared. Mostly because someone is actually watching us."

He opened his mouth but didn't say anything. He wrinkled his nose and nodded. "That's fair."

I turned my gaze back to the texts still coming in. Looking at the group chat, I froze the second I realized what was happening. "Rachel is texting us again."

"Seriously?" He moved closer and we both started to read the texts. They were older, an hour ago maybe. The new texts were in the new group chat that was made without Rachel, and the girls were freaking out in there.

I scrolled back to find the beginning of the conversation.

Hey girls, just wanted to check in and see how you all were doing.

A storm crossed my face. "Why is this person doing this? Why do they want us to suffer?"

Vincent scrolled down and we both read as Sage started screaming at them, caps lock and all. Then Sierra called them a sick #$%^ and threatened to take the pictures and the texts and show the cops. Lainey said nothing. Close to the bottom Rachel had written a stupid text that made no sense.

Just wanted to see how you all were doing. Was hoping we could hang out again real son.

I narrowed my gaze and shook my head. "Real son? Is that a typo or a signature, like keep it real, son?"

Vincent laughed. "Pretty much everyone we know is far too privileged to write keep it real."

Lainey had sent the last message. She had sent it forty minutes before I woke up. *Real son? Did you just have a typo in your threatening text to us? LOL!*

I moaned. "Don't antagonize them, Lain."

Vincent gave me a look. "We should go to her house right now."

"Why?" I shrugged. "You think they would react this fast?"

"I do." He nodded, jumping up and dragging me from my bed, still in my shorts and tee shirt from the day before. He grabbed my keys from the dresser and headed out the door.

We sprinted down the stairs and across the front lawn of my house and blasted past Robert and the stiffs in suits who napped a lot.

When we got to the driveway he called out to Hugo, "Meet us at Lainey Allen's house." He jumped in my car, not opening the door for me. He started my car like a savage and floored the gas to bring her to life.

"I should be driving. She doesn't like other drivers."

He rolled his eyes. "I drive better than you do."

"No—" I was about to argue further, but he skidded from my driveway sideways and managed to pull ahead without jerking. It was terrifying, and yet exhilarating to ride with someone who drove like a racecar driver.

"Did you take driving classes?" I shouted at him as we sped along the highway, him weaving in and out of traffic.

He nodded. "My driving instructor was a CIA trained driver. In case I ever encountered anything unsavory."

"No way. Wait? What? Unsavory?"

He nodded. "No one wants to be held captive for ransom. My dad liked to inspire me to never get caught by kidnappers by telling me he just won't pay." He shook his head, keeping one eye on the road. "I didn't like those odds so I paid for trainers in all sorts of Bond-like things. I learned to fight, survive, and drive. And Hugo is also a little bit more of an ex-mercenary than he is a driver."

"Hugo reminds me of Lurch." I slumped back in the seat. "Damn. Your own dad said he wouldn't pay?"

He nodded. "Not even a dime. He would go and find himself a nice orphan and raise him on his own to take over the company. He said he would do better than me anyway since the kid wouldn't have the negative effects of my mother to pollute him the way I am." He laughed but it had to be hurtful. My dad was a crabby dick on the best of days, but he loved me and he would pay no matter what.

"Your dad is an asshole."

"He's an asshole. He's nicer than his dad was though so I am lucky there." He shrugged and turned onto the other marine road where Lainey, Sierra, and Sage all lived. I held on tight as he maneuvered my car the way it was probably meant to be driven.

After a few miles he stopped and spun into a driveway, skidding along down to the house and screeching to a halt. My tires smelled like they were burning, but if my car could smile, it might. We jumped out, running for the front entrance. Lainey came to the door, opening it with a weird look on her face.

"What are you guys doing here? My dad is gonna kill me when he sees those tire marks."

Vincent nodded at her house. "Let me come inside and just check to make sure—"

BOOM!

A blast from the backyard cut him off. We all looked into the house as Lainey turned to run back inside. Vincent grabbed her. "Is your sister home?"

She nodded, shouting for her, "MAZY!"

Vincent pushed Lainey back out and ran into the house. I couldn't see or smell smoke, but I dialed 9-1-1 anyway.

"9-1-1. What's your emergency?"

"Fire please, my friend's house has had an explosion in the backyard I think. The Allen residence in—"

"Location first, miss." The snippy lady cut me off.

"Crimson Cove."

"Okay, and address." She sounded like I was a bother.

I glanced at Lainey. "What's your civic?" I held the phone up to her face.

"482 East Marine Drive," she said, still looking back for her sister.

"Okay, I got that. Fire is on the way." She hung up on me. I looked at Lainey. "Fire trucks are coming." Vincent came running out with Mazy and an orange cat. Lainey grabbed the cat and walked to my car. "Can you close the roof and windows please?"

I opened my mouth to tell her not to stick her cat in my car on the leather seats but I didn't. I sighed and pressed the button. The roof and windows closed, and she opened the door and put the cat in there and nodded at Mazy. "Come get in Lainey's car so we can go see what that was."

Mazy looked like she might argue but she didn't. She sniffed and got into the car. Lainey locked the door and closed it, shouting at her through the window. "If you open this, the alarm will sound."

Mazy seemed disgruntled but not as mad as her cat.

I winced for my car but I didn't get to worry long. Vincent came running back out. I hadn't even realized he had gone back in. He breathed heavily as he spoke, "The staff are leaving through the side yard. The backyard looks like this." He lifted his phone and showed us both the picture. It was a burn mark on the back grass that said, "REAL SOON!"

Lainey gasped and started to cry. I froze. I didn't have tears anymore. The fear in me was becoming a thing. A real living thing. It was shutting off abilities I needed, vital functions.

Lainey backed away, looking around at the massive manicured estate. Screams came from the backyard. I took off, not sure what help I could be, but I ran for the side of the house, stopping short where the staff was screaming and crying. A small lady named Giselle, who made the best pastries I had ever eaten, crossed herself and whispered a prayer while staring at a bush across from her.

On the ground next to the huge bush was Andrew's dad, Mr. Henning. He was clearly dead and had cuts or stab wounds everywhere. His body looked weird, like it was angled peculiarly. I cried out, lifting my hands to my lips and stepping back.

Lainey and Vincent came around the corner. His hand covered my face, pulling me into him as he dragged me back.

"He's shaped exactly the same way Rachel was. Even the stab wounds are the same, in the same places," Lainey whispered. Vincent slapped his hands over her mouth and pulled her back with me.

Tears streamed her pale cheeks as she stumbled, being led away by Vincent. He left us and walked back, shooing the staff from the body. "Go to the front yard. Stand by the car in the front yard."

They moved like sheep, listening to the shepherd. Women cried, men acted confused. I was lost. Lainey was right; his body was shaped the same way Rachel's was. Someone had broken his bones brutally to make him lie like that.

I dropped to my knees, wincing as the wound beneath the bandage hit the ground. I wrapped myself around Lainey, holding her tightly and staring as everything seemed to fall apart.

CHAPTER TWENTY-THREE
All the sinners in the house say,
"HEYYYYY!"

We stared at the ocean. Every one of us was silent and confused.

Lainey leaned into me but didn't speak. She and Mazy and the orange and white cat, Jewels, were staying with us. Their house was not only a crime scene but also the entire back part of the deck and sunroom had sustained fire damage.

Sierra rocked back and forth in the sand, her lower lip inside her mouth. She made a sucking noise.

Sage shuddered every now and then but never took her eyes from the darkening sky and the still sea. All the storms had passed through the town.

Everything was calm and I suspected it was the calm before the storm.

Rachel was dead.

Mr. Henning was dead.

Lainey's house was burned.

Our dads' business was suffering.

There were so many possible links between us all it was impossible to try to list them. We needed to start ruling out people but everyone had a motive.

Everyone but us.

Andrew's dad had never been anything but nice to me.

I looked back, hearing a noise but sighed when I saw Jake and Vincent walking down the boardwalk. They didn't wave or try to run. They didn't play. They walked somberly and sat down next to us on the sand, huddling even though the air was pretty warm for evening.

"His dad died of a stab wound in the back. He bled out somewhere else and was moved. He's been dead for eight hours," Jake muttered, sounding like he was a million miles away.

I pressed my lips together and closed my eyes. Every bit of me whispered a small prayer for their family.

"I did this," Lainey muttered.

Sierra shook her head, wrapping an arm around Lainey's shoulders. "You didn't do this. None of us did this."

"I taunted him or her or it." Her pitch rose as she started to believe what she was saying.

"No, Lainey. Whoever this sick bastard is, they did this. They did this to Rachel, and they did this to Andrew's family, and they are doing this to us. We are victims." Sage lifted her head to the sky. "What is the worst thing you have ever done? Say it now. The very worst thing you have ever done in all your life." Sage turned to me as she spoke, "I'll go first. I stole from the secondhand store downtown. I had eighty dollars in my pocket, and I stole from needy people." Her eyes darted to Vincent behind me. "And I hurt someone I cared about a lot."

Vincent's voice came up from behind me next. "I never gave someone worthy of it a proper chance, and I never let myself believe I was deserving of good things."

I looked down, ashamed of what I was about to say, "I have snooped in all your houses. I have seen your secrets. And I have an electronic journal in my phone with all of those secrets catalogued. In order." I winced as they all peered at me.

"I cheated on my midterms last year. I was having an anxiety attack for no reason and couldn't focus on the test. So I cheated. I had my phone with me and I knew the teacher wouldn't even suspect me, so I Googled every question." Lainey seemed mortified.

"I had sex with our soccer coach," Sierra owned hers. She shrugged it off.

My jaw dropped as Lainey gasped. "He's married and old and you're a minor. That's illegal."

Sierra sighed. "He's only twenty-one and he's engaged. Not the same thing. It was a couple of months ago. I was already sixteen. Age of consent." She winked at Lainey who blushed brutally.

"I secretly dated my best friend's boyfriend in Manhattan," Rita said next. "He died in a car accident and I never told her. He and I were dating the entire time, but I didn't want a commitment so he dated her to have someone to bring to events."

Sage's eyes darted behind me. I knew she was looking at Vincent. I felt sick.

Rita sighed. "But when he died, I let her think he was awesome. I even sent her a letter from him, handwritten. He had sent it to me months before so I had someone write her the exact same letter, and I mailed it so it came after the accident." She lowered her gaze, but Sage reached over and squeezed her hand.

"I also had sex with Andrew's mom," Jake blurted. I started to laugh, completely inappropriately, but everyone joined in. "She was hot and she seduced me, and it was awesome and I am not even sorry." Jake covered his face, shaking his head.

Vincent slapped him on the back, nodding his head. I grimaced but still laughed.

"My point I am making is this"—Sage looked at us all—"we have never done anything so horrible that we deserve any of this. Not one of us has done something so bad that we have earned this punishment. Now we know each other's darkest secrets. We know the darkness of the hearts we are surrounded by. We are not bad people." She sniffled. "My brother has been missing for a week. He isn't at our other houses, his passport hasn't been used, he's not answering his calls, and his phone is off. My parents have to file a missing person report now because the FBI is listing him as a person of interest." She wiped her eyes. "We need to find out who is behind this. I know it's not Ash and he might even be hurt. So we make a vow now, here on this beach. We will keep each other's secrets, and we will protect each other so no one else dies."

She pulled her hairpin and stuck it into her finger, drawing blood and lifting it up. She squeezed a couple of droplets into her mickey of Grey Goose and swirled it. She passed the pin and the bottle to Sierra who stabbed her finger and did the same thing. Each of us stabbed ourselves and put our blood into the vodka, and when we were done Sage drank it and passed it on.

The whole thing seemed a bit cultish, but with the fact we had two dead people and no suspects, I was willing to hedge my bets with a random group of kids. We each brought something different to the table.

And I knew the darkest secrets of every person here and it was time to share that.

"We have one issue here in Crimson Cove. We have the juiciest secrets and they are all ammo. So we need to start taking away the ammo by removing the label 'secret' from everything." I looked down, pressing my thumb into the passcode spot and opening my phone. "Want to hear what I have collected on everyone? So we can start creating a list of suspects and know what we are dealing with?" I asked softly.

Lainey nodded. "Just hit us with it. I know my family is in there."

I sighed and nodded. "Lainey, your dad has every single key to every house he has every sold. He finds out people's passwords on alarm systems when he helps set them up the first day they get their new home. I think sometimes he goes in the houses but I'm not positive. He is having an affair with your mom's best friend, Judith. They were high school sweethearts. When you and Mazy are old enough he's going to leave your mom for Judith."

Lainey nodded. "I knew all that already."

"Judith's son, Mike, is your brother."

Lainey's jaw dropped. "Holy shit."

I bit my lip as tears filled her eyes. "I have a brother, Linds?"

I twitched a subtle yes.

"Then my parents and Judith have to go on the list. Someone could have been blackmailing them or anything. Put them on the list. They have sinned, they could be weak."

I quickly added their names to a list I had already started. It consisted of only the hipster, Ashton, and Vincent.

My eyes darted to Jake. He shook his head. "I don't want to know."

I laughed. "Your parents don't have anything that I could find. They're squeaky clean and Andrew's mom was the only thing I knew about you."

He sighed. "Okay, good."

I glanced back at Vincent. "I don't know a single bad thing about your father that everyone else doesn't already know. I have to assume he keeps his really bad shit locked up tight, but should we say it's safe to add him to the list?"

He nodded slowly, his green eyes burning. "Add me too."

"Your name is already on there." He flinched when I said that.

I looked back at Sierra. "You want it?"

She paused and then nodded.

"Your dad is having an affair with Sage's mom, has been for years. They are actually in love. He understands her sadness at missing her husband who was his best friend. Your mom has been having an affair with your dad's brother for years, but we all probably know that. She doesn't keep it as hush-hush as she should."

Sierra glanced down and cringed. "Yeah, I knew all that too."

Sage turned pale as she wrinkled her forehead in distress. "How did you know? How did I not know?"

Sierra peeked at her from her hung head and offered a remorseful face. "I didn't know how to say it. I found out about six months ago."

Sage turned back to me. "I don't want to know anything else about my family."

I nodded. "Fair enough. That's all there really is."

She sneered. "You mean besides Tom's affairs?"

"Obviously. Everyone knows he has them."

Sage started to cry again. She covered her face and shook. "Put Tom down twice."

"Okay." My eyes darted to Rita. She waved her finger in my face. "I haven't been here long. You can't possibly know anything."

I bit my lip. "Do you want me to just write your dad's name down or do you want to hear it?"

"MY DADDY WOULDN'T EVER DO ANYTHING!" Her Jersey was showing hard. If she took her earrings off I was running. She seethed, "YOU DON'T SAY SHIT ABOUT MY DADDY!"

I typed his name into the next spot on the list. "Okay."

Rita narrowed her gaze. "What about your family, Miss Smarty Pants?"

I shrugged. "I haven't spied on them."

"Her dad is known for his temper. He changed his name about three years before he met Lindsey's mom, due to jail time spent for fraud and assault. His real name was something really common like Brown or Smith. Lindsey's mom was a saint and never knew this story. But Louisa does. Lindsey's lovely stepmom blackmailed Mark into marrying her. She was broke and destitute, a hooker and grifter, down on her luck. Her sister Lori is her maid and cook and doesn't know Mark's secret, but Lori knows Louisa has something on him," Vincent spoke from behind me.

My cheeks flamed and I felt sicker than I ever had. But I sighed and wrote my father, Lori, and Louisa all down.

Rita sighed. "Just say it. If that's true about your daddy, you can say it about mine."

I swallowed hard. "Your dad was asked to leave his firm, threatened with charges, and lost all his clients except one. He got caught doing insider trading. The firm let a flunky new guy take the fall, but your dad had to leave New York. His last client was Crimson Cove Inc. He became our mayor in a landslide vote about three months after he had to leave New York."

I didn't dare make eye contact with her, but I could see her nodding. "I knew that. Is that everything?"

I grinned wryly. "Like you said, you're new. I haven't

had much time to investigate."

We all sighed.

"I have all the secrets of the other prominent townspeople. I can make a list so we can be sure to have every known suspect. Vince, can we ping Rachel's phone?" I didn't glance back at Vincent; I couldn't look at him. I knew it was hypocritical, but I was so angry I couldn't breathe freely.

"I can get someone to try."

Taking the vodka bottle in my hands, I stared down at my feet when I spoke, "I'm sorry to all of you. I don't expect you to forgive me." I lifted the vodka and drank a big gulp of it. Shuddering from the metallic taste, I passed it to Lainey next and stood up, walking through them all, and headed for the house.

The talking started the moment I was gone. I heaved a sob from my lips as I realized the terrible thing I had done. I had outed their parents for the worst things they had ever done. I had snooped into people's private things.

I was the worst person there.

Blinding tears filled my eyes and I hugged myself and stumbled up the path. I got to the pool house and slipped inside, closing the door and sitting on the couch.

I sat alone, in the dark and wished I could get back the feeling of safety and security.

I wished I liked the dark and didn't need Vincent to be in it. I wished I were comfortable in my skin again and not constantly aching for his touch.

He felt like all the wrong choices for me, though my heart begged me to let go of what he had said about my family. But all I thought about was that he knew the worst thing about us and had kept it secret.

I sobbed silently, gripping myself.

A shadow came over me as someone slipped past the window. It was a hooded figure. Their back was turned to me.

My heart started to race and my mouth went dry as I slid along the huge couch to the side that was in the shadows.

The dark silhouette of the person moved a little and

then stopped. They turned abruptly, staring in the pool house window. I stayed frozen, hoping they couldn't see me. My hands shook as the person moved in the window to where the door was.

I got up, just as the handle turned, and stepped into the shadows even more. I slid along the wall silently, stepping into the drapes and hiding myself with the thick dark fabric.

The door opened. I heard the groan but no one made a sound.

I couldn't see, but I knew I was hidden so long as they didn't turn on the light. My heart raced so loudly I assumed the person in the hood could hear me. I didn't dare swallow as saliva gathered in my parted lips.

My whole body froze.

The door creaked more into the dark space and someone else's breath joined the silence. They breathed hard for a minute and closed the door.

Somehow, miraculously, I didn't cry. I didn't scream or panic. I stayed perfectly still, not even blinking.

I listened so hard I could hear my friends at the beach, but I couldn't hear someone else in the space with me.

Had they left or were they inside, hiding in here?

How would I get out if they were in here?

"Linds!" Vincent shouted from outside. I parted my lips to call for him, but I couldn't. In the frozen state of horror, my mouth refused to make a sound. I wanted to warn him in case the killer was here and was going to get him. I wanted to be braver than I was, but I couldn't.

My throat was so parched it started to hurt, needing the spit I had gathered in my mouth.

A floorboard creaked as the handle turned again. I cringed with my eyes shut tight. The door opened and closed again, but I didn't dare breathe.

I didn't know if they were still inside and waiting for me to make a move or what.

The light flicked on and my throat tightened.

Every inch of me stiffened.

"Linds?" Vince said my name softly. "I saw you come in here, you okay?"

I started to cry, clinging to the drapes and sobbing. Breaths tore from me as I swallowed and gasped. I pulled back the curtain, jumping when I saw him.

I expected him and still jumped.

"There you are." He wrapped his arms around me. "You're shaking? What's wrong?"

I glanced at the window, seeing the shadow there again. "Killer," was all I could get out.

His head snapped around and he caught the shadow crossing the window. "Holy shit!" He ran for the door, but the lights cut out and the handle wouldn't turn.

I started to shake harder as I lowered myself to the floor, waiting for the moment the fire would start to crackle and burn us in there or I would hear the screams of our friends as he killed them all savagely.

It was our turn.

"The door is stuck. Is there another door?" Vincent shouted at me, but I sat perfectly still, gripping myself.

I was never going to be the journalist I had wanted to be. I was never going to be the brave and wonderful girl my mother saw me as.

I realized then and there that the letter, and the expectations she'd had for me, felt out of my reach. My mother was dead, and I would never make her proud of me.

I was going to die in there.

I closed my eyes and let the white noise of Vincent shouting at me, and the sound of the blood pounding in my head, fill my ears.

CHAPTER TWENTY-FOUR
He's a **KILLER** of a kisser

Warmth surrounded me. My eyes were still blurry, but if I blinked a lot I got clear flashes of what was before me.

I was wrapped in a blanket and Vincent. He gripped me so hard that my skin was bruising, or at least felt like it was. His fingers dug in and his mouth moved fast. I caught words like shock and trauma and police. I smelled things like Louisa and my dad and the beach. As I scanned the room I realized there were many people still here. We weren't alone. We were in the house. I was safe.

My heart still raced, but I lifted my head and forced myself to look at Vincent. He stopped talking mid-sentence and cupped my cheeks. "Linds?" His words sounded like he was in a tunnel, but I tried to nod my head.

"You okay?"

I shook my head. "The killer—"

"You're safe. There is no one on the property now."

My head jerked to the right, looking at the windows to see if the figure was searching for me. I wasn't safe even if I was in my living room surrounded by people.

"He's probably out there." I blinked and gasped as if surfacing and breathing for the first time in hours. I swallowed and started to twitch my head in a no. "The killer is here still," I whispered. "He's here, I'm sure of it."

My dad's eyes widened. "It's a him?"

I nodded. I was certain it was a man. "He was big, too big to be a girl. He was broad. His face—it was hard to see but it was a guy."

He turned and talked to the guys in suits. The stiffs who should have seen it all coming. Why weren't they guarding the property? Why did they nap so much? Why weren't they taking this seriously?

Louisa gave me a worried smile. "You okay, Linds?"

My eyes narrowed on her and I immediately started to seethe. Vincent lifted me from the couch. "She seems better, I'll take her to her room." He walked around the sofa and carried me out of the room as everything came rushing back in.

"Put me down."

He shook his head, not meeting my gaze.

"PUT ME DOWN!"

He walked faster and headed to the games room and then outside.

The cool breeze coming off the ocean made my skin crawl as my breath hitched on the ocean air. I went numb as soon as I saw the pool house across the yard. I clung to him, shaking my head as tears filled my eyes. "VINCE!" I wriggled, but I couldn't get free of him. "PLEASE DON'T DO THIS!"

But he ignored me. As if he was on autopilot or completely shut off, he walked straight to the pool house and opened the door. He stepped inside as tears and panic suddenly blinded me. He closed the door, trapping us both inside.

He slid down the door, sitting on the floor, cradling me by force. I fought him, but he slipped a hand up over my lips and held me so tight I couldn't move at all except to flutter my feet.

It was then I had a dark and terrible thought. One that had points and clues and moments of clarity that seemed to fit perfectly.

I started shake and went quiet so I could think of a way to escape him—the one I had let touch me and kiss me, and the one I had let read my mother's letter.

All of the moments that proved my greatest fears became loud inside my head, listing off:

- Of course he had been the person calling me outside the window as the dark figure had appeared and then disappeared.
- He knew to go to Lainey's house after she taunted the killer. Maybe he had done it to make himself look really innocent or to make me take him off my list. He had to know he was on it. Of course he was.
- He was drunk at the party but it could have been an act. I never asked where he had gone after I left him cupping his balls on the docks.
- He texted me while he watched me sleep.
- He had access to my house at all times.
- His liking me was an act to get close to me to use me. His feelings weren't real. I was a pawn somehow in this.
- Vincent was the killer.

Silent tears and soft whimpers slipped from me as he started to speak in a hushed tone, "When I was fourteen I learned how to drive. The first few months were fun, learning how to predict what a vehicle does in all types of weather. I loved driving and I loved pushing the limits. But the real training didn't start until I was closer to fifteen."

I shuddered, shaking my head, uncertain of where this was going. Uncertain of how to survive this moment.

"One night, we were doing a course through a city. I got to go on a movie set in Chicago and drive a cool set car. It was a Lamborghini and I thought I could handle it. I sped through the raceway like a maniac, maybe showing off a little 'cause I was too young to actually be driving so I wanted them all to see how good I really was." His voice dropped to a whisper, "It had been raining, and I wasn't as good of a driver as I pretended I to be. I skidded, lost control, and crashed into a building." He sucked his breath. "I don't remember what happened; I know the car caught fire. I was stuck. I couldn't get out and there were flames all around me. I screamed and screamed and then everything was black, and when I woke I was in the hospital. Somehow someone had gotten me out, and I had a broken wrist to show for the entire thing." He laughed softly.

His soft story made attempts at calming me down, but I swallowed them and continued to remind myself he was dangerous and I was in trouble. I had to find a way to knock him out or stab him with something. I didn't even think I could stab someone. I needed to scream but his hand was still over my mouth. I could bite him.

His eyes fell on me, glinting in the dark. "The next day my instructor made me get behind the wheel of another Lamborghini. I fought it, I even cried at one point. I tried everything I could to not drive that car but he made me. I flashed my wrist and said it was impossible to drive. He laughed and made me do it. And the next day he made me drive again. And it went like this for a week before I was comfortable with the car and was driving it just how I used to. I learned about my limitations, but I also learned to conquer my fears."

He scanned the dark room. "This is just a building. It isn't anything you need to fear. You need to come in here every day and take back your power."

I started to cry softly, making sounds and breathing raggedly. He wasn't the killer, just crazy. Relief filled me as maybe a little pee left me. I shook my head, breathing through his fingers as he removed them.

He stood up, sliding back up the door and lifting me with him, setting me on my feet. I trembled as I clung to him. "This is nothing but a dark room, Linds. You have to get back behind the wheel or you will never drive again."

He flicked on the lights and I flinched, shying away from the room I had once been completely comfortable with. When I was little it was my dollhouse. When I was twelve it was my slumber party house. Recently, it had become the place people went to make out during pool parties.

"Whoever is doing this to us is trying to strip us of things, strengths. I see that now. This is a game for them. We cannot let that happen. If they wanted us dead, I think we would be dead. Because up to this point we haven't been prepared for them. They are playing with us. But now that we see that, we can take back some of the power." He flicked the lights off again and I nodded weakly. It would take me some time to get back to hiding in the dark and feeling safe, but Vincent was right. I couldn't give up.

I reached over and took his hand in the dark, squeezing. "Thank you." He had scared me straight, proving his point. I was scared of the boogeyman suddenly. Something I had laughed at as a little girl.

I let him pull me from the room and we walked back into the house. When we got inside the games room I paused. "Louisa—I have to tell my dad it's okay for him to kick her out."

Vincent's eyes lowered. "I should have told you. I'm sorry."

I shook my head. "No. I understand. I never told anyone any of the secrets I knew. I didn't want to hurt them."

He lifted my jaw, brushing his lips lightly on mine and whispering, "I would die before I hurt you on purpose."

I believed him.

He was a joker and a pervert and so many other bad things, but the good traits in him were beyond amazing and they might have even outweighed the bad.

He remembered what my mom smelled like. He risked himself to save people from fires, even though he had nearly burned to death once. He made me get behind the wheel again.

I was finished with doubting him. So I leaned into him, melding until it felt like we were one. "I love you, Vince. I think deep down I always knew I had feelings for you, but I think because you were Sage's and I believed I could never get a guy who was so—"

"Rude, arrogant, destructive—"

"Intense." I lifted my eyes to meet his and nodded. "You are intense and I think I always saw myself as a different kind of mess, not the kind that would match you. You match Sage with your stylish ways and how you do all the right things when people are looking, but do all the wrongs when they're not. And you're confident and cocky so when you do get caught for something bad you shrug it off.

I'm not like that."

He opened his mouth to speak, but I pressed my finger over his soft lips. "I liked that we played cat and mouse and we mocked each other, and I loved the level of comfort I had with you. I just never realized what those feelings were ultimately attached to." I blinked and said it because my mother's voice inside my head made me, "They were always attached to my heart. I remember my mother loving you. She always said what a sin it was that your parents didn't see what a great little boy you were. I thought she was crazy. But now I think she was adept at seeing people."

He sighed and nodded. "We don't have to conquer the world, Linds. But we have to be together. You see that, right?"

"I do. I hate that you and Sage have so much baggage and that's always going to be a thing. I am the girl who broke the best-friend code. I love Sage and I would never hurt her."

He rolled his eyes. "I wish you could see inside my heart and know how little you are breaking the code."

I stood on my tiptoes, lifting my other hand to his face and pulled him down to me. "I think I see you for the first time." I closed my eyes and kissed him with everything I had. He scooped me up and set me on the barstool. His arms wrapped around me as he pressed himself against me.

"Linds!" my dad called to me.

Vincent pulled back, separating us and yet still heaving his breath and looking at me like he might eat me whole.

Dad hurried into the room, giving us both a look. "Oh, sorry. I didn't know you were in here. I thought you were in your room, but you weren't there and I was worried." He gave me a look and I saw so many things in it.

Vincent leaned in and kissed me on the cheek. "I'll wait out there." He walked from the room, nodding at my father respectfully as he left.

My dad rushed to me, hugging me until all my breath whooshed from me and my back cracked a little. "I don't know what the hell is going on, but I was so scared."

I nodded, hardly able to move and muttered into his chest, "Me too."

He pulled back, gripping my arms. "What happened?"

"I came up from the beach and went into the pool house. I was sitting there and I saw a figure outside—a guy's face—but I couldn't make out details. He was looking in the windows, like he had seen me come in there. I hid in the shadows and then in the drapes, and he came inside I think. I heard the door and then I heard Vince calling me. Vince came inside, and he turned on the light and the killer wasn't there, but we were locked in and the lights cut out." I frowned, realizing that was the last of my clear memories. "I think I blacked out."

"You went into shock, Lindsey Marie. You were pale and your pulse dropped and Vincent wouldn't let go of you."

I sighed and shook my head. "I don't remember that. What happened after I blacked out?"

He sighed and ran his hands through his thick hair. "Vince was screaming and the lights had cut out and there was a pool chair under the handle on the outside of the door. The security guys searched the property but they didn't find anything. The breaker on the pool house had been switched off, but other than that and the pool chair, we didn't find a single thing out of place."

"We need to get cameras in the house."

He shook his head. "Louisa doesn't like them, dear. And I'm not fond either."

"I don't care what she likes. I suspect she might be behind some of this." I couldn't stop the rest of it from falling out, "Do you love Louisa, Dad?"

He winced and shrugged. "She's—well, I mean one day you're going to be gone to college and it'll just be me here alone."

I gave him a look and I muttered, "There's nothing wrong with being alone." I hopped off the barstool and walked to the hallway. "Did you call the police?" When he didn't answer me I glanced back at him. "Dad?"

"We have a situation. It's delicate and being handled."

"Let's agree not to lie to each other anymore. You don't love Louisa and I can read your face like a book." My insides tightened. "What happened?"

"Henning was murdered right after Gerry and I found out it was him who told the Blacks everything. He was getting revenge on us for cutting him out of the business recently. He had tried to work with us but we didn't like his ethics. He was bankrupt and desperate so he went for the Black family fortune and connections to pull himself out. He's the one who found the land deal in South Carolina for the Van Harkers."

I started to feel hot.

"Gerry left a message on Henning's cell phone, saying he was going to kill him if he saw him again. And I might have sent some texts to that effect. We were both just so furious. Neither of us meant it. I mean, he cost us millions. We were livid."

I swallowed hard. "Oh no."

"Oh no is right." He nodded. "Henning's cell phone is missing now. Gerry messaged Vincent and asked him to check the body for a cell phone but Henning's phone is gone."

I remembered that. I had seen Vincent give a quick look for his cell phone. He'd said it was to see who Mr. Henning had called last, in case the killer was a contact or an appointment. "The killer has it?"

He nodded as he walked to me. "It would seem. It's not at the house, his office, or on his body. We checked the car. We can't find it. Clearly, he was killed to make us look guilty, maybe for cleaning up the whole Rachel thing. Maybe whoever killed her wanted you girls to hang for it."

I shivered. "Dad, I'm so sorry. I should have cleaned it up myself."

He shook his head. "No. Don't be sorry you called me—ever. You don't know what the world looks like, not the real one. You and your friends have no idea how hard it is to stay on top." The comment was weird. He leaned in and kissed my forehead. "Your friends have left, except Lainey obviously. She went up to sleep with Mazy and that damned cat. Lainey doesn't seem like she's doing very well. Which makes sense. They are all scared and shaken up. I suggested you girls spend the rest of the summer lying low or out of the country. Vincent said his mother has some spare rooms—"

"I want to stay here. If I leave I might never be able to come back." And fear would rule my life.

He appeared defeated but he cocked an eyebrow. "If this gets even a fraction more out of hand, you are going to boarding school in Switzerland."

"Okay." I cringed. I walked out of the games room and met with Vincent in the hallway. "I'm not leaving here. Stop giving my dad ideas."

He looked like he might argue. His green eyes were hard and determined, but I shook my head. He sighed and took my hand in his, lifting it and kissing my palm.

"Want to go watch a movie in my room?" I asked. "That's lying low, and I don't think I can sleep anyway. I still feel weird. A movie is a good way to ignore everything."

He nodded. "All right. But I require things for movies—snacks and such."

I led him down the hallway to the kitchen to get a snack. My dad shouted after us. "Theatre room is much better for movies, Linds."

I smiled, liking where that was going. My dad was being a dad, and I was trying to sneak my boyfriend into my room. It was the most normal moment I'd had in a week, or all summer.

We grabbed candy, chips, and sodas and headed for the movie room. I flicked on Netflix and started scanning, looking for a comedy. Selecting *Austenland,* I grinned at Vincent's scowl. "This is an actual movie? Someone made this? Are you being serious?" He sighed.

"It's very funny. More comedy than chick flick. I swear."

"I feel like that's a giant lie." He groaned, defeated as I snuggled into him in the oversized armchair. He looked down on me, still appearing rather stern. "But I get to pick the next one."

"Deal." I turned the movie on just as my phone buzzed in my pocket. I pulled it out, wincing when I saw the group chat was going again. I opened my texts and froze, seeing the new comment from Rachel.

Any of you bitches try telling anyone including the police anything that's going on from this point forward, you lose a parent. Mr. Henning was just the beginning. We dance for our dinners here, ladies, you just don't know that yet. So let's play a game. You stop trying to guess who I am and start trying to guess who I am going to kill next. You have one week to prevent a death. I'll give you a hint. There is a pattern. Night, night, bitches. Sleep tight. Don't forget to cry yourselves to sleep tonight.

I angled the phone so Vincent could read it as I had a small panic attack and tried not to hyperventilate again.

"Oh shit," he whispered. "They were listening outside the sunroom? Or maybe they bugged it?"

I nodded and we both glanced around the room nervously.

"This is just the beginning," I whispered back.

EPILOGUE
A KILLING I will go

I pressed send on the text and grinned, sitting back in my chair. Those five bitches were going to pay for every little thing. I lifted Henning's phone and played the message one more time. Mr. Allen was so crazed for a friendly realtor. His true colors were vibrant and spicy. "Henning, you son of a bitch. I will kill you for this. Do you hear me? I will kill you. You are going to be nothing but a bum in a suit when I am done with you. This isn't over, buddy. This is just starting."

I laughed and turned it off. People were so easy to predict.

Getting up, I paced around the attic, listening as the Blacks' movers packed their house below me. I had a week left in the house before the new people took ownership of it. There still wasn't any word of whether or not they were planning on living in it, or if they just wanted to own it and wait for the market to come up so they could sell and make some cash.

It meant I had a week to find out if I was packing up everything.

I turned in a circle, proud of the systematic spread of spider web-styled planning I had before me. I imagined it was the way a writer planned a book: a picture of a face with facts below them and lines connecting them to the other people.

Only my lines were weaknesses.

My lines were the strings holding up the puppets, the marionettes who danced for me.

The six girls were the center of the spider web. The

lines from them all would be my way of dangling each of them until they died, strangled in the lines.

A slow smile spread across my lips as I glanced at the face of Rachel Swanson with the giant red X across her photo.

She was my best work yet, but I knew I could do better.

THE END

The mystery continues in *Second Nature and Third Time's a Charm*.

If you liked the comedy and romance in this book, check out *White Girl Problems*.
If you liked the suspense and want something a little scarier, check out *The Seventh Day*.

If at First

This YA book is written by one of many personalities currently residing in the evil mind of international bestselling author, Tara Brown.
The author went to Hogwarts, she was Ravenclaw and Luna was her best friend.
She crept through the wardrobe into the snowy landscape of Narnia, but might have been a little afraid of the forest.
She helped Nancy Drew solve every crime, and maybe she eyed up Ned Nickerson when Nancy wasn't looking.
She stays up late watching Gossip Girl and Pretty Little Liars and wishing they were combined to make a murder mystery TV show. And yet she's addicted to The Walking Dead and reading Stephen King. All of this is done while eating wine gums.
She is the writer and personality when YA and Middle Grade are needed as far as Tara Brown is concerned. The books here are for the brave of heart, they are not soft or delicate. She doesn't speak in flowy poetic lines. She makes up words like poopsock and hamtard and there is no glitter. She's bold, spicy, and filled with adventure--and of course love.
Tara Brown is an absolute romantic at heart. And so are all her personalities.

Printed in Great Britain
by Amazon

16824645R00133